To Lisa Lindstrom and Neil Snyder
Your real-life love story is more beautiful than
any romance I could write.

Intercepting Daisy

Also by Julie Brannagh

Guarding Sophie (novella)
Chasing Jillian
Holding Holly (novella)
Covering Kendall
Catching Cameron
Rushing Amy
Blitzing Emily

Intercepting Daisy

A LOVE AND FOOTBALL NOVEL

JULIE BRANNAGH

AVONIMPULSE

An Imprint of HarperCollinsPublishers

Excerpt from *This Earl is on Fire* copyright © 2016 by Vivienne Lorret.
Excerpt from *Torch* copyright © 2016 by Karen Erickson.
Excerpt from *Hero of Mine* copyright © 2016 by Codi Gary.

EPub Edition SEPTEMBER 2016 ISBN: 9780062443335
Print Edition ISBN: 9780062443328

Avon, Avon Impulse, and the Avon Impulse logo are trademarks of HarperCollins Publishers.

AM 10 9 8 7 6 5 4 3 2 1

Acknowledgments

I MIGHT WRITE for a living, but I do not have the words to adequately express my gratitude to my agent, Sarah Younger of Nancy Yost Literary Agency, and my editor, Amanda Bergeron of Avon Impulse. I could say thank you for their patience, their enthusiasm, and their encouragement a million times, and it wouldn't be enough.

Thank you to Elle Keck, Amanda's assistant, who's done a lot for me too. I am a very lucky author and so grateful for her help.

Speaking of lucky, thank you to the copy editing staff at Avon Impulse. They could write a bestselling tell-all on my issues with punctuation, correct sentence structure, and grammar.

Thank you to my husband, Eric. I could never do this without you. I love you.

Catherine, the flight attendant in *INTERCEPTING DAISY*, is named for one of my readers after she won a drawing. Congratulations, Catherine Edwards! I hope you'll love this!

Thank you to the lovely Amanda LeBlanc for helping me find a flight attendant to talk with for my research.

Thank you to the amazing Jenny Eilts for answering all of my kooky research questions, giving me a great peek into the life of a flight attendant, and being a delight. Your airline is lucky to have you!

Thank you to every flight attendant on every flight I have ever been on. You've gone above and beyond to help terrified-to-fly me get to her destination, and I am so appreciative. A special shout-out to Alaska Airlines; you've all spoiled me for every other airline.

I'd like to thank Charlie Whitehurst for signing with the Seahawks and staying here long enough for me to wonder what the life of a backup QB might be like.

Thank you to the Seattle Seahawks for interviews they have given in various forms of media. Not only are they a tremendous help with my research, I look forward to fictionalizing a certain quarterback's giving up his first-class seat during a flight to a soldier. I hope he's okay with that.

Thank YOU for buying my book! I hope you'll enjoy it. I could never express how much you mean to me. I'm on Facebook at https://www.facebook.com/JulieBrannagh. Stop by and say hi! XXOO

Chapter One

GRANT PARKER HEARD a loud crack as he rolled over in his date's bed and onto something buried in the sheets. He looked at the sleeping form next to him and sighed in relief when she didn't stir.

He extracted an e-reader from under one of his hips as he sat up and stared at a large horizontal fracture in the screen in the dim light from her bathroom. Crap. Grant couldn't remember her name, but he was willing to bet she remembered his. Even more, she was probably going to be pissed about the broken e-reader.

Shaking his head to clear out some of the cobwebs, he knew he needed to get his ass out of here. He had a hundred bucks in his wallet. He'd leave the money to replace the e-reader (along with a note) ten seconds before he walked out the front door of her apartment. Still too drunk to drive, he would call Uber as soon as he got outside.

He'd met her at a bar last night. She was exactly what he'd wanted: a woman who wanted one night with him. They'd had a lot of drinks, and they'd taken a cab to her place. Minutes later, they were naked. He'd had her twice before they both fell asleep from sheer exhaustion. He wondered what the biggest aphrodisiac was for the women who fucked his brains out on a regular basis: that he played pro football or that they were delighted to discover he was an excellent lay. She'd have several orgasms to remember him by.

The Sharks' PR department worked overtime to craft his squeaky-clean image. Grant had arrived in Seattle as a result of being drafted out of his small, conservative Christian college's football team. The Sharks had cut their former backup QB after a DUI and a sexual assault arrest. Grant was in the right place at the right time. Grant's parents were also the nationally known pastors of a megachurch in Texas, which seemed to seal the deal for the Sharks.

It was clear in Grant's Combine interview with the team's head coach and the general manager that any hint of bad behavior in his personal life would not be tolerated. The team believed Grant's background and football skills would go a long way to smoothing things over with angry fans. Grant wanted to play for Seattle. It was the perfect situation.

The Sharks' PR department circulated pictures of him to the local media with approved dates—girls from the local Christian college, for instance. He'd take them to dinner and a movie or a game. He'd walk them to their front door by ten PM, kiss them on the cheek, and make sure they were safely inside before he got in his car and went looking for what he really wanted: raw, anonymous sex with someone he knew he had no intention of seeing again.

He didn't lie to anyone he was with. He had told each woman before they went to her place that he was in for one night and one night only. He told them he didn't have sex without protection, which he provided. They nodded, smiled, and tried every sexual enticement in their arsenal to change his mind. It seemed that the women he dated always wanted what they could not have. If he met someone who boinked his brains out and told him to leave as soon as he got dressed, he'd be back for more. So far, it hadn't happened.

He knew he was playing with fire for being so public. He knew he should find a woman who was interested in a mutually beneficial (and highly confidential) arrangement. He wasn't callous or cavalier toward anyone else's feelings. He just wasn't interested in getting tied down to anyone, at least in the short term. If he got caught having multiple one-night stands, his carefully constructed image would blow up in his face, and any chance he had of succeeding Tom Reed, the Sharks' starting QB, would be gone.

He understood his behavior could be chalked up to doing the forbidden, to the idea he was getting away with something he shouldn't do. What kind of idiot would jeopardize eight million dollars a season for standing on the sidelines with a clipboard sixteen Sundays a year by taking such a risk? The Sharks organization wanted their fans to believe Grant spent his evenings with his playbook and turned in early. Alone. Preferably after reading a few pages of the Bible and saying his prayers. He was a normal, healthy guy with a normal, healthy sex drive. Was this a crime?

Grant wanted to watch the Sharks' starting QB Tom Reed on the sidelines holding a clipboard as Grant threw TD after TD. He wanted to be the guy in the hundred-foot-tall mural screen painted on the side of Sharks Stadium. He also wanted to be the guy who'd get his pick of twice as many women who all wanted to do him. After all, the ladies wanted the real thing: a starter.

He clicked on the small button that activated the e-reader. It still worked, despite the cracked screen. He saw the title of the last book she was reading, *Overtime Parking*; a picture of him crossing the tarmac at an airport to get on the Sharks' team plane was on the cover.

He'd been the subject of a lot of press, but someone had written a book about him? He hadn't seen this yet. He was surprised his agent or the team publicist hadn't told him about it. He'd have to call them both tomorrow. Maybe he should take a look at a page or two to figure out if this was an unauthorized biography.

He touched the unbroken part of the screen with his fingertip, and the text appeared.

And I shoved Parker's football pants down with both hands. He was naked beneath and sporting a gigantic erection.

"*Want it?*" he said.

"Yes." I unzipped my jeans and wriggled until both jeans and underwear slipped to my knees. I unhooked my bra and pushed my sweater up around my neck. I lay back on the hood of his car in the team's parking lot, spreading my legs, entirely exposed to him. In full view of anyone walking past. The parking lot was full of cars; it was a matter of time before we were discovered.

I reached down to touch myself, to move my fingers in the wetness I felt dripping out of me. I wanted to show him I could come from staring at him and stroking my clit. I wanted him to see it all and to want me as badly as I wanted him.

"Fuck me," I said.

He yanked my jeans and my panties off and pushed my legs up over his shoulders. I couldn't concentrate on anything besides his arms caging me, his mouth on mine, his hard, massive dick entering me seconds later. I arched into him, my nipples scraping against his rock-hard chest. He grabbed my ass to pull me into his pistoning hips. Somehow, it was even more thrilling to know we might have an audience, and I ground into him as a result.

"Oh, God. Fuck me! I have to have you!" I told him as I moved against him. He pounded into me, over and over. I heard flesh slapping against flesh and the muffled groans of satisfaction deep in his throat. I wrenched my mouth from his, raked my nails down his back, and let out a loud cry.

"More!" I cried out. "Harder!"

"Oh, I'll give it to you harder," he growled as he thrust again. I wrapped my legs around his hips as tightly as I could. My clit rubbed against his pelvis as I moved against him. The hood of his car was cold but slippery against my back. It was going to be covered with our juices by the time we were done. There was nothing like the smell of sex; it surrounded us in the cold night air. I reached down to grab his ass with both hands, pulling him closer.

"Faster," I cried. "More!"

"I'll give you more," he said roughly. "I'm going to fuck you, and then I'm going to fuck you again. Right here. Where everyone can see us. They'll know how dirty you are, how badly you want it. How you'd fuck them too."

He was breathing hard. He thrust faster, and I could feel myself coming, lust and adrenaline coursing through my bloodstream as I reached between us to rub my clit. "That's it," he said. "You want it. You want everyone to see you coming all over me, don't you? Come for me. Come now."

I let out a scream as my entire body convulsed around him. The waves of pleasure and release went on and on. I must have blacked out for a few seconds; I could hear applause and whistles as I came to. I saw a knot of guys a few feet from us; I was beyond caring that I was laid out like a naked, panting feast in front of them. I was limp in his arms, and he grinned down at me. He turned, made a slight bow to the onlookers, and turned back to me. His dick was already getting hard again as I watched.

"Ready for round two?" he said. "I'm going to do every nasty thing to you you've ever dreamed of. In front of them. And you're going to love every minute of it."

Grant stared in shock at the broken e-reader's screen. What the hell was this?

Chapter Two

THE CHARTER FLIGHT Daisy Spencer was working that afternoon had been smooth until they were an hour outside of Seattle. They bounced their way into the landing pattern for Sea-Tac Airport as the pilot's voice came over the intercom.

"Ladies and gentlemen, this will be a rough one due to weather in the Seattle area. Everyone needs to sit down and buckle up, including the flight attendants. I'll let you know when you can get up again. Also, please stow all loose items such as electronics in your seat back or under the seat in front of you until we've landed. Thank you."

Daisy would have liked to chalk this up to a typical day at work, but she'd received "sit down and buckle up" instructions with forty-five minutes left to go in flight only once before. That one had ended with the euphemistically termed "rough landing" and a quick evacuation via the emergency exit. The fire department had coated everything that moved in flame retardant due to leaking jet fuel.

The pilot had his hands full at the moment as the plane shimmied its way through strong winds and lashing rain while descending from cruising altitude. The jump seats were located behind the cockpit and facing the passengers; Daisy glanced around the half-partition that shielded the flight attendants from view. The Sharks' front office guys, who always sat in the front of the team plane, were clutching their armrests. One appeared to be praying. She saw a few of the players in the rear clasp hands across the aisle as the plane descended through a wall of dark clouds the last thousand feet to the runway.

Daisy's heart was pounding. Anyone who wasn't afraid in this situation was out of his or her mind. She had confidence in the pilots—she knew the captain wouldn't hesitate to abort the landing and divert elsewhere if he couldn't land safely—but she was still scared. She wasn't seeing her life pass before her eyes or anything. She remembered every emergency procedure she'd learned in her flight-attendant instruction. If they managed to deploy the emergency slide after landing, they'd have little time to evacuate the plane. Staying calm meant survival for everyone right now.

The silence was broken by the sound of dozens of men reciting the Lord's Prayer as the pilot fought to stabilize the wildly pitching jet. He was a thirty-year veteran of the airline and flew bush planes in Alaska previously. He was used to a lot worse conditions. The side winds still buffeting the plane were a big concern, however.

"Flight attendants, prepare for landing," the copilot barked into the intercom.

Daisy's coworker Rachel reached out to grab her hand. "Almost there." She'd been through worse too, but it would be a relief to arrive safely.

"Yeah," Daisy said.

"We'll be fine," Rachel said, her hand sweaty from nerves. "Breathe, Daisy."

The wheels of the jet touched the runway beneath them and bounced. The plane shimmied again as the pilot applied the brakes; Daisy knew he was using every bit of experience and skill to get the plane to stop before he ran out of runway. They heard the whine of the brakes as the passengers were shoved back into their seats. She could feel the jet still moving side to side in the strong winds, but the pilot managed to slow the plane. A minute or so later, he turned onto the path to the area they'd be disembarking at.

"Ladies and gentlemen, welcome to Seattle. I'm leaving the seat-belt sign on because the weather has really deteriorated in the past hour or so. It's forty-five degrees here, raining hard with a pretty good side wind, but we made it." His comments were interrupted by enthusiastic applause. "We may see some lightning in the next forty-five minutes, so we'll be exiting the plane as quickly as I can get it parked and then get you onto your buses."

Daisy didn't have time to reflect on the fact they'd narrowly avoided the worst possible outcome. She let out a long breath and unclenched Rachel's hand.

"Time to get back to work," Rachel said.

Daisy reached out to grab a plastic garbage bag from the galley. She and Rachel would have to set some kind of land-speed record cleaning up the cabin before they were told they could open the jet's doors, but it had to be done. The other two flight attendants in the back would help, but it would still have to happen in minutes. They hadn't been able to do the pre-cleaning of wrappers, plastic cups, milk and juice cartons, and other trash that collected when sixty-plus professional athletes, twenty-five coaches, support staff, and various others traveling on the Sharks' flight needed refreshments on their way home from Oakland. She saw the Sharks' head coach unbuckle his seat belt, scoot to the edge of his seat, and reach out one hand.

"Daisy, I can help. Let me have that."

"You're not supposed to get up until the seat-belt sign is off, sir."

He gave her the nod and wriggled his fingers. "Got it. I'll take that. And why don't you get me another one too?" He dumped a plastic cup full of wrappers in the bag, turned in his seat, and handed the bag behind his head to one of the assistant coaches. "Put your trash in this, and let's pass it to the back of the plane. Hopefully, the guys will get the message."

Four empty plastic bags were handed back. She could hear the rustling of paper and plastic as the passengers cleaned up after themselves. As the plane continued its slow progress, Daisy could hear a few of the players talking and nervous laughter.

"Damn. I thought we were done for, bro."

"Pretty bumpy. That pilot earned his money. The fucking wings were wobbling too. Scared the shit out of me."

"Still want to learn to fly, Anderson?"

"Hell no. I want to go home and kiss my wife."

This was greeted with a burst of loud laughter.

"I'll bet you're doing a lot more than kissing her," another deep voice chimed in.

"Not discussing that with you right now, Collins."

The plane came to a halt, and the pilot turned off the seat-belt sign. "I'd like to thank everyone aboard for flying with Pacifica Airlines. I still see lightning on my weather readout, so we'll make sure you're safely on the buses before it arrives. Please take extra care with the steps today due to the rain and wind. We look forward to flying with you again soon."

"How about next Friday night?" one of the players called out. "We have a business trip to Green Bay."

Daisy smiled as she picked up a few wrappers that had managed to escape the surprisingly tidy group. They might have had a scare, but they were ready to get back on a plane again. So was she.

"Thank you, guys, for cleaning up," she said to nobody in particular. "We really appreciate the help."

Matt Stephens, the owner of the Sharks, gave her a broad smile as she approached him. Daisy didn't spend a lot of time keeping up with football, but any woman with a pulse knew who the startlingly handsome Matt was. She also knew that he was married and, according to all reports, crazy about his wife, Amy.

"Thanks for getting us home safely." Matt reached out to shake Daisy's hand.

"The pilot's your man for that, but thank you," she said.

Daisy was a bit surprised that Matt never sat with the front office guys and coaching staff when he flew with the team. He seemed to prefer the sometimes-boisterous player seating. Matt's brother-in-law Brandon McKenna, who'd retired from the Sharks a few years back and took Matt's job on a nationally broadcast pre-game show, sat next to him.

"He saved our ass—butts today," the tall, blond Brandon said. He reached out to loop his arm around Matt's shoulders. "Let's go home, bro."

"You don't need to ask me twice," Matt said. "I wasn't sure we were getting off this damn flight alive."

"If I got killed in a plane crash, Sugar would kick my ass," Brandon said. His dimple flashed as he impulsively kissed his brother-in-law on the forehead. "We're outta here."

Daisy moved away from them and reached out for another full plastic bag from Grant Parker, the Sharks' backup quarterback. He looked into her eyes and raised an eyebrow—the universal guy signal for *Hey, how you doin'?*

Grant wasn't hard on the eyes, either. His tousled, wavy, sun-streaked, chestnut-colored hair brushed his shoulders. His eyes were the color of melted dark chocolate and twinkled when he smiled. He had the required three-day scruff of whiskers most men under thirty sported these days. Instead of the bulked-up muscles of most of his teammates, Grant was tall and lean. He also bore a somewhat disconcerting facial resemblance to a major religious figure. This hadn't slowed the party in her panties down one bit.

Imagine what the pastor of her parents' church would have to say if she told him she had lust in her heart for a guy who looked like Our Lord.

She made an extra effort to remain somewhat professional while he was around, despite the fact that she wanted to squeal like a fourteen-year-old girl confronted with her favorite teen idol. She'd been working on the Sharks' charter flights for two seasons now. The other guys on the team, the coaching staff, and the Sharks announcing crew and other media—they were fun to fly with, and she enjoyed chatting and laughing with them, especially after the team won. Grant was another story. She'd like to toss herself in his lap and run her fingers through his hair, for starters.

He spent his flights listening to music on his headphones and working on his tablet. There might be an occasional conversation between him and his teammates, but for the most part, she'd noticed he kept to himself. Her interactions with him were limited to "What would you like to drink?" and "What would you like to eat?"

Of course, this hadn't stopped her from embroidering a rich fantasy life about Grant in her head. She would love to know what he was like when he wasn't at work, so to speak. She'd read stories about him in the Seattle papers and had seen him shown on the local sports reports. She wondered how much was true and how much was creative fiction.

He was a pastor's son. He spent most of his spare time during the season making charitable appearances on behalf of the team. He told reporters that he hadn't met the "right girl" yet, despite the fact that he'd been seen out to dinner at Seattle-area restaurants with more than a few women from the local Christian colleges over the past few years.

Mostly, he (or his representatives) wanted Grant to be seen as an asset to the Sharks, a great addition to the community, and Tom Reed's worthy successor. Daisy wondered if Grant was curious about what it might be like to be out with someone who'd be interested in a bit more than sharing a root beer float and seeing a G-rated Disney movie with him.

Grant glanced up at her again.

"Need some help with the rest of this?" he asked. "Just point me toward the Dumpster. One of my jobs growing up was taking out the garbage."

"Thank you so much, but we'll let the cabin cleaners deal with it," she said. "You need to get on the bus before the lightning storm starts."

She heard the dull thump of the rolling stairs being shoved up against the side of the jet. The baggage guys were going to have a hell of a time unloading the jet in this weather, especially since she heard the boom of thunder from a few miles away.

The passengers grabbed backpacks, purses, and other items from the overhead bins and filed off the plane as she and Rachel stood at the jet's doorway and told each person good-bye. She got several hugs as the players filed past. One of the bigger guys reached into his backpack, pulled out several new Sharks-logo ball caps, and handed one to each flight attendant as he passed them.

"You ladies need some gear," he said. "I'll bring more next week."

"Is that a threat, Morrison?" one of his teammates asked.

"They're spending time with us. They need swag," he insisted.

"My son will love this. Thank you so much," Rachel said.

"Oh, no, ma'am. That's for you. I'll bring him something else." He sauntered down the stairway leading to the tarmac, where a small group of airline employees stood in a covered area waving the Sharks' flag and calling out, "Go Sharks" and "Welcome home."

Grant Parker was bringing up the rear. He stowed his headphones and tablet in his backpack and reached out to shake Daisy's hand.

"Nice to see you again," he said. Maybe she imagined that he'd squeezed her hand. "Will I see you on Friday's flight?"

"Yes. I'll be here." It was amazing she could get any words out at all.

"Good. I'll look forward to it," he said. She saw his lips curve into a grin. He was still holding her hand, and the fact that her pulse sped up as a result had nothing to do with today's flying adventure. "I know this is pretty sudden, but I have a question."

"Of…of course," she managed to stammer out. "What can I do for you?"

He pulled his cell phone out of his pants pocket as he released her hand. Damn it. She'd like to stand there and hold his hand for an hour or so. That wasn't weird or anything.

"Can I get your cell number, Daisy?"

"Uh, sure. Yeah," she said.

She rattled off the digits as he punched them into his phone. "Thanks," he said.

He was halfway down the stairs before she realized he'd asked for her number and she'd never asked him why. It seemed a bit sudden, but truthfully, she was still so rattled from the flight he probably could have asked her for the password to her checking account, and she would have blurted it out. She leaned out of the doorway of the plane to see if he was still around. The players and coaches were sprinting across the tarmac as she heard another roll of thunder in the distance.

Daisy could still feel the imprint of Grant's hand clasping hers. Of course, she'd done a lot more than shake hands with him in her imagination.

And in the book currently burning up every digital retailer's best-seller lists.

AN HOUR LATER, Daisy wheeled her suitcase into the suburban townhouse she'd scrimped and saved to buy. The weather was even worse. The steady pounding of rain, lightning, thunder, and howling wind had made the ride home from Sea-Tac a less-than-fun adventure with slick roads and pooling water. She needed a change of clothes and a glass of wine, and at the moment, she wasn't sure which she wanted more. She'd left the blue skies and low seventies of San Francisco's airport for the torrential rains of Seattle. She loved the area, but she was looking forward to some sunny days.

Her roommate, Catherine, was working a flight home from London. She'd arrive home late tomorrow afternoon, but till then, Daisy had the house to herself. Maybe she should add a hot bath into her evening's plans. She pulled off the low-heeled pumps she wore to work, carefully draped her damp uniform over the bedroom chair, and grabbed her iPad as she sat down on the bed.

Most single women in the Seattle area spent their time off enjoying the thousand and one things to do in the area. She liked going out and meeting new people, but lately, she was consumed with one thing. Actually, a person. The only chance she had to talk to him was when they were surrounded by a hundred other people who needed her attention and who weren't going to sit patiently while she did her best not to make a fool of herself over him. She thought about him when he wasn't around. She dreamed about him. Even more, she fantasized about him. There were other guys in her life, but she couldn't seem to forget about him.

One night after a bit too much wine, she opened up her laptop and wrote down one of those fantasies. A few days later, she found herself writing again. Before she knew it, she had written something a Google search called a "novella"—her raunchiest, filthiest, most graphic and unrealistic fantasies about the churchgoing, chaste Grant Parker of the Sharks. He'd flip out if he knew the things she thought about, and she'd die before she'd tell anyone else (besides her roommate) about them. Nobody else in her life had any idea.

According to Amazon.com's best-seller rankings, however, she'd told thousands of strangers. She'd copyrighted the work under her initials for some attempt at privacy. She'd snapped a picture of Grant with her tablet one afternoon as he walked across the tarmac to board the team's jet for a game in Denver and used it for the cover image. She'd figured out how to edit, format, and upload her book through a self-publishing service after researching it online. A few clicks later, she was a published author. She still couldn't believe she'd done it. Even more, she couldn't believe the book was selling.

If Grant ever found out about this, she'd die.

Another several-thousand-dollar royalty payment had been direct deposited into her checking account this morning. It joined the one she'd gotten last month. She was going to have to talk to an accountant about paying taxes on the money. Maybe she should donate it to a charity or something.

She glanced at the sales rankings one more time: number five. In all of Amazon. Her smutty little book was trouncing authors who actually did this for a living. And the reviews were as explicit as her fantasies.

If anyone found out what she'd done, she'd be lucky if she could get a job as a waitress in a coffee shop. In Iceland.

THE ADRENALINE PUMPING through Grant Parker's body after the rough flight had drained away during the drive home. The weather was shitty, but he could take it easy behind the wheel of his car. He didn't have the same control over the jet he'd been in an hour or so ago. Flying was part of his job, and for the most part, he enjoyed it. He wasn't sure he wanted to die in a plane crash, though.

He kept seeing his parents' faces as the Sharks' plane bounced around. Mostly, his mom's. He didn't want to think about them grieving for him. He had a tough time making friends due to the shyness he'd battled most of his life, but he had a couple. They'd miss him if the worst happened. Maybe they'd pour one out for him at the bar they all liked to go to while they were in college. But the last few hundred feet or so from the runway, he wasn't thinking about them. He was thinking about one of the flight attendants.

He'd noticed Daisy the first time she'd flown with them. She was pretty, but he was more attracted to her outgoing, funny personality. She seemed to be able to talk to anyone, and she'd made an extra effort to talk to him. Even if it was part of her job, he appreciated it.

He had gotten a glimpse of her sitting up front. If she was the last person he saw, his life had been pretty good. He'd decided that if the flight landed safely, he was asking her out.

He didn't have a date yet, but at least now he had her number.

Half an hour later, he dropped his garment bag in the living room of the Bellevue high-rise condo he'd moved into last year, after Sharks security suggested he might want to live somewhere a bit more inaccessible. A woman had broken into his previous house while he was on a road trip. She'd told the cops he was the father of her unborn twins. He'd never met her before. A DNA test proved he wasn't the father of her children, but his parents were horrified. He wondered what they might have to say if they had any idea how he spent his evenings off.

Wait until they heard about *Overtime Parking*, he thought. Even worse than his parents finding out he was the subject of someone's most explicit fantasies, the possibility that the book might become public knowledge made him groan aloud. He'd gotten enough crap from his teammates and the local sports radio hosts over the woman with the twins. Of course, the guys thought giving him shit showed that they cared.

His teammates didn't seem to care when he threw himself into a window seat on the flights to away games, pulled out his tablet and his headphones, and sealed himself off. He socialized with the guys at times, but he preferred to keep his private life private.

Of course, the Sharks' PR group capitalized on his visits to the local children's hospital, his interactions with the Make-A-Wish kids visiting practice once a week, and his speeches at local churches. He was fine with the media talking about that. The public ate it up. They wouldn't believe how he spent the vast majority of his time off.

He'd discovered early on in his dating life that many women who claimed they loved long walks on the beach, picnics, and bike rides on sunny days on online dating sites also wanted the nastiest, crudest, no-strings-attached sexual encounters he could offer. He wasn't complaining. He knew he wasn't the only guy in the world who was interested in getting what he wanted and then getting out, but it would be nice to meet a woman who had her way with him and then threw him out.

He didn't want feelings. He didn't want tenderness. He wasn't interested in the melding of souls, at least not right now. He wanted to bury himself balls-deep inside a beautiful woman, roll out of her bed, pull on his pants, and go home alone. He was pretty sure there was a reason for this that he didn't understand, but he wasn't willing to plumb his psyche right now for the motive behind why he'd avoided attachment to others (especially romantic partners) so much. If the author of *Overtime Parking* was a woman, he'd happily reenact every scene in her book. No matter how potentially compromising or how shocking.

Chapter Four

DAISY NEVER MADE it to the hot bath she'd been dreaming about. She woke out of a sound sleep a few hours later to the sound of a crash and someone saying in a British accent, "Dammit. Damn suitcase wheels." It didn't take the brains of a duck to figure out who it was. She threw the blankets back, jumped out of bed, and hurried down the stairs.

"You're home early," she called out.

"Bloody hell," her tall, slender, red-haired roommate said. "My flight home got cancelled, so I deadheaded back to Seattle through NYC. And the wheels on my bag decided to go tits up too. I love dragging a suitcase through JFK." Catherine heaved a sigh. "It's not all bad. It seems I might have an extra day or two off as a result." She reached out to lock the townhouse's front door. "Sorry I woke you up."

"No, you're not," Daisy said. The two women grinned at each other.

"Nice to see you," Catherine said.

"I'm relieved to see you too. There were a few minutes earlier I was pretty sure I wouldn't get to."

Daisy pulled breath into her lungs. The first time she'd had a near-miss on a flight, she'd laughed it off. This time, she'd kept thinking about all the things she still wanted to do in life, like fall in love. It still hadn't happened. What if it never did? She knew all the safety statistics on flying, but they didn't account for the fact that she still had a lot of living to do.

"But here you are. Fancy that." Catherine reached out to pat Daisy on the back while she shoved her suitcase away from the front door. "How about a piece of fruit?"

"I'd rather have a pint of Ben & Jerry's, but that'll work."

Catherine had been with Pacifica Airlines for eight years. She didn't mind working international flights. As a result, she worked a few days a week and spent the remaining days dealing with the jet lag. She'd moved into the spare bedroom in Daisy's place when Daisy had told a few of her coworkers she was looking for a roommate. It was always a good thing to split expenses, and Daisy genuinely enjoyed Catherine's company. It was also nice to have someone to complain to when her love life wasn't going as well as she might like.

Catherine had had the same problems until she'd met her boyfriend, Declan. Spending one's time flying back and forth from Seattle to London sounded like fun, but it was hard to find someone to date as a result. A few coffee dates turned into dinner dates. The dinner dates turned into a relationship. Catherine met Declan's parents. She joked that they were in no hurry, but Catherine had already told Daisy that Declan was *the one*.

Daisy was thrilled for Catherine. She'd like to meet *the one*, but so far, it hadn't happened.

Daisy met lots of single guys on flights. She met married ones as well but did her best to avoid them. Many of her fledgling relationships didn't last long due to her schedule. Daisy wasn't so worried about finding a guy to have a family with; she'd have plenty of time to have a baby later on. Right now, she just wanted to meet a guy who could handle her independent lifestyle. Men claimed they liked a woman who wasn't underfoot all the time but were irritated when Daisy couldn't drop whatever she was doing (or reschedule work) to be with them.

If Daisy had a rough time meeting guys the rest of the year, August through February was tougher. She sacrificed one or more of her days off every other week to work the Sharks' road game flights. She told everyone else that it was extra money, but she was more interested in the opportunity to be anywhere near Grant Parker for a few hours. She didn't want to dwell on the fact that she was attempting to get the attention of someone unattainable, as opposed to a guy who might want to date her.

Catherine reached out to grab the teakettle they kept on the stove to fill it with water. "How about a cup of tea?"

"That would be great," Daisy said. She grabbed a pear out of the bowl and reached out for a napkin to blot up the juice. "How was London?"

"I didn't see much of it this time. I went to Harrods Food Hall, though." Catherine turned to face Daisy, waving a plastic-wrapped box of tea bags in the air. "How's the best-seller list?"

"I have no idea what you're talking about."

"Of course you don't." Catherine's voice dripped with playful sarcasm. "I checked it on my phone. Number five. And you're beating Nicholas Sparks."

"At least the people in my book don't die at the end."

"You could say that." The teakettle on the stove whistled. "Did you talk to him on the flight home today?"

She didn't have to spell out who "him" was. They both knew.

"Just a little convo," Daisy said.

"Ask him out for a cup of coffee." Her roommate put a mug of tea on the table in front of Daisy. "Tell him you'd like to rip his clothes off and do unspeakable things to him."

"He's probably heard that one before."

"Not from you, he hasn't," she said. "You'll rock his goody-two-shoes world."

"He'd probably tell me he was praying for me."

"He'll need some prayer by the time you're done with him."

THE STORM RAGED on outside but Grant really didn't want to spend the rest of the evening cooped up in his condo. He'd actually played two quarters in today's game after Tom Reed had been injured. He was torn between happiness he'd gotten to play for two quarters and concern for a teammate he liked and respected.

Maybe he should go downstairs to one of the restaurants at the base of his high-rise building, have a late dinner at the bar, and see what developed. He wrenched off the tie he still wore from his flight earlier, unbuttoned his collar, and grabbed his jacket as he slipped his cell phone and keys into his pocket.

The winds were so strong outside he felt the elevator car swaying in its shaft as he descended. It occurred to him that staying in his condo might have been a better idea. If the power went out, he'd be climbing fourteen stories worth of stairs on already-tired legs.

He could handle it. The elevator opened onto a lobby packed with those who'd sought shelter from sideways rain and winds. The milling, talking crowd didn't seem to take much notice as he wound through them and headed toward one of the restaurants claiming to offer gourmet comfort food.

The hostess standing next to the front door (and the bustling lobby) gave him an apologetic smile. "Hey, Grant. How are you doing tonight?"

"I needed to get out of my place for a while. Is there an available table inside?"

"We're slammed," she said. "The power is out at several other restaurants, and everyone came here instead." She bit her lower lip. "There might be a seat at the bar. Will that work for you?"

The bar was fine. He wasn't going to attempt to try to find food anywhere else.

"I'll take it," he said.

"Follow me, then," she said.

She reached out to grab the door and motioned him inside the dimly lit restaurant. He'd noticed before that she didn't wear a ring. He'd never made a move on her, despite the fact that he ate here at least twice a week. She was attractive, but there was something about her he couldn't quite put his finger on that warned him away. She was friendly but not flirtatious. In other words, she wasn't into him.

He didn't bother with women who didn't show interest. If there was one thing he had in common with his teammates, it was that he really didn't chase. Why put himself out there when there were so many others who were happy to let him know they wanted him?

He elbowed his way into the bar area and slid onto an empty barstool. He'd have something to eat, enjoy a couple of drinks, and go back to his place to sleep it all off.

After a game, most of his teammates went out to dinner with their agents or their families. He knew he would be invited if he expressed interest. The other guys on the team had formed a tight connection, but he hadn't made much of an effort to join in. Most of the time, this suited him just fine. He really didn't need a bunch of people in his face all the time. Not hanging out with his teammates also ensured he wasn't questioned about his personal life. Things were great until he woke up at three AM alone and wondering why he didn't seem to make the easy friendships with others that most people valued in life.

He was probably still shaken by his experience earlier—the idea that he could be gone and he should have made more of an effort in life to expand his circle a bit. He didn't want to think about people crying over his death, but he'd like to think that a few people might miss him.

Maybe it was a function of getting older, or maybe he was tired of the superficial relationships he seemed to have with everyone else in life besides his parents. It felt weird to admit that he was sometimes lonely.

He wasn't going to start putting notes in his teammates' lockers ("Do you like me? Check yes or no,"), but he could start by inviting a few of the guys out for a beer or some type of get-together more often. It would be nice to know he had a few friends in the area. If he'd made an overture or two before tonight, he might be enjoying some time and dinner with a friend. Or friends.

It also wouldn't hurt to date a woman more than once. He'd already checked his phone three times to make sure he still had Daisy's number. He should have called her the minute he got home from the flight. He wanted to talk to her. Talking to her, however, wasn't the problem. He was having trouble with the asking-her-out part. What if she said no?

She probably thought he didn't notice that she blushed when she talked with him or that her eyes strayed in his direction while she was interacting with some of his teammates.

He pulled his hand out of his pocket so he wouldn't check to see if her number was still in his phone again. If Daisy turned him down for a date, it was actually going to hurt.

He caught the bartender's eye.

"I'd like a dinner menu, please."

"Got it," the bartender said. He moved off down the bar.

Grant knew the guy recognized him as living in the condos upstairs. Right now, though, he saw several people waving twenties in the bartender's face so they could get a drink. It might be a while before he got that menu.

He glanced around and spotted an attractive woman. She sat alone at a table several feet away. She was tall, blonde, and alluringly dressed. She wore a bit too much makeup. She caught his eye, raised one eyebrow, and nodded at the empty seat across from her. She looked familiar, but he couldn't figure out where he'd met her before. He got up from his barstool and made his way to her table. If he talked with her a little, he might be able to remember why he knew he'd seen her before.

"Hello," he said.

"Hi. Want to have dinner with me?"

"I think I will." He pulled the chair out and sat down. She shoved a menu across the table to him. "I'm Grant," he said.

"I'm Harley," she said. She cocked her head to the side, and her eyes narrowed as she stared at him. She managed to recover from whatever seemed to startle her, however, and held out her hand. He reached across the table to shake her hand briefly. "My friend was supposed to be here. She probably decided not to leave the house when she found out how bad the weather is." He heard the faint chime of a text received on the smartphone she'd left face-up on the table. She hit it with one finger and squinted at it. "Yeah. She just cancelled."

"I didn't want to leave either. You must have driven here before it got so bad."

"I live upstairs," she said.

He glanced up from the menu and looked into her eyes. He couldn't shake the feeling he'd met her before. Maybe she'd moved in recently. He spent so much time at the facility during football season that he didn't keep close tabs on the people in his building.

"You didn't have to go outside, then."

"Nope," she said.

He wasn't exactly a dazzling conversationalist right now, so he was surprised to watch her slip her cell phone inside what he knew was an expensive handbag. She must have wanted to chat.

The server arrived to take their order.

After handing his menu to the server, he sipped the ice water another server put in front of him. The woman across the table from him caught his eye.

"I think you know my friend," she said. "The one who didn't show up tonight."

"Is that so?" he asked.

"Pretty much," she said. "You spent the night together a few months ago."

He reclaimed his glass and took another swallow while he tried to figure out what to say in response.

"I'm not going to make a big deal out of this," she said.

"Okay," he said. He wondered if the restaurant would be willing to box up the macaroni and Gruyère cheese he'd ordered in case he needed to make a quick retreat. If she wasn't going to "make a big deal out of this," why had she brought it up in the first place? Something was wrong.

"I have a question, though," she said. Another server dropped off a basket of warm bread and butter. The scent made his stomach growl. It wasn't like he hadn't eaten already today, but he'd happily down the whole thing.

Harley pushed the bread away from her like it was contagious.

"Shoot," he said.

"She told me that you made quite a speech before you had sex with her. Something to the effect that this was one night only, she shouldn't expect to hear from you again, and you weren't changing your mind." She watched him pull a piece of bread out of the basket she'd pushed to his side of the table, smear some butter on it, and put half of it in his mouth. "Do the Sharks know you're this sexually active?"

He managed to swallow before he choked on the bread.

"Excuse me?"

"I've heard you're busy."

He was so shocked at her comments he wasn't sure how to respond. "As long as I'm doing my job, I don't think they care," he said.

"Isn't it a bit risky to engage in so many one-night stands?" she said. "Do you often forget the women you've slept with before?"

"I don't forget them," he said.

"If the Sharks' PR group's campaigns are any indicator, they seem to believe you're not having sex a lot. They also want other people to believe it as well."

He pretended like he didn't feel the hair rising on the back of his neck and took another bite of delicious bread and whipped butter with a hint of sea salt and truffle oil. This was a bit more than a sticky situation. He eyed Harley across the table. She wasn't making small talk; she was asking questions for a reason. And he was missing something.

"What's your point?"

"Why not be honest? Why are you lying to people?"

He finished his slice of bread and hoped his entrée would arrive soon. He didn't want to spend five more minutes with the woman across the table from him, but right now, he wasn't interested in causing a scene in front of a hundred people who so far were ignoring him.

"Most people see what they want to see," he said. The server arrived with their entrées and asked Grant if he'd like another beer. "Not right now," he said. "Thanks."

He waited until the server left and looked into Harley's eyes. "Are you honest about yourself with everyone you meet?"

She took a small bite of her salmon. "What about the people who'd like to get to know you as a person, not just as a football player?"

"They're really not interested. They want an autograph or a picture with me." His baked macaroni and cheese with a crispy panko bread crumb crust was waiting for him. "I'm used to it."

"Don't you think it's a little cynical?"

"You never answered my question. Are you honest about yourself with people you meet?"

"Of course. Most people are—at least the ones who don't have something to hide."

Despite his best efforts to remain unruffled, anger swelled inside him. He didn't need to justify himself or his life to someone he didn't know, but he realized he had no graceful way out of this. At the very least, he could make it quick. He caught a server's eye and nodded. The woman quickly approached his table.

"Would you please box this to go?" he said, handing his still-steaming plate to the server. He grabbed the credit card out of his wallet. "This is for the check."

Harley's mouth dropped open. "You're leaving?" she said.

"Yes," he said. He gave her a nod. "Thanks for dinner."

"I guess you don't recognize me," she said. "I'm Harley McHugh, the new sports reporter at KIXI-TV."

Shit. For a minute there, he thought he'd slept with her and forgotten about it. So she was pissed because he didn't recognize her from her job. Of course, she had looked familiar. He'd probably met her at practice before and didn't make the connection. He reached out his hand to shake hers again. "Good to see you," he said. She didn't shake his hand. He rose from the table. "Have a nice evening," he said.

It took him less than five minutes to sign the credit card slip, make his way across the still-crowded lobby, and get into an empty elevator car with his to-go bag. A minute and a half after he walked back into his apartment, the power went out. Luckily, the building had generators and his cell phone still worked. He sat down on his couch with a bottle of beer and stared out at the view of Lake Washington as he dialed his agent. He could see the whitecaps buffeting the 520 Bridge from here.

Blake answered on the third ring. "Hey, Parker. My flight got delayed, so I'm still at Sea-Tac. Is everything okay?"

"No," Grant said. "It's not." He kicked his shoes off and swung his feet up onto his coffee table. "I think I need your help."

Chapter Five

GRANT COULD THINK of a lot of things he'd rather be
doing right now. None of them involved unburdening
himself to someone he had a professional relationship
with. He had a tough time sharing his thoughts and feelings with a friend. Thinking about doing so with someone paid to represent his interests wasn't fun. He'd gotten
a little attention from the media over the years, but something about his conversation with Harley had every nerve
ending tingling. It wasn't from desire. *Sheer terror* might
be a better description of what he felt.

She knew something. Or, she wanted him to think she
knew something so she could trick him into revealing
something stupid she could report on. Whatever. Maybe
Blake had an idea of how to fix this.

"What's up? Want to talk about today's game? You
looked sharp."

"Thanks," Grant said. "Maybe we could talk about the game later. There's something I need to tell you about." He let out a nervous-sounding laugh. "I don't know how to say this."

"You're not pregnant, are you? I thought we had that talk," Blake said.

"Nope, not pregnant." Grant took a deep breath. "It's my social life."

"I heard you've had a few dates."

"Just a few." Grant took a swallow of his beer. "Actually, more than a few. And they weren't quite what the team thinks they are."

His agent went silent for almost a minute. Grant could hear flight announcements in the background. "Okay. One question," he said.

"Go ahead."

"They are all of age, right? You're not dating anyone who's not legal."

"No. Everyone I've been with is a consenting adult," Grant said.

"Great. We can deal with this," the agent said. "And no judgments on sexual orientation, either."

"I'm straight," Grant said.

"So, what's the problem?"

"They're not the good Christian girls the team says I'm out with."

"Please tell me money is not changing hands."

"No. No money. Well, no money until I broke this woman's e-reader last month. I left a hundred bucks for a new one before I took an Uber home from her place."

"At least you're responsible."

"Yeah. Uh, Blake?"

"Yup?"

"I've slept with a lot of women who I don't see again."

His agent let out an exaggerated gasp. "Oh, no! That's never happened in the history of the league. Are you some kind of manwhore? I'm shocked."

"Come on—"

"I'm giving you shit, Parker. Truthfully, I'd be more shocked to learn you weren't sleeping with every woman who made herself available. What do you think the rest of the team is doing?"

"Most of them are married now."

"Yeah, okay. If you think the single guys are going without, you're nuts. So what's the issue?"

"One of the local sportscasters seems to have found out about it. Harley McHugh—are you familiar with her?"

"Sportscaster Barbie? Who isn't familiar with her? What did she say to you?"

"I saw her downstairs earlier. She started asking some nosy questions about my social activities."

"How many women you've slept with?"

"That's the idea."

"You're using protection, you've been tested for STDs, and you haven't fathered any children, right?"

"Yes. And no on the kids part."

Blake let out another long sigh. "Okay. I'm aware the Sharks' front office fell in love with you because they thought you'd never have the kind of issues your predecessor had in Seattle. You've let them think you were playing along while you were doing something else. It's not great, but you are an adult, and your social life is really not their business to begin with. Here's the deal: we're going to have to figure out how to minimize the damage if Sportscaster Barbie—oops, Ms. McHugh—actually stumbles onto something. Are you dating anyone right now?"

"Not really." Grant took another swallow of beer. "I asked one of the flight attendants on our charter for her number, but I haven't called her yet."

"It would be better if she had nothing to do with the team, but this is a good start. Is she a one-night stand, or would you be interested in dating her?"

"I'd like to go out with her."

"Which flight attendant?" Blake had been on the team's charter flights before.

"Daisy. She's cute, blonde, and kind of funny. I think she might be into me."

"I remember her," Blake said. "Call her tonight. Ask her out for this week. If you have anything in common, keep dating her. In public. I'll work on what to do next." He snorted a bit. "If she doodles your name on her Trapper Keeper, you're in, buddy."

Grant closed his eyes with relief.

"They're calling my flight, Parker. How about I talk to you tomorrow?"

"Yeah. There's one more thing."

"What's that?"

"Someone wrote a book about me."

Chapter Six

LATE WEDNESDAY NIGHT, Daisy hip-checked the hotel room door open as she dragged her wheeled suitcase across the threshold. It had been a long day capped off by mechanical trouble with the flight home to Seattle she was supposed to work. She'd be staying overnight in Los Angeles tonight with the rest of the crew and heading home in the morning. She was looking forward to a quiet evening of room service and relaxation.

Staying in and getting some rest was definitely counter to the old-fashioned stereotypes about flight attendants. Daisy was supposed to be out on the town, dancing at a club or tearing things up. She enjoyed having fun as much as the next woman, but right now, her feet hurt, and she wanted to spend an evening that didn't involve dealing with someone's screaming infant or unbelievably drunk people.

She stared at her rollaway bag. Of course, she'd forgotten to bring her yoga mat. She'd started yoga a couple of years ago, after her doctor had encouraged her to try some gentle stretching each day. Yoga also helped when her schedule allowed her to play with the amateur soccer team she'd belonged to for four years now. She was an alternate goalkeeper, which meant she had something in common with Grant Parker: she woke up the day after a game aching all over. She was going to play as long as she could hobble out onto the pitch.

She dropped her tote bag onto the bed and sank down next to it. She'd need to be at the airport by six AM, so the best thing she could do was change into her pajamas, order some room service, and get eight hours of sleep. As she reached into the tote and pulled out her tablet, the small wireless keyboard she'd been traveling with for the past month or so brushed against her fingertips.

She'd been writing off and on since childhood. She kept a journal, which she'd switched from paper to digital a couple of years ago. She wrote short stories, letters to the editor, anything that might help her express herself. The crazy "book" she'd written about Grant Parker was the longest manuscript she'd attempted. She dropped the tablet on the bed next to her and let out a groan.

She shouldn't have pushed Publish. She should have kept it all to herself, because it was inevitable that he would find out who wrote all this crap about him. Why couldn't she have chosen something safer and less ridiculous, like writing erotica about some woman who had a fling with a dinosaur? She wouldn't have to worry about facing a pissed-off dinosaur. It's not like they still walked the earth or anything.

If Grant Parker discovered who she was (and that she'd written an appallingly explicit description of everything she'd like to do to him and with him), she'd—well, her life would be over. The worst thing about all the crap she'd written, besides the fact she'd bared her soul, was the knowledge that she wished she had the guts to start a manuscript she could admit to.

Daisy wasn't sure she wanted to write anything literary, but she could certainly write about the crazy things she'd seen while doing her job over the past ten years. She couldn't use her real name, and she'd have to change names, locations, and other identifying information, but it might be fun to write a memoir of sorts.

The idea had taken root and blossomed over the past several years. She could write on her off-hours and keep her stories to herself or publish if she wanted to. The choice was up to her. Mostly, she wanted a little more from life than she had right now.

She'd have to start to make any attempt at all, though. She pulled the keyboard out of her tote bag, reached out for the bedside telephone with her other hand, and brought the receiver to her ear.

"Room service, please."

Chapter Seven

THE SUN WASN'T yet over the horizon Thursday morning when Daisy scrambled into the shuttle that would take her to LAX, but she felt warmth in the air. The only good thing about being on the road at four AM was the fact that Los Angeles's infamous traffic was somewhat lighter. LA was a paradise of palm trees, cloudless blue skies, and eighty-degree weather. Surprisingly enough, though, she longed for the overcast skies and cool, clean, pine-scented air of Seattle.

Her phone vibrated as the shuttle pulled up to the curb. She grabbed it out of her pocket as she moved through the electronic doors and found a seat in a waiting area. It was her roommate, who'd arrived home from London yesterday.

"Aren't you supposed to be sleeping or something?" Daisy joked.

"There's a woman on the *Today Show* claiming that she wrote *Overtime Parking*."

"Seriously? What? Who is she?"

"She's from California. She says she got the idea after she slept with Grant Parker a few times." Daisy got up from the seat in the waiting area and headed to the gate area.

What the hell? Daisy wasn't sure how to react—should she be mad because someone else claimed her book or relieved that nobody would know she'd written it? Letting someone else claim it as her own work was the easy way out. But the relief was short-lived. She also felt a hot stab of jealousy over the fact the book-stealing woman claimed to have slept with Grant.

It was ridiculous to feel jealous over some guy who'd asked for her number and still hadn't called her. What was up with that? She realized her phone was in her hand, and Catherine was still talking.

"Why would she say she wrote the book?" Daisy interrupted.

"Maybe she has a thing for him and thinks she'll get his attention."

"She'll get attention, all right." Daisy let out a long sigh.

"I'll keep watching this for you. Have a good flight."

"Thanks. I'll see you in a few hours."

Daisy hit End and stared at the clock on her phone. She'd better get a move on; being late was out of the question. The flight would be full of business travelers who were hungry and impatient to get to their destination and a few who'd want a drink to take the edge off. If she made sure she was stocked up and ready, things always went better. She picked up the pace as she moved through crowds of people who seemed to have nothing better to do at four thirty AM than stand in front of a television, staring slack-jawed at the weather report.

There were three passengers sitting in the waiting area when she skidded to the gate. The gate agent was unlocking the Jetway door for Rachel.

"Nice to see you," Rachel joked.

"What happened to you this morning?" Rachel hadn't been on the crew shuttle.

"I overslept."

Daisy and Rachel boarded the plane to start their workday.

"That's never happened before," Daisy joked.

"Oh, hell no. Some idiot in the next room was on his phone and yelling about something half the night. Imagine how late I would have been if you had had to bail me out of the LA jail."

They stowed their luggage and got to work. It was important to make sure the first-class breakfast supplies were there, but Daisy knew she'd better double-check the alcohol and the makings for drinks like Bloody Marys and mimosas. She was elbows-deep in the alcohol drawer when she heard a familiar male voice behind her.

"Hey, Daisy, is that you?"

She almost hit her head on the warming oven as she straightened up to look at him. Grant Parker grinned back at her. "Good morning," he said.

"What are you doing here?" she said. She wanted to bite her tongue. What a ridiculous thing to say. Plus, it was five AM, and Grant looked like he'd stepped out of the pages of *GQ* or something. He wore a pressed, button-down sports shirt in a subtle light-and-dark blue check, jeans, and a pair of black Chuck Taylor high-tops. He'd rolled the sleeves up to his forearms. His hair was pulled into a loose bun at the base of his neck. A few sun-streaked strands of hair had escaped and caught in the stubble on his cheeks. His smile was warm. And his eyes sparkled as always.

There weren't many times in Daisy's life she didn't know what to say, but this was one of them. He was gorgeous. And he was the last person she thought she'd see this morning.

"I had to make a last-minute trip to LA last night." He got a little closer. "I kind of hoped you'd be here."

He reached out to take a piece of celery out of her hand she'd almost stabbed him with. She could figure out why he'd been pre-boarded so early. He'd probably been recognized, and the gate agent was afraid of a riot. Daisy wanted to talk to him, but for some reason, she couldn't think of a thing to say. She took a breath before she passed out. He smelled good too, like freshly showered guy. She wanted to lean forward. She could bury her nose in his shirt front and take a long sniff, but that would be even weirder than her standing here like a statue.

The pilots had finished their pre-flight check and were in the cockpit already.

"Hey, Parker. Nice to see you," one of them told him.

"Good to see you too, guys. How's it going?" Grant said.

"So far, so good. We need to get you back for practice this morning, don't we?"

"I'd appreciate that. I need to be at the facility by one PM for meetings." Grant laid the piece of celery onto the galley counter as he reached around her to bump fists with the pilots. He nodded at the guys and took Daisy's elbow in his fingertips. "Got a minute?" he said to her.

"Of course she does," one of the pilots called out.

"Go talk to him, Daisy. We'll handle things up here," the other one said.

Handle things? They'd get into the snacks and make a mess. She'd end up getting quizzed by those two later about what Grant wanted, but she followed him out of the galley.

"Lucky me that you're here today," he said. He smiled. Her knees knocked in response.

"Usually, I'd see you tomorrow for the team flight," she said. "It's nice you're here too."

She still couldn't think of anything remotely interesting to say. He'd taken her hand in his. She told herself to breathe. His hand felt warm and dry, and he stroked his thumb over the back of her hand as he spoke.

"I'd better hurry up. The other passengers will be mad if I keep you all to myself."

Grant gave her another nod. It wasn't like she'd never been asked out before, but she was suddenly nervous. *Suddenly?* Hell. She'd been nervous and excited since she heard his voice. And if he wanted to stand here and hold her hand all day, the other passengers were going to have to get over it. She looked up into his sparkling eyes.

"Are you busy later on?"

"Not especially," she said. She didn't want to look desperate, but she'd cancel almost anything if he was asking her out right now.

"Would you like to have a glass of wine or a coffee with me? Maybe around seven?"

"Sure," she said. "That would be fun."

"How about I text you later, and we can set up a place?"

"I'd like that," she said. Rachel caught her eye from a few rows behind where they stood and winked at Daisy. She was pretty understanding, but there was a limit. "I have to get back to work."

"I'll text you later," he said. "Let's hope it's a good flight home."

"Absolutely," she said.

Grant sat down in the front-row window seat. She gave him a little wave as she hurried away. She wanted to break out in a wild dance of joy in the center aisle, but she managed to control herself. She now had a date with Grant Parker? Maybe she was dreaming.

Daisy was so busy that she didn't have a chance to talk with Grant again during the flight. Less than an hour after the flight landed, her phone chimed with Grant Parker's contact information and the fact that he'd like to get together with her at Purple, a wine bar and restaurant at the base of a high-rise in Bellevue.

And now, as she stood in front of her closet, she was having major buyer's remorse. She wasn't sure what to wear.

She was so excited and nervous she could hardly breathe. A squadron of butterflies had invaded her stomach. She'd fantasized about this guy, dreamed about him, and wished she could spend even an hour chatting with him. The chatting part might be a challenge if she didn't calm down a little. She might open her mouth and blurt out something really cringe worthy or ridiculous. Who was she kidding? Of course she would. She had wondered so many times what it would be like to be alone with him.

She knew he was shy after observing him on so many team flights. She was a dork. What if both of them were too afraid to talk and spent the time struggling to make conversation?

"It's just a first date," she muttered to herself. "You've been on a million of them before." Maybe not quite a million, but a hundred would not be much of an exaggeration. They tended to go one of two ways—they were either promising or unmitigated disasters. She wasn't sure why. Dating was different now than it had been when her parents met or when her friends who'd been married ten years or more first met. Lots of guys weren't interested in anything beyond a hookup. She wasn't necessarily opposed to sleeping with a man she was attracted to, but liking him went a long way toward helping her decide she wanted to get physically involved. Guys didn't seem to care, especially when they found out what she did for a living and obsessed over whether or not she was a member of the mile-high club.

She wasn't a germophobe, but she wasn't having sex in an airplane bathroom unless she used a few cans of disinfectant on it first, and probably not then either.

She had to be dressed and at the restaurant in an hour, and she still hadn't decided what to wear. Her heart was pounding already. She made herself take deep breaths before she started hyperventilating.

"Relax," she said. "This isn't the rest of your life. If he asks you out again, then you can fall apart."

GRANT GLANCED AT his Apple Watch. It was two minutes later than the last time he'd checked and ten minutes before Daisy was due to walk into the restaurant. He pretended to check his e-mail as he tried to look casual. This was the first date he'd had in a year that he'd actually had to plan, and he hardly knew what to do with himself.

His hands shook. He wanted to fidget. He was nervous, and he couldn't figure out why. It was a date. He'd been on a lot of them before. This was no different.

Actually, it was. He'd wanted to spend time with Daisy since the first time she handed him a miniature bag of pretzels and smiled at him. He could tell himself he was doing this in order to stave off whatever was coming from the media about his private life, but he could have found someone else if he needed to see and be seen. He wanted to get to know her.

She was as warm, friendly, and extroverted as he was shy and introverted. She wouldn't have trouble talking to him, so he'd better step up his own game. He'd once compiled a list of date-friendly topics of conversation on his phone, but there usually wasn't a lot of talking before he ended up in bed with someone. Grant knew his parents had dated for four years before they got married and slept together for the first time, which he couldn't imagine doing. He'd asked them once what they talked about while they were dating. He was hoping for some ideas on what to talk to a date about—well, when he had one that actually required conversation. They'd told him about how they met and fell in love several times, when he was still living at home and beginning to date. In those days, he'd invite girls from church out for ice cream or a movie. His parents had been overjoyed by this.

"We talked about the sermon we'd heard at church. Sometimes we did a Bible study together," his mother said. "I got to know your dad spiritually before we were physically involved."

He still remembered the blush that spread over his mom's cheeks as he watched his parents smile at each other. He knew they'd had other dates—roller skating, going to baseball games, or seeing G-rated movies—and he wasn't about to tell them the details of his dating life. He wasn't sure why he felt the need to be untruthful with them about his private life, but he knew that concrete proof he wasn't living the life they would have liked would cause more friction between them. He saw his parents so seldom now. He'd like the time he spent with them to be enjoyable.

He felt a rush of cool air as the lobby door opened and Daisy entered the restaurant. She had on a red knit dress with a matching fabric band around the waist and a swirling skirt that ended well above her knees and moved when she walked. Her blonde hair was down and loose around her shoulders. She wore some strappy, spike-heeled shoes. He typically saw her in the conservative skirt, white blouse, protective apron, and low-heeled shoes of her airline uniform. The difference was pronounced. And he was immediately thankful he'd put on dress clothes. He wanted her to know he'd made that effort too. His heart beat double time as he saw her smile at him. She looked gorgeous. Even better, she didn't bother glancing around the lobby to see who else was there. He was the center of her attention. He couldn't wait to talk with her.

She grinned at him. "Hey," she said.

"Hey, yourself." He leaned forward to kiss her cheek and took a deep breath. She was wearing perfume, but he couldn't figure out what it smelled like, besides something nice. He gestured toward the hostess, who stood ready with a couple of menus and an inscrutable smile.

"You look beautiful," he said. "Ready?"

"Yes. I'm starving," Daisy said.

He also hadn't met many women over the past couple of years who actually admitted to eating or being hungry. This date was already spectacular.

Grant followed Daisy into the restaurant's dining room. The space was dominated by dark wood, large windows that let in the fading light of an evening in fall, and soaring ceilings. A floor-to-ceiling open wine cellar featured hundreds of bottles. Overhead penlights offered sufficient illumination but still encouraged intimacy. Tables for two and four dominated the space. The hostess stopped in front of a table for two, indicating they should be seated as she handed them each a menu.

"Your server will be here in a moment for your drinks order. Enjoy your dinner," she said.

"Thank you," Grant said as he pulled his chair a bit closer to the table. He leaned forward. "Have you been here before?"

He saw Daisy's mouth twitch a little, as if she were stifling laughter. "I thought there was some kind of law that every single person in Bellevue had to go to Purple at least once."

"I've been here a lot too," he said. He didn't mention that the restaurant delivered to those who lived in the condos. He'd discovered this when a few of his teammates (who also lived in the same building) had invited themselves over to play video games a few weeks ago. It had been an easy way to feed four ravenous men.

Purple was upscale enough that people would pretend not to stare at him, but it didn't have a dress code. He wanted to impress her, but he didn't want to scare her off.

Daisy laid her menu down on the table. "So, I'm a bit mystified. When did coffee or a glass of wine turn into dinner?" She grinned, but he saw one of her eyebrows arch.

"I don't get much of a chance to talk with you when we're flying to a game," he said. "I'd like to."

She sat back in her chair. He wasn't a body language expert, but he watched her crossed arms relax as she laid her hands in her lap. She bit her lower lip. He had to smile when she reached up to smooth her now-marred lip gloss with one finger. He was willing to bet that the normally never-at-a-loss-for-words Daisy was having a tough time coming up with something to talk about.

"Do you know what you'd like to eat?" he asked.

She picked up her menu and opened it again. "I think I'd like the chicken Marsala. What are you going to eat?"

"I think I'll have that as well. How about a bottle of the wine they're recommending?"

"Sure," she said. "I'd enjoy that."

She was giving all of the classic symptoms of nerves—not knowing what to do with her hands, playing with her silverware, not looking into his eyes unless she had no other choice. She looked like she wanted to jump up from the chair and run out of the restaurant.

"I have an idea," he said. Her head jerked up. She'd stopped running her fingers through the horizontal fabric tucks in the waist of her dress. "Maybe we should pretend that we've never met before, that I'm Grant, who works in a cubicle somewhere, and you're Daisy, who works for the business next door. What do you think?"

"I'd like that," she said. "I wasn't sure if you wanted to talk about your job or not. You probably get sick of people asking you about it."

"I don't mind so much," he said. "There's other stuff to talk about, though, and I'd like to get to know you. What do you like to do when you're not flying?" He leaned forward a bit more. A few seconds later, he saw her lean forward too.

"I enjoy a lot of different things, but I have to be able to schedule around being here or not do them. I'm in a women's soccer league. I try to get a certain schedule so I can play in games, but sometimes I can't. My teammates are understanding about it. I worry they're not happy I can't be at every game." She shrugged a little. "I run. I tried rock climbing a couple of months ago. I'm still not sure about that one."

"What didn't you like about it?"

"I'm afraid of heights."

"But you fly for a living."

"I don't really think about being up that high when I'm flying," she said. "It doesn't seem to bother me as much. I'm not staring out the window or anything." She took a sip of water. "I work with a guy who became a flight attendant because he was scared to fly."

"You're kidding me," he said.

"No. It took him a few flights, but now he's the guy helping the passengers calm down when things get bumpy." She smiled at what must have been a private memory. "Most passengers hold it together, but I've worked flights before when someone had a real meltdown."

"How do you all handle it?" he said.

"The bumpy stuff?" she said. "The flight I was on with you guys—that was scary. The only reason I wasn't freaking out right along with you was I've flown with that pilot a hundred times before. He started out flying in the military, and then he flew bush planes in Alaska. He's seen every situation that can happen with a plane, up to and including losing more than one engine." She let out a sigh. "Turbulence is like hitting a bad patch of road in the car. It's a case of taking a deep breath and remembering that the pilots know what they're doing, they have the guys in the tower and the weather stuff right in front of them, and they'll divert to another airport if there's really a problem." She glanced at him again. "See? I'm talking about work. Maybe we should talk about what you like to do when you're not working in that cubicle you mentioned earlier."

The server arrived at the table and took their order. Mostly, Grant wanted the guy to walk away so he could chat with Daisy some more.

"Are you as hungry as I am?" she said to him.

"Absolutely," he told her. "Speaking of things I like to do, I've always been fond of eating."

"Do you know how to cook?"

"Oh, hell no," he said, and he was rewarded with the sweet sound of her laughter. "Well, I really can't say that. I can cook enough to feed myself, but anything more involved doesn't happen. I get some of those pre-made meals delivered each week. The rest of the time, I go out."

"Would you like to learn to cook?"

"Are you offering, Daisy?"

"I'm not an expert, but I can teach you to boil water and make toast," she said.

"Sounds like fun. If we burn everything, we can go out again."

"Perfect," she said. "What else do you like to do?"

"I like the outdoors too. I tried rock climbing for the first time during the off-season last year. It's fun, but I had to stop."

"How come?"

"There's a clause in my contract that I can't participate in any activity that might injure me before training camp. It's part of dealing with my job, but it can get old."

"So no race-car driving," she said.

"No race cars, no motocross, no shooting myself out of a cannon. I'll have to come up with something quieter, like knitting."

"Knitting needles can be dangerous," she teased.

"Absolutely. I could jab myself in the finger or strangle myself with one of those circular needles I've seen my mom knit with," he said.

"I read a few months ago that your parents are pastors. Is that true?"

"Yes," he said. He needed to change the subject as quickly as possible. He didn't want to spend the evening answering questions about his parents. He loved them, but he wanted to find out about her more. "Their church is in Texas." He took a sip of water. "Do your parents live here?" he blurted out. "What do they do?"

"My parents live in Redmond. My dad works for Bank of America, and my mom just retired from teaching high school English."

She picked up her water glass and took a sip. She didn't seem any more willing to answer questions about them than he was about his own family, but he wanted to hear more about her.

"Were they surprised when you became a flight attendant, or was it something you'd been planning for a while?"

This all sounded like a job interview to him—general questions about their backgrounds and interests, nothing about what he'd like to discuss. He was having a great time with her, but he wished he could think of something more original to talk to her about. If he was planning on making a move, he usually didn't bother with dinner. He'd meet up with a woman at the bar; a few drinks would be consumed, and he'd call an Uber to get to her place. It occurred to him that he'd been on so many dates during which there was little to no conversation involved that he had no idea what to do next.

Actually, that wasn't accurate. He knew what to do next. But for once in his life, he knew it wasn't the right move. He wanted to get to know Daisy before they went to bed for the first time. That realization sent a cold shiver up his spine. Getting to know her meant that they would have to talk, and that meant that he'd be revealing himself to someone else.

Her lips curved into a smile. "Welcome back," she said. "You were a little lost in thought there."

The server chose that moment to arrive at the table with their bottle of wine, a basket of bread, and a small container of whipped butter. He poured a half an inch or so in the bottom of Grant's glass. "Try that and let me know what you think of it," he said.

Grant swirled the glass and sipped the wine. The tastes of black cherry and oak burst over his tongue, accompanied by a pleasant fullness. Hopefully, Daisy would enjoy it too.

"It's good."

The server filled their wineglasses and put the bottle back down on the table. "I'll be back shortly with your entrées," he said.

She took a sip of wine and put her glass back down on the table.

"Do your parents come to your games?" she asked.

"Nope. Sundays are for church," he said.

"They've never been to a game?"

"They show up when we're playing on Monday night or Thursday."

"What happens when you become the starting quarterback? Won't they take a week off to see you?" She swirled the stemless wineglass in her fingertips. "My parents and I have had our disagreements over the years, but they'd show up at something like that if they had to walk to the stadium."

He picked up the wine bottle and poured a bit more into his glass and took another sip. The wine was really good, and he was hoping it would help him calm down.

"They really don't like going to the games. The noise gives my mom a headache, and they're offended by the cheerleaders. It's a good thing they can't come in the locker room, or they'd be upset over the language too. They're not bad people. It's just the difference between my world and theirs, I guess."

"That's awful," Daisy said. "I'm sorry."

"You didn't do it," he said.

"I know, but I really am sorry. I've been reading the sports news since I started working on the team's charter flights. You're at the top of your profession. I can't believe they're not more interested in that."

"They're proud of me, but if I wasn't playing on Sundays, I could be at church with them," he said.

"You wouldn't have the platform to speak to people and make appearances you have now if you didn't play football," she said. "Have they considered this?"

He picked up his glass and took another sip. They'd almost killed the bottle, and their entrées hadn't shown up yet.

"I don't think it's on their radar yet."

She raised an eyebrow.

"So we've established that you enjoy the outdoors instead of binge-watching Netflix or playing video games around the clock," she said.

"Don't get me wrong. I enjoy video games. Every time I leave my place, I'm signing autographs and posing for pictures. Some days I'm fine with it. Other days I'd like to spend some time hiking or whatever, get some time on my own. Once in a while, I get a break, but there's nothing like being out in the middle of the woods, enjoying the quiet and not hearing, 'Hey, I know you. Aren't you that guy from the Sharks?'" He aligned the silverware next to his plate. "Do you have days when you're really not in the mood to deal with the flying public?"

"Everyone has days they don't want to deal with the flying public, let alone other people. Mine don't seem to happen that often." He watched her relax farther into her chair. "I always feel energized after talking with people. Most people are interesting, and I love finding out what makes them tick. Ninety-nine percent of the passengers on my flights are nice people. The one percent are the ones you have to watch out for." One side of her mouth curved into a smile. "They'll wreck your whole week."

"Want me to tell you about the people who come up to me who are still mad the team I played for in college lost the Sugar Bowl my sophomore year?"

"What? That's crazy."

"Oh, it happens," he said. He reached out for his glass and extended it to her in a toast. "Let's drink to the nice people."

"To the nice people," she said as they touched glasses. The server arrived with their entrées.

"Would you like another bottle of wine?" he asked.

Grant glanced at Daisy, who shrugged her shoulders. "I drove here," she said.

He was pretty sure she'd navigated the *I drank too much and need to get home* challenge before, but he was surprised that she'd made it clear she didn't intend on ending her evening at his place. Of course, this made him want her there all the more.

"How about a bottle of sparkling water instead?" the server said.

"Yes, please," Grant said.

AN HOUR OR so later, Daisy grabbed her bag off of the restaurant floor to pull it onto her lap. She'd been on more than a few first dates in her life, but this was the most interesting one yet. She hadn't been sure what he would be like when he wasn't on the team plane. She'd expected Grant to be a player—spouting lines, trying to get her drunk so she'd go home with him, or acting like a conceited ass. He was a little quiet, but she was charmed by his sense of humor and admission that he had a tough time coming up with things to talk about on a date.

"There's no test later," she said.

"Got it. I'd like to get to know you, though, and I sound like I'm interviewing you for a job instead of a date," he said. She saw his lips twitch into a smile.

"Are you going to ask me what I'd like to be doing in five years?"

"Not unless you want me to."

"We haven't covered benefits or salary yet, either," she said.

Her teasing comment made him laugh aloud. A couple of people at neighboring tables turned to see what they were laughing at. She delighted in the fact he sported a full-on grin now instead of the shy smile she'd seen all through dinner. Even more than imagining him as the object of her most explicit sexual fantasies, she'd wondered what he was like as a person, and slowly but surely, she was finding out. She also felt the first stirrings of guilt.

Obviously, he was a good-looking guy, and he was quiet but self-confident. His self-confidence was leavened with a good amount of humility and humor. She got the impression that he didn't talk about himself with many people. She was surprised and touched he'd chosen her. And she realized she didn't want to betray his confidence. If he knew who she was, though, he'd think she already had. He most likely knew about the book she'd written about him; maybe she should confess now. He'd think she was a weirdo and probably not want to see her again.

And rightly so.

But she really wanted to see him again. The part of her that wanted to spend more time with him won out over the part of her that knew she should confess.

"That's the second date," he told her. "We'll have to get together again and talk about it."

"I'd enjoy that," she said.

He reached across the table for her hand. "You'd like to do this again?"

"Absolutely."

His hand was large and calloused, probably from gripping a football, but warm and comforting. He squeezed her hand in response. "Are you parked in the garage downstairs? I'd like to walk you to your car."

GRANT REACHED OUT for Daisy's hand as he led her out of the restaurant. He could have invited Daisy upstairs. They could have opened another bottle of wine, had a few more drinks, and let the expected happen between two single adults who were attracted to each other. It wasn't that he was uninterested. He'd like to spend the night with her. But he'd spent some time this afternoon thinking about how he wanted to proceed with Daisy and decided that he should take things a little slower than he had in the past.

Daisy was everything he'd hoped she'd be. She was as outgoing and funny as she'd been on the team's flights, but he found out she was also sweet, thoughtful, and a great listener. It didn't hurt that she was beautiful, but he knew he'd be able to talk to her in or out of bed.

Maybe he should have made his move. He was trying to be a little respectful. They'd just had their first date, after all.

Mostly, he wanted to see how things went if they dated a few more times before sleeping together. Maybe he should take her to one of the few outdoor activities his contract didn't disallow, if he had any time at all between the additional film study he had at the start of any season and practices.

He knew he wanted to see her again the minute she'd walked into the restaurant tonight. He'd make the time.

He and Daisy stepped onto the elevator to the parking garage. She reached out to poke the button for the floor her car was parked on, and she slipped her hand inside of his again. He squeezed it.

"Will you be in town over the next few days?" he asked.

"I'm working for the next several days," she said. "Thursday looks good."

"How about late Thursday afternoon?"

"That would be great," she said. "What did you have in mind?"

"Rock climbing?" he said.

She let out a laugh. "I'll consider it."

The elevator doors opened, and he put one hand over the door so they could exit safely. She indicated a late-model blue Nissan Rogue in a nearby stall. "That's my ride," she said.

He could have hit the Stop button and kissed her in the elevator, but there was probably a security camera. He didn't really care, but she might not like being the center of attention when the snip of video got leaked to the local press or put up on YouTube. He wasn't letting her drive away without kissing her, though.

She paused in front of her car as she turned to face him.

"I had such a nice time. Thank you so much for dinner," she said. She shuffled her feet a little. He'd observed her so many times while she did her job. She always seemed at ease, even during the turbulence they'd experienced on the last Sharks flight. Maybe she had the same butterflies in her stomach that he had in his.

He moved a little closer to her and slid his arm around her waist. She tipped her head back to look into his eyes. He had to smile at the flush making its way over her cheeks as she licked her lips. Yes, Daisy wanted to kiss him too.

He touched his forehead to hers for a few seconds. Her skin was so soft. He could smell her perfume. He couldn't identify the flowers in it if someone offered him a million dollars, but it was nice. The parking garage was not exactly the backdrop for romance. Next time, he'd say good-bye to her at her front door instead.

"I had a great time too. I'm already looking forward to next Thursday," he said.

"Maybe we could go bungee jumping."

"Sounds perfect," he said. He heard her laugh again. "Right after that, we'll go zip-lining at Sharks Stadium."

He felt her shiver. He wasn't sure if it was the fact she was wearing an almost sleeveless dress, the idea she'd be that far off of the ground and speeding along a relatively slender cable, or that she was as attracted to him as he was to her. He needed to make his move, and he'd better do it before someone came screeching around the corner in search of a parking spot. He reached up to take her face in his hands.

"Maybe we should have a glass of wine in front of a roaring fire instead," he whispered, and he watched her eyelids flutter as they closed. He touched his mouth to hers, adjusted a bit, and kissed her.

She tasted like the wine they'd been drinking with a fresh, honeyed overlay that must have been all her. Her lips were soft and cool beneath his. He felt her arms slide around his waist as he deepened the kiss. He slid his tongue into her mouth, tasting her again. As he felt her tremble, he knew it had nothing to do with the cold. He pulled back a little and laid his cheek against her smoother one.

He wanted to kiss her until they both were breathless. He wanted to spend the rest of the evening with her, and maybe tomorrow too. Mostly, he wanted to figure out how to entice a woman into falling in love with him, and he wondered if he'd been going about it all wrong. The woman who currently regarded him with a soft expression as she reached up to stroke his face deserved more than he'd offered to women before.

"Thursday," he said. "I'll text you."

"Should I get more life insurance?"

"No. We'll have a great time." He pulled back a little and looked into her eyes. "I promise I'll figure something out that doesn't land us both in a body cast."

She dug through her purse, extracted her car keys, and hit the button to unlock her car. He made sure she was safely inside. She started her car, opened the driver's side window, and looked up at him again.

"Thursday," she said.

He watched the taillights of her car vanish around the corner seconds later.

Chapter Eight

DAISY WALKED INTO the dimness of her townhouse twenty minutes later. She'd spent the entire trip home attempting to convince herself that this had just been a dinner date. The typical post-date deconstruction with Catherine would have to wait. Judging by the silence, she was already in bed.

Daisy could text one of her friends. Most women in their early thirties weren't in bed at ten or so on a Thursday night and were always up for a convo about a date. She felt a little weird about discussing it with anyone else besides Catherine. She'd known most of her friends since she was in elementary school, but she knew the temptation to tell their friends she'd been out with Grant Parker would be insurmountable.

She and Grant had been in a public place earlier. If anyone recognized him at the restaurant, the chances were good that his being out on a date was already on social media. There was no reason she needed to keep her evening's activities quiet, other than the usual: she'd been out with a guy she had a thing for, who was going to lose it when he discovered she was the reason he was most likely being tormented on a daily basis by the press and his teammates. Then again, maybe he'd never find out. She didn't have to tell him. The woman who claimed she'd written *Overtime Parking* would be happy to take the blame. She wasn't getting any of the cash.

She knew she had to tell him. The happiness over their date was tinged with the guilt she felt. She really liked him. He'd kissed her like he liked her too. But she was afraid of what he was going to say when he found out.

If Daisy was better at lying, she would have asked Grant how he felt about the whole thing at dinner earlier. One of the nationally televised morning shows had contacted Grant's representatives earlier in the week to ask if he would appear on-air with the "author." His agent announced a couple of days ago that while Grant was flattered by the author's attention, he wasn't interested in a meeting.

She'd seen something on the news about how a few of Grant's teammates showed up at the daily Sharks press conference yesterday with a Kindle and proceeded to stage a dramatic reading of a few pages of the (inexpertly censored) book. Thirty seconds of hilarious footage showed up on sports channels from coast to coast and the YouTube video was closing in on half a million hits. Grant seemed to laugh the whole thing off when she saw coverage of his week on the Sharks website, but her conscience was on fire.

She wanted another date with him, but maybe she should be an adult and tell him. She'd tried to tell herself she wasn't sure why she'd published the book in the first place. That wasn't true. She knew why. She loved the reality of seeing something she wrote actually in print. It felt great for about a day, until she glanced at the online sales rankings and almost barfed.

She knew that Grant was well-known in the Seattle area, but she had never imagined what that kind of fame was like. Everything that happened to him was newsworthy, including a ridiculous erotic fantasy. She could do something embarrassing or silly in her spare time; her family and friends would laugh about it and most likely tease her for it, but it didn't end up on the news. Even if Grant was not the most famous member of the Sharks, his every move was discussed and criticized by sports fans.

Speaking of money, her earnings from *Overtime Parking* weren't going away either. She never thought she was going to have to account for or pay taxes on the $50,000 in royalties that had landed in her checking account over the past month. Maybe she should give the money to charity. Or, maybe she should sock it away as something to live on when the airline found out that she'd done something this dumb.

Maybe the airline wouldn't care. And maybe pigs might take up flying.

She threw herself down on her bed, aimed toward the walk-in closet, and booted her shoes off, which landed with a satisfying thump. Right now, a little TV sounded a lot more fun than doing a load of laundry or emptying the dishwasher. She grabbed the remote off of her bedside table, pointed it toward the TV, and hit the power button.

The local news came on. She recognized one of the women sitting behind the anchor desk. Daisy had met Harley on a flight before, but they'd never actually had a conversation.

"The Sharks are preparing for Sunday night's nationally televised game, but that's not the only thing on their minds. Sources have told KIXI that the author who came forward to claim responsibility for publishing a racy book about the Sharks backup quarterback, Grant Parker, is not the actual author. We tried to obtain more information from the self-publishing service in question, but they cite confidentiality issues. We'll have more news as it becomes available."

A dark-haired female news anchor's smile didn't quite reach her eyes. "Why should Sharks fans want to know who's responsible for the book?"

"The Sharks' PR group has spent years assuring fans that Grant Parker is a great role model for their kids. What if he's not? And how will this affect the Sharks' locker room? You have to admit it's juicy."

Chapter Nine

GRANT STROLLED INTO the Sharks' locker room the morning after his date with Daisy to a knot of teammates waiting for him at his locker.

"Guys," he said. "What's up?"

"You had dinner with Daisy the flight attendant last night," Clay Morrison said.

He didn't bother asking them how they found out. Social media never slept.

"Yes, I did. Is there a problem?" Grant said.

"I'd like to take her out," Clay said.

"Maybe you should start shaving first," Seth Taylor called out from across the room.

The normally easygoing Clay clenched his hands into fists. Grant watched fresh color spreading up his neck, his ears, and his cheekbones.

"I was shaving before your balls dropped," Clay snapped. "Fuck off, Taylor."

The two men met in the middle of the locker room seconds later. Seth poked a finger into Clay's chest.

"You might want to settle down, son."

"I don't think so," Clay said.

Caleb hurried over to grab Clay's arm. "Take it easy," the big man said. "You too, Seth."

"She doesn't wear a ring," Clay said.

"Maybe she's not into guys," one of the wide receivers called out.

"She went out with Parker, didn't she?"

"I'm still here," Grant said. He kicked his street shoes off and dumped them into the bottom of his locker.

"How'd it go?" Kade Harrison said.

"None of your business," Grant said.

He grabbed some men's leggings off one of the hangers in his locker and struggled into them. If he kept his muscles warm while he ran, it really cut down on cramping and injuries later. Right now, though, he'd like to get his ass out of here so he didn't have to recap his date for these knuckleheads. He pulled on shorts over the leggings, stripped off the shirt he wore, and grabbed for a Heat Gear T-shirt and a hoodie. Late fall in Seattle wasn't typically the nuts-freezing cold other cities in the league suffered with, but the wind off the lake penetrated his bones. He'd like to get a couple of miles in before he had to lift and not expire from hypothermia.

"It didn't go well, then," Seth said. "He's telling you there's a chance, Morrison."

"I don't think so," Grant said.

"Well, then, maybe you should enlighten us. Did you get to second base?" Kade said.

"Don't talk shit about Daisy. She takes good care of us," Kyle called out. "Maybe we should ask Parker if he asked her out again instead."

Fifty-two sets of eyes swiveled to focus on Grant Parker.

"And?" Zach Anderson said.

"We have another date next week," Grant said. He pulled the hoodie on and grabbed for his headphones. His teammates nodded at each other. He'd asserted himself, and now every guy on the team knew she was off-limits.

"It's back to trolling the bars for you, Morrison," Taylor said.

DAISY'S WEEK PASSED in a whirlwind of trips to various West Coast airports and counting the days until she would see Grant again. She hadn't had a chance to talk with him during last Friday's team flight, but he sent her a text the next morning.

Looking forward to Thursday

She was, too.

She awoke from a fitful sleep in the wee hours of Thursday morning. The quarter moon made a pattern on her bedroom wall through the blinds covering the window. She'd felt a little weird earlier in the evening but had hoped it would pass if she got a good night's sleep. It appeared she was wrong.

She'd kicked all of her blankets off, her stomach hurting. Daisy reached up to feel her forehead; it felt unusually warm as she shivered with cold. She tried to sit up to grab the blankets, but it wasn't a good move.

Daisy threw herself off the bed and ran to the bathroom.

Ten minutes later, she was lying on the bathroom tile and scrabbling around for anything to wipe her mouth with when she heard Catherine's voice.

"Are you okay, love? Do you need help?"

"I'm sick. Don't come in here," Daisy said.

"Don't be silly. I got a flu shot. Everyone who didn't was sick on my flight the other day."

Everyone was sick on Daisy's flight the other day too, but she was hoping it was a fluke.

Catherine stepped over Daisy and rinsed the washcloth that was always on the bathroom sink. "How about a washcloth?"

"Thank you," Daisy muttered as Catherine put the now-damp washcloth into her hand. "Please tell me I'm not dying."

"You're not dying." Catherine crouched down next to Daisy and felt her forehead. "You have a fever, though. Good job on making it to the loo in time."

"Yay, me," Daisy said. The bathroom floor was freezing, but she was close to the toilet. Right now, it was the little things. Maybe Catherine would bring her a blanket if she asked nicely. "Do I have to get up?"

"Let's get you off that floor. Come on."

"But it's close to the toilet." Daisy wondered if there was some kind of connection between barfing and the tear ducts. She wiped her mouth and flipped the washcloth over so she could wipe her face with it. She was a tear-dripping mess.

"I can get you a basin," Catherine said. She reached under Daisy's arms and pulled her to her feet. After some frantic gesturing by Daisy, Catherine left the bathroom when the inevitable happened again.

"Are you sure I'm not dying?" Daisy moaned.

Catherine pressed the freshly re-rinsed washcloth into Daisy's hand. "You're not going to die. I'll get you a basin, you're going back to bed, and we're calling Operations to tell them you're ill."

"I can't go out with Grant later if I'm barfing."

"Are you always this whiny when you're sick?" Catherine teased. "Come on, you big baby. Let me get your blankets sorted. You'll feel much better when you're tucked up in bed."

Half an hour later, Daisy had changed her clothes, was back in bed with a large and empty plastic bowl, and had made her call to the airline's Operations group. She wasn't the only one who was sick. She wasn't thrilled to be feeling like crap, but even worse—she wouldn't be seeing Grant later.

After a lot of thought, she'd decided she was going to tell him she'd written *Overtime Parking*. No matter how many times she tried to tell herself he wasn't going to find out that she'd written the book, it was inevitable. One of those trashy tabloid TV shows managed to get the woman who claimed she was the author to submit to a polygraph test. She didn't pass, so the search was back on. Daisy couldn't figure out why there was so much curiosity about her real identity. The book just kept selling.

Grant had to be getting a ton of crap over this. It wasn't his fault. She should have the guts to tell him what she did.

Catherine bustled into Daisy's room again. "Okay. Declan says his mom used to give him this when he was sick." She put a can of 7-Up on Daisy's nightstand and shuddered a little. "It's not diet. And I made you some toast with butter."

"No Marmite?"

"I was afraid you'd throw it at me." Catherine sat down next to her on the bed. "You can try it when you think you might keep it down."

"Maybe next week."

"Try the drink first. Sip slowly." Catherine reached out to pat Daisy's hand. "Are you going to text Grant?"

"Later." She let out a sigh. "I was going to tell him when I saw him tonight."

"Are you sure about that?"

"I feel so guilty. I didn't mean for this to happen. It's just a goofy thing I wrote. I had no idea people would freak out so badly over it." At first, she'd thought he might think it was funny, but after getting to know him a little better, she realized he'd more likely be bothered by the fact that it had sparked a media frenzy.

"Maybe you can see him later this week, when you're feeling better," Catherine said. "Maybe he'll think it's cute."

"Maybe he'll think I'm a crazy stalker."

"He might surprise you," Catherine said.

GRANT OPENED HIS eyes to the overcast, grayish light of a late fall Thursday in Seattle. He'd spent the past several hours lying on his bathroom floor between bouts of illness. It wasn't sexy or comfortable, but it was a hell of a lot easier than running for the toilet. When he wasn't ill, he was burning up with fever.

He'd also awoken during the night in a panic after a horrible realization. He'd figured out why Harley McHugh looked so familiar to him: he'd slept with her once about two years ago. She'd been in a bar, he'd been a bit lonely, and she'd made it clear she wanted him.

He'd all but run out of her apartment when he discovered she liked to bite during sex. Not a love nip. An actual bite. He'd reached up to feel the bite on his shoulder and saw blood on his fingertips. He shuddered just thinking about it. He usually had no problem with women who were somewhat aggressive in bed, but he drew the line when a tetanus shot was required afterward.

He should send some kind of thank-you note to the builder for the heated floors in his condo, which kept him from freezing to death. He managed to pull himself off of the tile floor, crawl into his bedroom, and grab his cell phone out of his pants pocket. He hit Contacts and stared at a number. His parents were in Texas. Dialing 911 might be a slight overreaction. He knew he needed a little help right now though. There was only one person in the Seattle area who wasn't going to flip out at a six sixteen AM phone call, and Grant touched the phone receiver icon by his name.

"Talk to me," Tom Reed said as he answered his cell phone.

"It's Parker."

"I know that. Your face popped up on my screen. What's up? You don't sound good."

"I've been throwing up since two o'clock or so this morning."

"And you're alone in your condo," Tom said. "Let me get the team doc on the phone. He'll want to come over and take a look at you. I'd bring you some juice and stuff myself, but I don't want my kids to get this. Want me to grab some stuff at the store and leave it with your building's concierge?"

"I can handle it," Grant said, which was a lie. If he could handle it, he wouldn't have been calling another person before seven AM. "Actually…I feel like shit."

"I'll bet," Tom said. "Get your ass back into bed, and I'll have someone over there as soon as possible. And if you need me to go get you some juice or Gatorade or some damn thing, call me back."

"Hey, Reed," Grant said.

"What?"

"Are you busy this afternoon?"

"Hell no. What's up?"

"Will you go to Children's and visit with a few of the kids? They'll be disappointed."

Most of Grant's teammates visited the local children's hospital on Tuesdays, their day off. He'd called the nurses and made a special arrangement to stop by after practice and before he was supposed to see Daisy. Grant hadn't been able to make it last Tuesday, having spent the day at the practice facility with his coach and the Sharks' general manager.

Tom Reed was going to be out for two weeks with broken ribs. As a result, Grant was now the Sharks' starting quarterback. He'd been studying for and working toward this day for several years, but he was rattled. Grant wasn't Tom. He wondered what was going to happen when the Sharks fans figured that one out too. He'd do his best every time he stepped onto a football field, but he wasn't going to be the lightning-bolt-for-an-arm thriller the fan base had been watching for over a decade now.

Getting the starting job was a vote of confidence from the Sharks' front office, but they had already talked about wanting him to spend more time with Reed this season. It wasn't that Grant didn't know the playbook, and he could drop back and throw a perfect spiral. But he knew the coaches were hoping that Tom's All-Pro personality might rub off a little on the introverted and more cautious Grant.

Grant hoped so too.

"Just when I thought you were a selfish bastard, you go and say something like this," Tom joked. "I'll be there. And take it easy. Call if you need anything else."

"I'll do that. Thanks for visiting the kids."

"It's my pleasure."

Tom hung up his phone. Grant knew he was probably dehydrated. He also knew he had some Gatorade in the refrigerator, but he wasn't sure he could stand up long enough to go and get it.

His phone rang again. He hit Answer.

"Hey, Parker. Reed called me. I'm on my way over. Can you walk to your front door to let me in?" the team doctor said.

"I'll crawl if I have to. I feel like I got hit by a truck. I don't get it. I had a flu shot."

"Sometimes the shot doesn't cover every strain of flu," the doctor said. "I'll be there in fifteen minutes. Don't worry; you're going to live."

"Thanks, Dr. Mike."

Two hours later, Dr. Mike drove Grant to the emergency room of Evergreen Hospital. Grant wasn't overly fond of hospital stays as a rule, but he was willing to try almost anything by now. According to the doctor, he needed IV fluids and something to bring his fever down. On his way out the door, he'd jammed his cell phone and the charger into his pocket with his wallet. He needed to text Daisy, since he wasn't going to be able to make their date.

What if she was as sick as he was?

LYING IN BED, Daisy heard her cell phone chirp with a new text message. It was probably Catherine wondering if she was still among the living. She reached out to grab the phone.

It was Grant Parker. *Tell me you're not sick too.*

Chapter Ten

GRANT SPENT THE next day and a half in a hospital bed. He'd had the flu before, but it had been nothing like this. Even his hair hurt. Anything else but Gatorade and water came right back up. The nurse had tried giving him some low-sodium chicken broth last night, which hadn't worked especially well. The doctor who visited twice a day had already told him he wasn't playing Sunday afternoon. He'd lost seven pounds and was as weak as a newborn kitten. Worse than the illness was the knowledge that Daisy was sick too. She'd replied to his text, admitting she also had the flu.

The nurse was a big Sharks fan and had let him keep his smartphone. He clicked on Daisy's cell number.

"Hello?" she said. Her voice sounded a little weak. "Grant, is that you?"

"It sure is," he said. He settled back against the pillows in his hospital bed. "How are you doing? Do you feel any better?"

"It's nice to talk with you." He could almost see her smile through the phone. "I feel better than I did yesterday. That's good, isn't it?"

"I'm glad you're feeling a little better." He pulled in a breath. "Hey. Let's have dinner next week. What do you think?"

He was rewarded with the sound of her laughter. "Are you sure? Maybe we should both quit hurling before we have another date."

"I'm fine," he assured her. "You pick. El Gaucho or the Space Needle."

He could hardly keep his eyes open due to needing yet another nap, but he belatedly remembered that a woman afraid of heights might not be thrilled about having dinner six hundred feet in the air.

He heard a little snickering laugh from Daisy. He wondered what he could do to make her laugh some more.

"How about a restaurant on Earth?" she said.

He laughed out loud. He still felt like shit, but at least she was well enough to make jokes.

"You're on," he said. "I'll text you."

"That'll be great," she said. "I hope you'll feel better soon."

"I will," he said. "Are you flying on Sunday?"

"I have to see the doctor before they'll let me go back to work," she said.

He tried to make his voice as casual as possible. His heart was banging around in his chest like the drumline at a Sharks game.

"Perfect. I'm not sure I'll be playing yet, but how about coming to my game? I'll leave some suite tickets at Will Call for you and your roommate. If you're still too sick, don't worry about it. I'd really like it if you were there, though." If he got on the field, it would be the biggest day of his life so far, and he wanted her to be a part of it. "If you can't do it, don't worry about it."

He heard a little gasp. "I'd love to be there. Thank you for asking me."

He didn't want to hang up, but he didn't want to overstay his welcome, either. Hopefully, he hadn't scared her off. He fell asleep shortly afterward. He woke up the next morning to see that he must have been texting in his sleep. There was a long string of emojis on his phone's screen. Maybe he'd fallen asleep with his thumb on the keys or something. Luckily for him, Daisy assured him via text that she found this hilarious.

He returned from the men's room to find a square glass vase filled with bright, colorful flowers, a six-pack of Gatorade, and a card. He tore it open.

Sorry it's not beer, she'd written. *Get well soon. Go Sharks! —Daisy*

Grant loved the flowers, but he loved the note even more. He had a game to get well for, but the thought of another date with Daisy was definitely on his mind too.

He grabbed his phone and fired off another text to her.

Thanks for the flowers and the drinks. We'll get beer soon.

His QB coach sauntered into the room a minute or so later and parked himself in the recliner next to Grant's bed. "Hey, Parker."

"Hey, Carl. Nice to see you."

Grant edged his ass onto the hospital bed while a nurse held the IV pole. The nurse settled the blankets over him once more, fluffed his pillows, and glanced over at the coach.

"He needs his rest," she said to Carl.

"Got it."

Her eyes narrowed. "I mean it."

Carl raised one eyebrow. "I heard you the first time."

Despite the fact that Carl had been assured that Grant was no longer contagious because he didn't have a fever, he wore a paper mask over his nose and mouth and latex gloves.

"Looks like you have an admirer," Carl said as Grant propped the little card up where he could see it.

"Just a friend," Grant said.

"Of course she is." He had braced an electronic tablet on the rolling table next to Grant's bed and hit Play so Grant could watch yet more game film on the Minutemen.

"This will come in handy the next time we play them," Carl said.

"I'll be on the field Sunday." Grant was playing even if he was missing a limb. He wasn't going to lie there and watch the third-string QB make a mess of things.

"You can't stand up and walk across the room. Johnny will handle it."

Johnny Freeman was a Heisman Trophy winner runner-up, QB of a national championship college team, and had done nothing so far in the NFL. The Sharks were his third team in three seasons. Everyone had to start somewhere, but the typical response to being traded once and outright released last season would have been *I'd better work harder.* Johnny relied too much on his natural talents and not enough on learning the Sharks' playbook. Coach thought he could fix what was wrong, but Grant knew it wasn't going to happen, and now wasn't the time to discuss it.

"No. He's never taken a snap in a pro game. I'll be there."

"Parker, we can't take the risk. Johnny will start, and Terrell will back him up as the emergency QB."

"I promised Reed," Grant said.

"Reed will survive," Carl muttered, just as the man himself breezed through the door.

"Talking about me, Coach? Hey, Parker." Tom Reed moved closer to Grant's bed and fist-bumped with him. "Got some stuff for you from the kids."

"Your kids?"

"The kids at Children's." He reached into a plastic bag and started pulling out pieces of construction paper, which he handed to Grant. "I told them you were sick."

The pieces of paper were crayoned drawings. Some were obviously meant to look like him wearing his Sharks uniform and holding a football. Some were stick figures with misshapen letters and numbers. Grant picked one out of a pile that had a heart in the middle of the page. "Get well soon. I love you, Emma," with Xs and Os for kisses and hugs.

Maybe the lack of solid food was getting to him. He fought back tears as he looked at the misshapen heart, imperfectly colored but drawn with love. He knew Emma. Someone must have helped her write the card. After she'd had open heart surgery a few weeks ago, she'd played tic-tac-toe with him. Of course, he let her win, and her smile was radiant. She'd also told him she wanted to marry him when she grew up.

"Are you sure? You might meet someone you like better than me," he'd said.

Her amber-brown eyes sparkled. "Nope. I wanted to marry my daddy, but he says I can't. He has to be my daddy. So I'm going to marry you."

Grant had reached out to take her small hand in his and kissed the back of it, being careful not to dislodge the IV needle taped there. "Well, then, I accept."

The next time he went to see her, he brought her some flowers, one of his away jerseys for a pretend wedding dress, and one of those rings with a diamond made of hard candy. It was too big for her finger, but she didn't seem to mind.

The last time he went to visit Emma, he couldn't get in to see her. She'd had another surgery and was in quarantine for some reason. He'd left a frilly Sharks hair thing for her with the nurse. He hoped she'd be well enough soon to wear it to one of his games.

Emma knew there were more surgeries ahead as she got older. Every time he'd seen her, though, she'd been smiling. And she wasn't scared of what was ahead. She was going to get through it. He could follow her example.

Despite the fact that he'd spent the past two days puking until there was nothing left, he was getting his ass out of this bed. He wasn't Tom Reed, but the team needed him. He was running onto the field with Emma's little drawing folded up in his sock or something. It would bring him luck, and he could tell her about it later.

He reached out for the button that called the nurse.

"What'cha need?" Tom Reed said.

"Food," Grant said.

GRANT HAULED HIMSELF out of a hotel bed in Bellevue on Sunday morning. The Sharks spent the night before every home game there. The team had dinner, a meeting or two, and a chapel service before bed check. He knew there were a few guys who sneaked downstairs to the hotel bar to grab a beer before the coaches did everything but tuck them in for the night. Maybe he'd join them when he didn't feel like he'd been run over by a truck. Still.

Game day had dawned clear and cold. The clear part was good—it would improve the offense's grip on the ball. The cold part wasn't the best; it wasn't great for any athlete's muscles, but at least the team wouldn't have to worry about cramping due to heat-related dehydration.

Grant heaved a sigh of relief. The conditions were almost perfect. He heard his roommate Kevin's deep voice from the other side of the hotel room. Kevin was the Sharks' newest running back. He and Grant had done some extra work this week on handoffs and a couple of trick plays the coaches were holding in reserve just in case. The team's typical starting RB was out with a calf strain. In other words, everyone else was going to have to step up today to match the guy's production. Grant was pretty sure Kevin had his own set of nerves going, but hunger seemed to have won out, at least at the moment.

"It's game day, bro. Let's get our asses downstairs for breakfast," Kevin said.

Grant strolled into the locker room at Sharks Stadium a couple of hours later. He wasn't 100 percent, but he was going to do his best to convince his coaches he was. The somewhat bland food he'd been surviving on since he had left the hospital helped with the other game day problem: nerves.

Players dealt with nerves in a variety of ways. Some threw up, either in the locker room bathroom or on the field itself. Some pulled their headphones on and tuned out everyone else until it was time to take the field. Some sat in front of their locker and said their prayers. Grant had spent years on the sidelines holding a clipboard. By the time he was told to get in there, he didn't have time to get nervous. He relied on the hours of study and practice to get him through. Today, it was all on him, and he hoped the baked chicken breast and brown rice the hotel chef had made for him would stay down. Or in, as the case may be.

After busting his balls about *Overtime Parking*, his coaches and teammates had finally backed off the subject.

Nobody on the team was interested in a distraction this week. He knew that the PR group had released some additional photos of his visits to Children's Hospital and put up a short blog post on the Sharks' website about the kids making cards for him when he wasn't feeling so well.

The front office seemed to believe that the publicity (and the resulting media-driven questions about Grant's private life) would die down after he made his debut as the Sharks' starting QB. At least they hoped it would happen. If he managed to pull off a win, his private life and reputation would be the last thing anyone would be talking about for the rest of the week.

Tom Reed sat down in front of his own locker next to Grant's. He wasn't playing today, but he'd be listening to the coaches' instructions to Grant through an earphone.

"Need a hand with the shirt?" Grant said to him. Getting the long-sleeved T-shirt stamped with the team logo on over the bandaging Reed currently wore might be an interesting feat.

"I'll let you know." Tom glanced over at Grant. "Hey, Parker. Are you sure?" He didn't have to spell out what he was talking about.

"I'll be fine," Grant said. He reached out to grab the long underwear he wore under his uniform when it was colder than a well digger's ass on the field. He checked to see that the wristband with the abbreviated list of plays the coaches had scripted was in his stuff too. He knew what they wanted to do and he had a two-way microphone in his helmet, but it never hurt to have a backup.

"You nervous yet?"

"What do you think?"

Tom reached out to bump fists with Grant. "If you didn't give a shit, you wouldn't be nervous. *Champions* are nervous." He looked at the floor for a few seconds, glanced up, and met Grant's eyes again. "Get your ass out there and take my job."

The locker room was loud with the commotion that ensued when fifty-three guys attempted to get dressed and taped in an hour, but at the moment it came down to two men sitting in front of their lockers, struggling to know what to say to each other.

"Are you sure?"

"Fuck, yeah." Tom swallowed hard. "There's never a good time to walk away. I love this. But I love my wife and my kids more." He let out a long breath. "I mean it. Go out there and earn it. Make me proud."

Grant shuffled his feet a bit. "I'm not you."

Damn right he wasn't. He had the physical attributes, but he didn't have Tom's lightning strike of an arm, his exhaustive knowledge of the Sharks' playbook since the team's inception, or the balls to tell the offensive coordinator and the head coach he was calling his own goddamn game. Grant was good enough to be a starter, but he wasn't good enough to succeed a legend. And he wasn't sure he'd ever be. His game was more about finesse, while Tom's was about gunslinging and going for broke. Grant preferred to pick defenses apart and take calculated risks. Calculated risks tended to cut down on the number of disastrous interceptions, but they didn't make football fans jump out of their seats screaming over a seventy-five-yard Hail Mary or the perfect strike to one of the league's burner-speed wide receivers some dumbass defender left wide open in the end zone.

"And your point? Goddamn it, Parker, you've been here the whole way. Don't be a chickenshit."

Grant knew other guys around the league who had made a run for the starting QB's job. It wasn't pleasant or friendly, especially if they failed. It was a steel-cage death match—two men entered, one man left. Some of the guys who didn't make it continued on another team's sideline, holding a clipboard and collecting a gigantic check each week for doing very little. They were every team's insurance against injuries to the NFL's marquee players. And those marquee players would do anything to undermine the other guy's chances, up to and including playing while hurt so their backup couldn't get out onto the field.

Reed might believe it was time to hang it up. He might want to right now, when he was injured and feeling every day of his age. But he could change his mind at any time, and he might torpedo Grant's career in order to keep the job he couldn't walk away from. It happened in the league every season. Grant didn't want to lose his chance because he'd underestimated the pull of a huge salary for six months' work and international fame.

Tom turned to face Grant and said in a low voice, "I'm giving you a gift. Don't fuck it up."

"Why me?"

"My kid likes you. And no, I'm not buying him one of your jerseys."

"I'll make sure he gets one."

"Nice to see you found your balls, Parker," Tom said. "Make them pay. And kiss my ass."

Reed grinned at him. They bumped fists again. Reed followed the group of guys on injured reserve who would stand on the sidelines during the game out of the locker room.

A few minutes afterward, Grant threw up in a locker room toilet before he ran out onto the field.

Grant tried to put it all out of his mind—Tom's comments and the fact Daisy was in the team's suite. She'd sent him a text this morning to let him know she would be there. He would see her after the game, but he wanted to impress her. His parents had also made an exception to their rule and decided to come to a Sunday game; they'd arrived in Seattle late last night with a member of the congregation who happened to own a private jet. He'd been getting ready for bed check at the hotel last night when his cell rang.

"Hello, son," his father said. "We're in Seattle. We'll see you tomorrow."

"You're here?" Grant said. He had a keen eye for the obvious. At the same time, a thrilled grin had spread across his face. His parents wanted to see him start for the Sharks.

"Of course we're here. We wouldn't miss this." His dad paused for a moment. "We might need some tickets."

"I'll make sure they're at Will Call for you. Dad, I'm really happy that you and Mom are here. Maybe we could meet up for dinner or something after the game." He could hear the low voices and slamming doors in the hallway; the coaches were coming around to make sure everyone was in their room for the night. He had to get off the phone, but there were a million other things he wanted to say. Hopefully, he could say them tomorrow.

"I'll see you then, Dad. I have to go."

"We're proud of you, son," his father said. "We'll be cheering you on."

Oddly enough, they'd insisted on sitting in the stands instead of the team's suite. Grant couldn't think about his mom's reaction to the language of many of the Sharks' fans or the fact many of those fans liked to drink while they were enjoying their Sunday afternoon. He had a game to win.

The first twenty plays went as well as he'd expected. The Sharks were attempting to establish a running game along with some short-yardage passing. They were mixing it up enough to keep the Minutemen's defense guessing— and frustrated. He scrambled a couple of times when the receivers he was most interested in were covered and found a surprisingly large number of coverage holes in New England's secondary. Ahhh, he could work with this.

The adrenaline of actually being on the field with seventy thousand screaming fans in the stands gave him the extra shot of confidence and energy he needed. He spotted a black and teal uniform in the end zone, gave the ball a bit of extra zip, and watched as Kyle Carlson stretched to grab it out of the hands of New England's cornerback. Touchdown.

He ran to congratulate his wide receiver, who was shaking hands with his teammates. Grant jumped into midair with Kyle, and they bumped hips and headed back to the sidelines. As they watched the kicker attempt the extra point, Grant was glad he had a few minutes to take a breath while he chatted with the QB coach on the next series of plays.

New England seemed sluggish and confused by the Sharks' defense, which was already having a career afternoon. The first play by the Minutemen's offense yielded a botched snap that turned into a safety. The Sharks had the ball back after another kickoff, and Reed slapped Grant on the ass as he ran past him onto the field.

"You lucky bastard. Pour it on," Tom shouted.

Oh, he'd pour it on, all right. Grant wondered what the hell was going on with the Minutemen's defense, who seemed to spend more time arguing with each other about the coverage and less bothering to work with their teammates. The Sharks' offensive line was taking advantage of their confusion by keeping their pass rush away from Grant. The first snap was a handoff to Kevin, who managed to run through a blocking hole the width of a school bus. Kevin made it to the one-yard line.

The crowd went wild. Grant could hear multiple voices in his headset—the head coach's, the offensive coordinator's, even Tom's. "Run it in," his coach barked.

"Watch their free safety," the offensive coordinator said.

"Step on their necks," Tom said.

Two and a half hours later, the game was over. The Sharks had won, 35–3. Grant pulled off his helmet and went to find the Minutemen's QB to shake hands. He was still trembling with adrenaline and the high of hearing people chanting his name. He hoped this was just the beginning of the best day of his life so far. The sun descended behind the arch of Sharks Stadium, and the Minutemen's QB appeared out of the gathering late-fall twilight.

"Good game," Grant said and extended his hand to shake.

The opposing QB grabbed his hand and pulled him into a hug. "We'll beat you next time, bro."

"I don't think so," Grant said.

"We'll see about that," the other guy said as he moved away from Grant to hug another one of the Sharks.

Media clustered around Grant as the Sharks' sideline reporter reached out to tug on his jersey sleeve. "Would you answer a few questions for me?" she said.

"Yeah. Right here?"

"I need to upload comments to the network," another reporter said.

"I'm on deadline," someone in the back called out.

The circle of reporters around Grant got larger. He was typically ignored after games—after all, he'd spent the time on the sidelines.

Today, he'd led his team to victory.

He glanced over the heads of the reporters to Tom Reed, who appeared to be laughing at Grant's current plight. He had a crowd around him too, and Grant could almost bet what was being said: How did Tom feel about standing on the sidelines while his backup went twenty-two for twenty-nine, passing for 250 yards and three touchdowns? Also, when was he planning on being back on the field again? Fans despaired of the fact they didn't get penetrating interview questions, but most players preferred to give the same clichés they'd offered at every interview throughout their careers. Vague and formulaic answers tended to cut down on problems later.

The sideline reporter nodded at her camera guy. Grant saw the bright light over his camera lens come on, and the reporter said, "We're here with Grant Parker. His first start for the Sharks was a success by anyone's standards." She recited the game stats one more time. "How does the first win of the Grant Parker era in Seattle feel?"

She was going for broke on her first question.

"Thanks, but Tom Reed is still our starter."

"We have a source that tells us Reed has passed the torch to you, at least privately. What are your thoughts on that?"

He didn't change his facial expression or his tone of voice, despite the fact that he knew she wanted to keep re-asking the question until she got the reaction she wanted. He wasn't giving it to her.

"Again, Tom Reed is our starter. We're hoping he'll be back on the field soon."

She gave him an almost invisible nod. In other words, she knew that if she didn't get off the subject of Tom and his possible retirement, Grant was walking away from her.

His teammates Kyle and Seth materialized out of the crowd and stood on either side of Grant.

"Good game, huh?" Kyle asked Seth in a loud voice.

"Oh, the best. How about our boy here? The stats looked pretty good today," Seth responded while slapping Grant on the back.

"We shouldn't tell him that," Kyle said. "He'll get a big head."

"I understand he's big all over," Seth responded. "It's true, ladies. Plus, he's single."

"Our man needs a date. Send your applications to Sharks headquarters," Kade Harrison chimed in. They both knew he was dating Daisy. As usual, his teammates were giving him shit. They wouldn't bother if they didn't accept him. He tried to look pissed, but he felt a smile breaking through.

Several of the guys had drifted over to the knot of reporters and were adding their own opinions on Grant's on-field performance, the fact he could use a date, and other conversational openings that had nothing to do with the current interview that had broken down in complete chaos. He hoped Daisy wasn't watching the TV coverage in the suite.

Derrick Collins's voice boomed out. "He's partial to blondes. I heard he likes chocolate chip cookies too."

"Hell yeah," Drew McCoy said. He reached out to ruffle Grant's hair. "Milk and cookies, puppies, and walks on the beach. He's all about that."

The group of men dissolved into laughter, shoving and fist-bumping.

"We're all about helping him get laid," Clay Morrison said.

"That's right. We're givers," Derrick said.

The sideline reporter who'd been attempting to interview Grant pulled the microphone away from Grant's face. She turned her back to the joking football players and looked into the camera.

"Congratulations to Grant Parker on his first win for the Sharks. Back to you, guys." She gave Grant another nod as she turned to face him. "Nice to talk with you."

"Thank you," Grant said.

He reached out to shake hands with her. Post-game interviews never did it for him in the first place, and his teammates' photobombing was actually funny. As long as he didn't get fined or bitched out by the head coach for the blown interview, he didn't care if the media walked away from him.

He knew he should try to make their jobs easier and tell the guys to back off. He'd gone from being ignored by the media for years to being the flavor of the week. Suddenly, everyone cared what he had to say. Maybe he didn't need them so much.

"You're leaving so soon?" Kyle asked the reporter who'd been attempting to ask Grant questions. The grin on his face was a bit calculating. "Don't you want to talk with us? We're interesting too."

"We've got lots to say," Seth said. "We're full of—what do you all call it? Colorful commentary? We've got plenty to go around. Want a taste?"

While the initial reporter stalked away with her cameraman, the other reporters kept filming and recording. They were hoping for something explosive. Mostly, they were getting an increasing number of Grant's teammates elbowing into the camera shot and demanding to be interviewed as well.

Four of the offensive linemen arrived on the scene.

"Guys. *Guys.* Coach is looking for us. You can flirt with the media later," Clay said. "You know how much he hates to be kept waiting."

"He can't give that post-game speech to an empty locker room," another of Grant's teammates said.

"Let's get out of here. See you fellas later," Derrick said to the media. He reached out to wrap a big arm around Grant's shoulders. "Places to go, things to do."

WHILE GRANT SPENT his day leading the offense up and down the field, Daisy and Catherine spent their afternoon in the Sharks' suite. She'd never been in a stadium suite before. With the price tag per ticket, she probably wouldn't be again. The team's suite was larger than her townhouse. It boasted a view of the team's fifty-yard line and was highlighted with recessed pin lights, wall sconces, and pendant lamps she was sure were made with Chihuly glass. A framed, signed Matt Stephens jersey hung on one wall, while another wall was dominated by a framed panoramic photo of Sharks Stadium during a game. She glanced around at handwoven wool rugs covering hardwood floors, custom cabinetry, and stone counters in the bar area and the island in a fully stocked kitchen area. The suite's windows slid open to allow for listening to the crowd's noise or breathing in the crisp fall air. Sumptuous leather chairs offered comfortable seating for conversation or watching the game. A clear glass door led to the private outdoor seating area. More chairs were pushed under a long metal table outside, perfect for resting food, beverages, and smartphones on.

A bartender stood ready to mix or pour one's favorite beverage behind the bar. Nothing as tacky as a tip jar marred the perfect wood and granite surface. Daisy was glad she had a little folding money in her purse. She could slip him some cash when she ordered a Diet Coke or something.

Servers dressed in Sharks-logo polo shirts and black pants were already circulating through the crowd with appetizers. A stone-topped serving area ran the length of the wall as well. Chafing dishes full of food were set up, along with team-logo china, flatware, and cloth napkins.

"Would you like me to fill a plate for you?" one of the servers asked Daisy.

"No, thanks. I can do it," she said. Catherine was already sitting in the outside seating area with a strawberry-blonde-haired woman dressed in a Brandon McKenna jersey, jeans, huge diamond stud earrings, and a killer pair of Louboutin shoes. Catherine had evidently recognized her from a flight. "Thanks for asking."

"Let me know if there's anything I can get for you," the server said. She moved away to ask a group of women (who were dressed in head-to-toe Sharks wear) if they'd like some food. Daisy had thought a pair of jeans and a plain blue hoodie would be an acceptable thing to wear to a Sharks game. She was wrong.

A medium-height, attractive blonde woman in a Matt Stephens jersey, a high ponytail, jeans, and an enormous diamond ring on the third finger of her left hand dashed into the suite. Cries of "Amy!" rang out as about half the women in the room rushed at once to hug her.

Daisy turned to the heavily pregnant woman standing next to her. "Do you know her?"

"Oh, hell yeah. My husband works for her husband." The woman smiled. "Amy's husband owns the team."

Amy Stephens hugged her way through the crowd. She stopped in front of Daisy and reached out to hug her too. "You must be Daisy. Matt said you'd be here today. He's also told me all about you, especially the fact our son loves you. I'm so glad you're here."

"Jonathan's adorable," Daisy said. "We had so much fun the last time he was on the team flight."

"I'm a little biased, but I'd have to agree. He's my love-bug," Amy said.

"Matt talks about you and your kids all the time."

"It's all lies," Amy joked. "Do you like margaritas?" At Daisy's nod, she glanced over to catch the bartender's eye. "Two margaritas, please. No salt." She leaned over to talk into Daisy's ear. "You'll need a drink before this starts. Trust me."

"I'm not sure what to expect. I don't watch a lot of football."

"I heard that too."

Amy hugged the woman standing next to Daisy and said, "How are you doing, Delisa? It's good to see you."

"The baby's kicking a lot, but I'll be fine." She let out a sigh. "One more month to go. He's going to be a line-backer like his dad."

Amy caught the bartender's eye once more and said, "Would you make a virgin margarita for Delisa, please?" The guy gave her a nod.

Amy grabbed their drinks, palmed some cash to the bartender for a tip, and reached out to take Delisa's arm. "Come on, ladies. Let's go sit with Emily. This could be quite an afternoon."

"Damn right. DeAndre was pacing the floor at our house yesterday," Delisa said. "He needs to run off some energy."

Catherine glanced up when Amy, Daisy, and Delisa settled in the row of seats behind them. "Remember my telling you about the adorable twins on my flight a month or so ago? Emily's their mom and Amy's sister."

"Hopefully, everyone's recovered," Emily said as she extended her hand to shake Daisy's. "I had things for the kids to do, but by about hour five, they were a little bored. Our boys don't like to sit still for long. They're just like their father."

"They were so cute. No problem at all," Catherine said. "I have to tell you I fell a little bit in love with them."

"You are really nice. I'm sure the passengers are still talking about the twins trying to help you all do your job by passing out the snacks. Corralling them again was quite a project."

"It's hard to resist a couple of angelic-looking little blond boys telling you that if you don't eat your dinner, you won't get dessert," Catherine said.

"They only look like angels," Emily said. "Like I said, they're just like Brandon. And let me tell you what my husband was doing while our boys were terrorizing the other passengers—"

"He was taking a nap with baby Charlotte, wasn't he?" Amy said.

"Of course he was. She has him wrapped around her little finger. Wait until she's older and learns the words Nordstrom and Tiffany. She's going to put a dent in Daddy's bank accounts." Emily's voice dropped. "She's just like me."

"Matt does that too. Jonathan can be racing through the house at top speed making a ton of noise, and I'll find Matt and our daughter, Jessica, asleep on the couch, asleep in the chair, whatever," Amy said. "Then he wakes up and calls out, 'Hey, Jon. Knock it off,' and our son stops whatever he's doing to crawl into Daddy's lap too."

"Daddy time," Emily sighed. "It's like a miracle."

DAISY STILL FELT a bit weak from her adventures with the flu, but she got to her feet when Grant and his teammates ran out onto the field. She thought Grant glanced up to the suite area, but she couldn't be sure. Just in case, she waved at him.

The game was a blur. As she'd told Grant, she didn't know a lot about football. Some of the women in the suite appeared to be watching intently. Others were milling around. It seemed most of them wanted to talk with Amy, and Amy introduced Daisy.

"Daisy is Grant Parker's date."

A tall blonde with too much makeup on couldn't hide her surprise. "I didn't know he was dating anyone."

A short brunette wearing the biggest set of diamond stud earrings Daisy had ever seen gave her a pasted-on smile. "How nice. Great to meet you." She waited until she thought Daisy was talking with someone else, caught the blonde's eye, and rolled hers.

Either Grant was not a favorite, or there was some sort of problem. Daisy waited until the crowds drifted away to load up on more food and drink at halftime. Maybe she could ask Amy what was wrong. She sat down in the chair next to her again.

"Amy, may I ask you a question?"

"Of course you can. Want me to explain some of what Grant's been doing on the field?" She patted Daisy on the back. "Stick with me. I'll have you calling plays and reading defenses in no time flat."

Daisy knew Amy was teasing her, but her expression was warm.

"I'd love to take you up on that," Daisy said.

"I'll tell you a secret," Amy said. She leaned closer. "You don't have to know everything to enjoy the game. But I don't think this has anything to do with what's on the field. Am I right?"

"I don't mean to sound like I'm still in elementary school, but what the hell is up with some of these women?" Daisy said in a low voice.

"Grant's dated a lot. He's probably had drinks or dinner with some of those women before. He didn't choose them. Now they're with someone else, and they're jealous."

"Should I be worried?"

"No. You are the first woman he's given suite tickets to since he signed with Seattle. You have nothing to worry about."

"Ever?"

"Ever," Amy said. "Ignore them. And let's have fun."

The idea that she might be special to him warred with the notion that Grant may have felt sorry for her because she'd gotten so sick after their first date. She'd drive herself nuts if she kept puzzling over it. Maybe she should sip her drink, eat some wings, and get over herself.

THE SHARKS' COACH outdid himself with his post-game motivational speech. Grant was used to standing in a locker room with a bunch of sweaty, half-dressed guys while a coach ran through a litany of sports clichés, but today was one for the ages. Coach Clark talked about how the season had gone so far. It had been two steps forward, one step back. The team would celebrate a great win. One week later, they'd lose due to stupid (and preventable) errors.

"Do you want to go home after the last game this season and know you didn't give it your best? Do you want to wake up in the middle of the night on December twenty-ninth and realize you wasted your season because you weren't all in? Do you give a damn about anything besides your next contract and endorsement money?" The coach paused to take a deep breath. "If you're in, I'd like to see it. And it'll show on the scoreboard." His eyes moved slowly around the circle of men surrounding him. "Are you in? I want to know. If you're not, if you're not willing to give the rest of the season everything you have and a little more, I don't want you here. If you don't give a shit, you can leave now." He nodded at the locker room door.

A few seconds of silence followed his comments. Grant and Tom glanced at each other. Tom's lips curled into a smile. He gave Grant a barely there nod. *Step up, asshole*, Tom's eyes said.

Grant stepped toward his coach. "I'm in," he said. He stretched out one hand to his teammates. His coach gave him the nod. He'd shown the rest of the team he was willing to lead them with one small gesture.

"I'm in too," Zach Anderson said.

"I'm in, goddamn it," Derrick Collins said as he grabbed onto his teammates' hands.

"I'm in," Drew McCoy said.

Seth Taylor almost knocked Drew over as he stretched a hand out and tried to yank his underwear on at the same time. "I'm in. For life."

Kyle Carlson strolled in from the showers in nothing but a towel. "I'm in too."

Grant glanced around at his teammates pushing and shoving to get to the front of the circle, grabbing their teammates' hands and calling out that they were in. After a lifetime of feeling like he stood on the sidelines watching everyone else, he'd stepped into the game. Maybe it was corny, but he didn't feel quite so alone anymore. They had a common purpose. And he was one of them.

He felt guys behind him put one hand on his shoulder. They wanted to be included in what was happening too.

Joining in was as easy as reaching out. Maybe he could try reaching out in other areas of his life, as well.

The fifty-three players for the Seattle Sharks surrounded their coach as he shouted, "You're in, huh? You'd better be. We're going to win it all. And the work starts now."

The noise was deafening as fifty-four men clapped, shouted, stomped their feet, and whistled their approval.

Chapter Eleven

GRANT FINALLY MANAGED to pry himself out of the Sharks' locker room almost an hour later. He'd sent Daisy a text telling her he was a bit delayed. *A bit*, hell. Every reporter who hadn't managed to get his or her questions answered on the field after the game had a burning need to talk with him. They all asked the same three or four questions.

His parents were waiting in the hallway outside of the locker room door. It was hard not to notice they stood alone while the families and friends of his teammates surrounded each player who emerged from the locker room with hugs, kisses, and praise. It reminded him of how often he'd stood apart from his teammates in the past. He didn't want to stand alone anymore, with the team or with his parents.

He hadn't seen his parents for almost six months. He'd had organized team activities and training camp and hadn't been able to drop it all and fly to Texas for a week. When he'd asked them if they'd like to visit during training camp and maybe meet some of his teammates' parents and families, they'd said they couldn't leave their congregation for that long.

His dad had all kinds of charisma when he was standing in his pulpit with a Bible in one hand, but he wasn't much for socializing or small talk with those outside of his congregation. His mom had never cared for organized sports. Again, he wished he knew the magic words that would bridge what seemed to be an ever-increasing gulf between him and his parents.

"Mom," he said as he hurried toward her. She reached out to hug him. Over the past couple of years, he'd started noticing how small she felt when he hugged her. She looked the same as always, but she felt different somehow. "I'm so glad you came."

"I'm glad we came too, honey," she said. "You did such a good job today."

"I did my best. Did you have fun?"

"It was very nice. Thank you for the tickets. Someone from the team walked us to our seats and asked if we'd like something to eat or drink. Your dad got some peanuts," she said. "They came back at halftime and asked if we'd like to sit in the suite. We didn't want to bother the other people."

"Mom, you could never be a bother," he said. "Maybe next time you'd like to sit up there? It's nice, and there's free food."

"I'll think about it," his mother said. She kissed his cheek. "We're so proud of you."

He kissed his mother on the cheek, shook hands with his dad, and said, "Thanks for being here today."

His father clasped his shoulder. "Of course we'd be here. You had quite a game."

"It went well," he said. "The other guys really stepped up." They wanted the win as much as he did. He wanted to make sure the coaches wouldn't regret their decision to start him. It was clichéd but true.

He pulled in a breath. "Would you like to go out for dinner before you have to go back? My date is upstairs in the suite, but I could get her and meet you here."

His mother shook her head. His father jumped in.

"It's really nice of you to ask, son, but we're going back home with the guy from my congregation. He offered us a ride. We don't want to be late." His dad patted him on the shoulder again. "Maybe after the season."

"Yes, honey. You're done for the year right after Christmas; maybe you could come and see us for a few days."

He wanted to spend time with Daisy, but he also wanted to talk with his parents some more. It was the biggest day of his life so far. He tried to arrange his face into a neutral expression as he scrambled to think of something else to say. He didn't think it would mean so much that his parents had come to his first game as an NFL starter, but it did. He'd hoped they'd accept his dinner invitation, and he was surprised how hurt he felt.

He'd tried to explain before that the playoffs started the week after the final regular season game was over and that he hoped to be in them. Most NFL players didn't make off-season plans until they knew their teams had been mathematically eliminated from any chance at the playoffs, and some did nothing until the Super Bowl was over but rest and recover. He couldn't leave his team in the lurch, and his parents didn't seem like they wanted to make the extra effort to see him again.

It was weird. He always thought most parents lived to see their kids, even the grown ones. He knew his mother had suffered multiple miscarriages before he was born. Maybe she tried to remain detached in case he didn't make it, either. He was here, though. He was healthy, in his late twenties, someone they could be proud of.

"Do you need me to take you to the airport or anything?" Grant said.

"Oh, no, son. We're meeting Wade outside in ten minutes. He's got a driver. We'll be there in plenty of time," his father assured him. He stuck out his hand again. "You played a great game. We'll see you soon."

Grant walked them down the long corridor to the locker room exit, kissed his mother good-bye again, and watched them drive away with their friend. Even worse than not wanting to have dinner with him was that they showed no curiosity about Daisy.

Out of all the women he'd dated before, Daisy was the only one he wanted to introduce them to. Maybe he'd fly them up when the Sharks played on Monday night later in the season, if Daisy wasn't out of town. Aside from the whole doesn't-go-to-church thing, at the very least, his mom would really like her. She was down-to-earth, smart, funny, and thoughtful. And his parents would be stunned he was with someone like her. He hoped they would think he'd made a good choice.

He reached out to grab the handle of the locker room door and hurried inside. He couldn't wait to see her again.

HE SAW DAISY right away when he walked into the suite ten minutes later, but he shook hands with several former Sharks players first who wanted to make small talk. She glanced at him, caught his eye, and smiled. Several of the players' wives had settled in for another drink while waiting for their guys to get to the team suite. The tall redhead he didn't recognize sitting at their table must have been Daisy's roommate, Catherine.

It looked like he might be taking two women out for dinner tonight instead of just one. Things could be worse, but he wanted to be alone with Daisy.

Grant moved away from the guys and approached Daisy's table. "I'm sorry you had to wait so long," he said.

"Not at all," she assured him. "I'm having a great time, and I've really enjoyed meeting everyone here."

"We don't want her to leave," Amy Stephens said. "How about a hot dog for dinner from the concession stand?"

"We could hang out here for a while, ladies. Brandon's plane is probably landing any minute now at Boeing Field," Emily said. "Does anyone else want another drink?"

"Is Tom on his way?" Megan Reed asked him.

"He was right behind me," Grant said.

Daisy reached back to touch his forearm while nodding at the tall redhead. "Grant, this is my roommate, Catherine."

He shook hands with Catherine. "Great to meet you," he said. "Would you like to join us for dinner? I have a reservation at Skillet Diner in half an hour. It's not formal, but the food's delicious."

"Thank you for the offer, but I have a date tonight. Maybe another time?" Catherine asked. "I drove Daisy here. Will you make sure she gets home?"

"Of course," Grant said. Daisy looked like she was stifling laughter.

Catherine grabbed her handbag and stood up from the table. "Ladies, I need to go change. Thank you for such a great afternoon. If I had known football was this fun, I would have started watching it a long time ago."

"I'll make sure you get tickets the next time we play in Seattle," Grant assured her.

A few minutes later, the suite was invaded by a group of men looking for their wives and girlfriends, and Daisy and Grant walked Catherine to her car. Catherine reached out to hug both of them before she slid behind the wheel of a metallic blue RAV4. They watched her taillights vanish around the corner.

Grant gestured toward a late-model silver Subaru Outback. "That's mine."

Daisy approached his car, and he hurried ahead to open the door for her. She glanced up at him. He saw the slow smile move over her mouth. Her eyes met his, and his heart skipped a couple of beats.

"I haven't had a guy open the door for me since I was in college," she said.

"Maybe you've been hanging around with the wrong guys."

He offered her his hand as she slid into the passenger seat. Her fingers curled around his, and he felt the jolt of happiness from the top of his head to his toes. He settled into the driver's seat, put on his seat belt, and glanced at her. "Ready?"

"Yes, I am."

The post-game traffic had thinned out a bit by the time they arrived in Ballard. The formerly quiet (and primarily Scandinavian) community had transformed into a hipster's haven in the past ten years. Thriving bars, restaurants, and live-music venues drew a younger and more active generation to the neighborhood. The opportunity to live in an area where you could walk to surrounding businesses and activities (and an easy commute to downtown Seattle via mass transit) kept them there. Grant preferred Ballard to the more urban Belltown neighborhood or Pioneer Square. He hoped Daisy would enjoy it too.

"Have you been to Skillet's food truck before?" Daisy said.

"I've been there a few times in the off-season," he said hedgingly. The food truck parked in a lot about a block from his condo on Wednesday afternoons. He'd raced downstairs more than a few times to beat the line of software-company employees looking for Skillet's famous Bacon Jam on a burger. One of the benefits of exercising for a living was the fact he could eat like he had in college and still not gain weight. "Do you go there?"

"I've visited a couple of times," she said. "I talked Catherine into going to Where Ya At Matt's food truck about a month ago. She didn't want to leave." Where Ya At Matt was another Seattle phenomenon—a food truck that served the best of New Orleans Creole cuisine.

"Isn't she British? I thought they hated everything spicy." He softened his comments with a grin.

"Oh, no. She loves Indian curry; she asks for more stars when we go out for Thai food. She decided she loves gumbo. I think the guy who owns the food truck might be kind of in love with her now too."

"How long have you known Catherine?"

"A couple of years. We fly for the same airline. She normally works for international flights, but we were in the crew room at the airport one day at the same time and started talking. She needed a roommate, and I had an extra bedroom," Daisy said. "When she's not flying, she's been seeing a guy who lives in Kirkland off and on for the past several months." Daisy turned a little in the passenger seat to face him. "I think he's going to propose. She'll get married and move out, and nobody will be tormenting me with beans at every meal and blood sausage anymore. She's also into this stuff called Marmite."

"What's Marmite?"

"Yeasty vegetable paste stuff." He could see Daisy shudder despite the darkness, and he had to laugh. "She smears it on toast."

"I guess you don't like it."

"It's an acquired taste."

"You'll miss her, though."

"Like an appendage," Daisy said. "She's the sister I never had. I know we'll still see each other, but it won't be the same."

"My college roommate got married last year. I've known Cam since his freshman year. Now he has a wife and a baby."

"Shocking, isn't it?" Daisy said. She watched the side of Grant's mouth turn up into a smile.

"I know. This adulting stuff is hard." Daisy was so absorbed in staring at him that she hadn't realized they'd arrived in Ballard. Grant pulled into a small parking garage, headed for a marked stall, and turned in. "The restaurant is about half a block away," he said. "Hopefully, we'll get there before the rain starts."

She reached for the handle on the passenger-side door.

"I've got that," he said and hurried around the back of his car to open the door for her. She didn't want him to treat her like she was going to break. She could open her own doors. She could pay for her own dinner, buy her own house, and be her own person. It was nice that he made such an extra effort, though.

He shoved some folding money in the *pay here* parking box and said, "I tried to figure out something more exciting for our date, but the zip line is closed tonight."

"No drag racing?"

He reached out for her hand. It felt so natural to slide her hand inside of his bigger, warmer one. "I saw this thing I still can't believe at the local demolition derby a few years back: jet car barbecue."

Raindrops bounced off of her nose. The few people still on the sidewalk were pulling up the hoods on their jackets or trying to walk beneath the awnings on the buildings. She could see the lit-up restaurant sign ahead.

"What's a jet car barbecue?" He'd gone to a demolition derby? She didn't know there was such a thing in Seattle.

"You know those tricked-out race cars that shoot fire out of the back?"

She was going to have to get out more. "Uh, no," she said.

"They chain up some old, stripped car to the back and hit the gas until it's a smoking wreck."

"What happens then?"

"Everyone watches more of the demolition derby."

"I thought you were going to tell me that they bust out the marshmallows, chocolate bars, and graham crackers."

"Oh, hell no. It's so hot you can feel it from half a mile away. There's plenty of beer, though."

She couldn't tell if he was teasing her or he'd really gone to such a thing. Then again, it didn't matter. He pulled open the door to the restaurant and gestured for her to precede him inside.

The restaurant had a high, exposed beam ceiling and hardwood floors. Lighting was bright, but not annoyingly so. Tables were on one side. A long, winding stainless steel bar with customer seating sat across from them. The décor was modern, casual, and youthful. This wasn't the place one brought Grandma for brunch on Sundays. The scent of food cooking that drifted out of the pass-through window to the kitchen was incredible.

The hostess directed them to a table for two away from the large picture windows that looked out over the street. She stared at Grant for a moment and pursed her lips. "Don't you play for the Sharks?"

"Yes, I do," he said.

"Okay, then," she said. "Your server will be right with you." She spun on one heel and walked away.

"I'm still wondering if that was good or bad," Grant said.

"Maybe she's flirting with you," Daisy said.

"I'd like to flirt with you," he said.

Time seemed to stop while she stared into his dark eyes. He reached out for her hand again. She'd lost interest in the food. It smelled delicious, but this had just gone from a casual dinner out to something a lot more exciting, at least for her.

Whenever she'd pictured spending time with Grant before she'd actually had a conversation with him, he wasn't doing a lot of talking. He was pretty much naked. And they were exploring the limits of what they could do to each other and for how long. She still wanted to do all kinds of things with and to him, but she wasn't positive he wanted the same thing.

He was flirting, he was holding her hand, but he'd acted like a perfect gentleman so far. She didn't think it was a lack of interest in getting busy. Maybe he was shy, or maybe he was saving himself for marriage. They'd kissed each other good-bye in a parking garage last time. Maybe this time, they'd pick somewhere a bit more romantic to make out than the front seat of his car or her porch.

Maybe she should concentrate on enjoying the moment more than worrying about what was going to happen (or not) later.

Daisy glanced at the menu. She wasn't really hungry, but she knew she had to order something. She'd already had drinks earlier, so one glass of wine with her dinner would do. She wasn't flying tomorrow, but she really didn't need to wake up with a hangover atop still feeling a little weird from the flu.

"What looks good?" he asked. He squeezed her hand. She squeezed back.

"It all does," she said. She wasn't necessarily talking about the food.

He laid his menu back down on the table and clasped her hand inside of both of his. She felt a little breathless. Hopefully, this had nothing to do with some kind of flu relapse and more to do with the fact her heart was beating faster at his touch. She'd listened to her friends talk about touching the guy they fell in love with for the first time—the crazy butterflies in their stomachs, their pounding hearts, their sweaty palms, the fact they just knew. She had all of it and more.

She was out on her second date with him. They didn't know a lot about each other yet. Well, he didn't know a lot about her. She knew what she'd read about him, stories most likely concocted by a publicist, the Sharks' PR group, or both. She was the first one to scoff at another woman who insisted she'd met *the one* on a first date. Would she feel the same way about him if he was a plumber or an insurance agent and didn't make his living on a football field in front of tens of thousands of screaming fans?

She didn't want to let go of his hand to eat. She didn't want to let go of it for any reason at all, and he wasn't making a move away from her, either. She was aware the front door was opening, and people were surging into the restaurant for the dinnertime rush, but she was content to sit in a pool of soft light holding Grant's hand as rain pelted the restaurant's windows.

A woman with a sleeve of tattoos materialized at their table and took their order. She stared at Grant the entire time. It would be a miracle if any food arrived at the table at all. Maybe that wasn't so bad.

The server collected the menus and walked away from them.

"I can afford dinner," Grant teased. Daisy had ordered a salad since she really wasn't hungry. Plus, she knew how the server felt—she wanted to do nothing else but stare at Grant.

"I know. I stuffed myself in the suite earlier," she said. "It was endless wings and margaritas. I had a great time. How was your afternoon? I guess it was a little more action-packed than the usual Sunday," she joked.

He took a sip of the iced tea the server had just brought to the table. "It's been one of the best days of my life so far."

"How come?"

"The game went well. We won. I knew I was going to see you afterward."

"Are you flirting with me, Grant Parker?"

"Yes, I am," he said. "You can't imagine what I'm going to say next."

GRANT WATCHED DAISY pick at her salad. He made a few attempts to eat, and the food was delicious, but his attention was riveted on her. He noted the sparkle in her eyes, the soft pink flush moving over her cheeks, and the darker pink of her mouth as it twitched into a smile. As she shoved a curtain of blonde hair behind one ear and took a bite of her food, he was entranced.

He'd told himself before their first date he was going to take his time and get to know her before he seduced her. They could wait and see if they liked each other. They didn't need to jump into bed immediately. But the longer he sat at the restaurant table, the more he realized he was full of shit. His resolve was taking a beating tonight. He enjoyed her company. Even more, he wanted her, and he was pretty sure she wanted him too.

Maybe he should make his move and find out.

The server approached their table with the bill. "Is there anything else I can get for you tonight?" She wasn't exactly diplomatic, but her attempts to hurry them out of her section worked well with his plans for the rest of the evening.

He reached into his pocket, pulled out his wallet, and handed the server a credit card he pried out of it with one hand. "This should take care of it," he said.

Daisy raised an eyebrow. "Didn't we agree I was treating you this time? Plus, you gave us those tickets for the game today."

"Another time. I got this," he said. "Where would you like to go next?"

She nodded at his half-full plate of food. "Should we get a take-out box?"

He almost laughed out loud. "It might make a nice midnight snack."

"I spend a lot of time wandering around the kitchen at my house thinking that pot roast and mashed potatoes might be just the thing in the middle of the night, you know."

"I'll bet you do." He signed the redelivered receipt, stuck his credit card and his copy of the receipt into his pocket, and got to his feet. "Let me help you with your coat."

There were a hundred places they could go in Seattle and its surrounding neighborhoods for a couple of hours tonight. It wasn't late. The rain was increasing, though, and wandering around one of the parks or the Seattle waterfront was out of the question. A nightclub or a movie might be fun, but they wouldn't be able to talk. He walked her to his car. He made sure she was settled inside and slid into the driver's seat.

"What would you like to do now?" he asked. "How about a drink?"

"I have a pint of Ben & Jerry's in the freezer at my house," she said.

"Let's go."

Chapter Twelve

GRANT PULLED INTO the driveway in front of Daisy's townhouse and shut off his car. The rain kept up a steady pitter-patter on the windshield as he reached out to take her hand in the darkness. He knew he should say something. He couldn't seem to say enough to her at the restaurant, and now he was tongue-tied.

He was nervous. He'd been in this situation so many times before—sitting in a car outside of a woman's place, getting ready to go inside and have sex with her. He hadn't been nervous with them. He hadn't wanted more from the majority of women he'd dated in the past. The vast majority hadn't wanted more from him, either. He was entertainment. They went on to date or marry a man who could give them what he thought they wanted: a home and a family. Someone to rely on. Permanence.

He wasn't sure he was ready for a wife, 2.2 kids, and a house with a white picket fence, but he needed to make some changes. He'd like to be with someone who'd still be there the next morning and who wanted to be with him. From the minute he'd met her, he knew that Daisy was different. He was attracted to how she looked, but even more, he was drawn to her sweet, funny personality. In the short time they'd known each other, he realized she made everything better, and he wanted to do the same for her.

He hadn't thought he could be someone to rely on until he realized he was a bit envious of his college roommate Cam's new family. He envied the guys on the team who'd managed to meet and marry women who made their lives better. He'd caught the surreptitious looks between husbands and wives, the wordless communication of love and a unified front.

He was torn between his enjoyment of his independence and the fact he didn't want to wake up at two AM alone and ill on a bathroom floor again. He also realized that he would have to give as much as he took from any woman. It wasn't a one-way street.

He squeezed her hand one more time. He didn't have to decide the rest of his life in the next ten minutes. He'd already decided that he wanted a change. It began tonight. He wouldn't be able to begin or sustain any relationship until he was all in. His coach had imparted an important life lesson for him again.

"Would you like to come inside?" she said.

He hurried around his car in the rain to open the passenger door for Daisy. He reached out his hand for her smaller one. The rain seemed to have doubled in strength in seconds.

She reached up to stroke his cheek.

"There's a raindrop on your eyelashes," she said.

He wrapped his arms around Daisy. He'd never been much of a rain fan. November in Seattle tended to be wet and cold. All he could think of at the moment, though, was watching the rain slide over her lips. He wanted to taste them. Seconds later, he sealed his mouth over hers.

He wasn't surprised that her mouth was soft and clung to his in response. He tasted water, but kissing Daisy was like nothing he'd experienced before. It had zero to do with the food they'd eaten or anything else she'd had since he'd kissed her last. He felt the rain sliding through and over their faces as he slipped his tongue into her mouth. Their sweet, gentle kiss became frantic with need in seconds.

They pulled each other up the walk to her front door. She fumbled for her keys as they continued to kiss. She tore her lips off of his long enough to grab her keychain out of the bottom of her bag.

"I got it—"

"Let me help," he said. He took one hand off her long enough to reach out for the keys, which fell from her hand and hit the ground with a jingle. She started to bend over as he sank to one knee. "I got this," he insisted.

He put one big hand in the middle of her abdomen as he snatched the keys off of her porch. He straightened again and peered into her eyes.

"At least we're under cover," she murmured.

Thirty seconds later, they were inside her house. She pulled him against the (closed and now locked) front door. The front porch light shining through the peephole in the door offered little relief from the darkness. She heard her house keys hit the tile entrance one more time. She could pick them up later. She reached up to slide her fingers into the dampness of his hair.

"Dropped your keys again," he breathed against her neck. His tongue glided over a particularly sensitive area, and she gasped.

"It can wait," she whispered.

She didn't care about the keys. Every time she'd fantasized about being alone with Grant Parker, all she cared about was that there was somewhere to lie down. Or sit down. Whichever worked best. Being naked at the time would also help. Speaking of naked, he'd slid one hand under her hoodie and cupped one of her breasts as they continued to exchange hot, hungry kisses that in her experience meant the evening would continue in her bed.

For a guy who was allegedly Mr. Chaste, he sure knew his way around a woman's body. He slid his hand into her bra as he stroked her nipple in a maddeningly slow fashion. She'd always wondered if there was some type of corresponding nerves between her nipples and her lady place. Those same nerves made her knees buckle as well. She felt a gush of moisture between her legs as he attempted to unbutton and unzip her jeans with one hand.

He wasn't messing around. Well, they were, but he made it clear he was going to make her crazy before they managed to get up the stairs to her bedroom. Maybe they should forget about going to her room. She could flip the gas fireplace on in the living room, pull him onto the carpet, and rock his world there. They weren't going to be walked in on, since Catherine had gone to her boyfriend's house. Then again, the fear of getting caught might make things more exciting.

"I can help," Daisy said. She unbuttoned and unzipped her jeans, sliding them over her hips as he slid his other hand into her underwear. He found the little button of flesh between her legs as he rubbed. Slowly. "God," she hissed through clenched teeth.

His tongue flicked over her collarbone as he continued to stroke her nipple. With one quick movement, he flipped her breast out of her bra, shoved the hoodie up to her neck, and fastened his mouth onto her nipple. She let out a moan, which sounded unnaturally loud in the silence of her house.

He sucked her, he rubbed her, and everything telescoped into sensation and feeling: the throbbing between her legs, the pull of his mouth and teeth on her nipple, the pounding of her heart, and the acceleration of her breath. He dragged his fingertips through the moisture between her legs and redoubled his efforts. She plunged one hand into his waistband and closed it around his erection.

She heard his groan against her breast. He sucked a little harder. She felt the rushing sensations in her head and more moisture between her legs and began tracing her tongue around the shell of his ear as she tugged on him. Up, down. Up, down. Her thumb slid over the bead of moisture on the head.

She felt his teeth scraping her hardened nipple. The suction almost brought her over the edge by itself, but the rubbing made an orgasm a certainty.

"I...I...don't stop," she choked out.

He said something, but it was muffled against her nipple. She felt his finger slide inside her as he rubbed with his thumb. He thrust once, twice, and the orgasm hit her in waves.

"I'll fall," she cried.

"No, you won't," he said. His voice was strained. He ground his hips against hers and moved against her as she quivered in his arms. Her body convulsed.

His mouth covered hers again. Their kisses were frantic, teeth and tongues and pressure. Cold air over her exposed nipple brought exquisite pleasure and pain. He was continuing to thrust inside her with one finger, and she felt herself clench around him again.

Her hand wrapped around his penis, she was still pulling on it, and she felt the jerking motion that preceded any man's orgasm. He wrapped his hand around her fist. A few more pumps, and she felt warmth spurting over their hands.

"Shit. Fuck. This is amazing," he groaned. She wrapped one arm around his waist as his head dropped onto her shoulder.

A few minutes passed. He pulled her closer, his warm breath coming out in puffs against the side of her neck.

"Are you okay?" she whispered as he gently bit her earlobe.

"I'm great. How are you?"

"Mmmmm," was all she could manage. She felt him shake with laughter.

"I think we made a mess," he said. "All we have to do is get to the bathroom."

Her jeans were around her ankles, and her underwear was halfway down her thighs. They'd managed to shove his jeans and his underwear off during the pre-orgasmic phase. Using one's hand on a guy while he was fully dressed could be a challenge. They'd been able to make things work, though. He was hard against her once more. She didn't want it to go to waste, even if her fist was somewhat sticky.

She wanted to ask him if he'd ever done this before—wanted anyone else so badly that he barely made it inside her place before they fell on each other like crazed weasels. Well, maybe the crazed weasels would have taken the two minutes or so to undress each other first.

"There's a powder room on the left."

He didn't take the hint. He reached out, picked her up by the waist, put one foot down on her jeans, and pulled her free. She wrapped her legs around him.

"Let's go."

Grant managed to make it upstairs to Daisy's room without tripping over anything or dropping her or the clothes he'd scooped up from the floor. His heart was still racing. They tumbled onto her bed, and he landed on top of her. He tried to brace his weight on both hands so he wouldn't squish her. It was always a good thing to be somewhat considerate.

He heard her laugh a little as she pushed the ball of clothing he'd wedged between them onto the floor again. "I don't think we need these right now," she said.

He normally would have made the usual comments before they got to her room about how this was one night, he wasn't in the market for any type of ongoing relationship, and he was not sticking around. Nothing came out of his mouth besides, "It's nice in here," which may have been the most stupid comment in the history of second-date sexual encounters.

Her room was dark, so he couldn't see a hell of a lot. Her bed was comfortable, though, and held her scent—flowers and sunshine.

"I'm glad you like it," she said. He heard the hint of laughter in her voice. Maybe she felt awkward too.

Her fingertips moved over his face; she tucked his hair behind one ear. His man-bun was out. He'd be spending a few minutes searching for the elastic when he left.

He obviously needed help of some sort. He shouldn't give a shit about where he'd left the little elastic thing he used in his hair while he was lying on a mostly naked woman five minutes after she'd helped him have an orgasm so intense he'd almost blacked out. What was wrong with him? Maybe all that passion had affected his brain function somehow.

Maybe he should quit thinking so much and get back in the game.

His eyes had adjusted to the darkness while they rested for a bit. He wasn't going to think about the fact he needed a break or what that said about him. He wasn't usually this tired after a game, and he wasn't that old. She stroked his face again. Grant breathed in her scent. Shit, she smelled good.

"Want to snuggle for a while?" Daisy asked.

He couldn't figure out which was worse—post-orgasm snuggling or talking. He'd been with women before who were all about the chatting. He preferred sleeping or leaving, whichever was easier. He loved sex, but he wasn't so into exposing himself emotionally. Right now, though, he felt like he was on his first-ever date. And he realized that if she wanted to snuggle, well, goddamn it, he'd do his best.

Grant didn't know who the hell he was right now.

He rolled onto his side, propped himself up on one elbow, and reached out to wrap one arm around her waist. Raindrops beat a soothing rhythm against her bedroom window.

"Are you warm enough?"

"Maybe we should get under the blankets," she said. "Do you need some water?"

"I'm fine. Are you thirsty?"

Shit. Maybe they'd start talking about the weather next or how she felt about the tolling lanes on 405. They were talking just fine during dinner. What the hell was wrong with him?

"No," she said.

They scrambled beneath the blankets, and he reached out for her again. He took a deep breath. Things were still happening below the waist, at least for him, but he didn't want her to think he was an insensitive bastard, either. He'd better work up something to say before he made his move again.

"Uh, Daisy," he said, clearing his throat. "I feel like a real asshole admitting this to anyone else, but I'm not exactly the king of witty convos after we—well, after I blow my load, so to speak."

He saw the flash of her smile in the darkness.

"So we're not discussing US foreign policy or climate change?"

"Probably not." He pulled her a little closer. "Did you want to talk about that?"

"You want me to come up with a subject, then?"

"If you'd like."

She put both hands onto the middle of his chest and pushed him into the pillows.

"I changed my mind about the snuggling," she said.

"You did?"

She straddled him and bent to cover his mouth with hers. She surfaced long enough to whisper, "Less talk. More action," and kissed him again. Her tongue tangled with his. He reached up to grasp her hips as she ground herself against him.

He wanted to flip her onto her back and dive inside, but the condom he had was across the room in his pants pocket.

"Do you have any condoms?"

"Yeah."

She braced herself on the floor with one leg and pulled herself off of him enough to open the bedside table and grab the box inside. He heard the snick of a cardboard box opening and the crinkle of a foil wrapper and then felt her hand moving over his abdomen in search of his dick. He couldn't remember the last time he'd put a condom on in the dark. He hoped she was better at it than he was.

"Need some help?" So his voice sounded a bit strangled. She'd managed to find Mr. Happy, or at the moment, Mr. Let's-Get-That-Thing-On-NOW.

"Don't worry about it."

She gripped him in her small, cool hand, sliding it up and down his dick a couple of times for the hell of it. He could already hang clothes on it. Mostly, he needed to suit up. The more time that passed, the more he knew he'd need to do a little catch-up before they started again. He felt goosebumps when he ran one hand over her ass. She was cold. Something was wrong. He felt her try to stretch the rubber over the head of his dick, but she didn't attempt to roll it down to cover him.

"Daisy?"

"Maybe I need some light," she said. "I think this is inside out."

The faint illumination from her bedroom window wasn't enough to see detail. She leaned over to flip on the bedside table light. He could see her frowning at the condom. If he wasn't already so aroused he wanted to explode, the sight of a naked Daisy would be enough to do it.

Her pale, lightly freckled skin almost glowed in the soft light. He noted her delicate collarbones, the pulse beating at the base of her neck, the rosy pink of the nipples he'd been sucking on. He loved her slightly rounded belly. He couldn't wait to explore it with his tongue and his mouth. His eyes trailed farther and stopped on a small but surprisingly detailed tattoo of a compass on her hip. He reached out to run his fingers over it.

Seconds later, he took her face in his hands and sealed his mouth over hers. Her silky-soft hair slipped through his fingers as he readjusted and kissed her again. He heard the moan that rose in her throat as he turned her onto her back, and she wrapped her legs around his waist and slid her arms around his neck. Her breasts rubbed against his chest; he felt the damp heat of her against his belly, and his breathing accelerated.

She pulled her mouth off of his and said, "I want you."

"I want you too," he managed to say.

He could have said a lot of other things. He could have told her he thought she was pretty before, but he'd never seen anything as beautiful as she was at that moment, desire in her eyes and the flush of arousal spreading over her body. He wanted to start at her toes and work his way up. He wanted to spend hours exploring and experiencing every inch of her. And he knew he'd want to do it all over again. Maybe he should quit thinking and start doing.

He moved against her. He was inside her with one long, slick slide. He pushed his feet into the mattress as he moved in a slow rhythm, thrusting deeply. He felt her readjust her legs around him, pulling him closer. She bit her lip and let out a moan as her body squeezed him.

"Faster?" he said.

"Uh-huh." He had to smile at her attempts to nod while she moved back and forth on the pillows. "That's good." She reached out to cup him in both of her hands, moving against him, grinding her wetness against his pelvis as he continued to thrust inside her.

He felt her hand slide between them as he kept thrusting. He pushed himself up on his hands to watch as she pulled her fingertips through her wetness and rubbed herself, her legs spreading wider, her breath coming faster.

"Oh, God," she cried out. "I…I…" Her back arched. He felt the first ripples of her orgasm, the tugging against him, and he couldn't last any longer. Stars burst behind his eyelids. He heard himself groan as he moved faster; waves of sensation rolled over him. He felt Daisy's arms slip around him as he collapsed against her.

They lay there for a few seconds. He was still trying to pull himself together as she wrapped her legs around his again and slid her fingertips over his sweat-drenched back.

"That was fun," she whispered. "I loved it."

"I had a great time too," he said, which actually meant, "You are the hottest woman I have ever had sex with, and I think you're beautiful." Unfortunately, Daisy probably didn't have a Grant-to-English translator.

He was still feeling the aftereffects. Twinging and stuff. It felt amazing. Usually, he came, it was over, and he could make sense of what had happened a few minutes later. This? He was fresh out of anything that would dazzle her. If he concentrated on breathing deeply, the blood might come back to his brain, and he could summon something meaningful besides, "Let's do that again. Right now. For twice as long."

Grant threw himself back into the pillows. Daisy glanced over at him.

"I need some water. Would you like some?" she asked.

"I'd love some. Thanks," he said.

She rose from the bed as she struggled into a robe she grabbed off of a chair. He heard her light footsteps on the staircase seconds later. He stared at the empty doorway for a minute or so.

He had to admit he'd felt relief in the past when his date was sufficiently exhausted to fall asleep and he could pull his clothes on and get out of her place as quickly as possible. He wasn't feeling relief at the moment. He wanted more. He wished she hadn't gotten up and gone downstairs, but maybe she was having as much trouble with her feelings right now as he was and she needed a little time alone to process.

Maybe it was a combination of spending his afternoon running around a football field, his previous bout of nerves, or another huge orgasm, but he felt relaxed. He was happy. If this was how things were when you were with a woman you couldn't wait to spend time with, sign him up.

He wished she'd come back upstairs so he could wrap his arms around her and listen to the rain on the roof of her place for a little while.

Come to think of it, maybe it was time he got his ass out of Daisy's bed and got dressed. He didn't usually stay overnight with any woman, or he hadn't lately. He was comfortable, though. He breathed in the light perfume that infused her bedding. The tat-tat-tat of rain bouncing off of her bedroom window was almost hypnotic as his eyelids drifted closed.

DAISY REACHED INTO the cabinet over the kitchen sink for two drinking glasses. She positioned one glass under the ice and water dispenser on the front of her refrigerator and pushed the button.

Grant was everything she'd hoped he would be in bed and out of it, and she was so freaked out about it she was hiding in her kitchen while she tried to get herself together. To think that they'd see each other again was pretty ridiculous. They'd been out a couple of times now; they'd slept together, and she was taking this waaay too seriously. Dating was supposed to be fun. She was supposed to enjoy the time she'd spent with him and not get all hung up on how cute he was or how much she wanted to see him again.

She'd tangled her fingers in his hair. She'd kissed that full mouth. His stubble had scraped the tender inner skin of her thighs. She shouldn't have slept with him. She shouldn't have gotten out of bed afterward, either.

She barely knew him. To feel this strongly about a man she'd spent just a few hours with was ridiculous. Well, she'd spent some of that time with him when they weren't dressed, which tended to hurry things along, emotions-wise.

He had to be seeing other women too. A guy like him probably had his pick. They weren't exclusive. He could do whatever he wanted. So could she. She put the second glass back down on the kitchen counter and dropped her face into her hands.

When she wasn't worried about getting her heart smashed like a loaf of bread in the bottom of the grocery bag, her guilt over not telling him the truth about *Overtime Parking* was reaching epic levels. She could have told him at dinner. She could have told him while they were sitting outside in his car, and all she had to do was open her mouth and blurt it out. She hadn't. She could march right back upstairs and tell him. Maybe that was the best thing to do.

She filled the other glass with ice water and carried them both upstairs. If she said it quickly, it would be over, and she wouldn't feel so guilty. His feet probably wouldn't touch the ground as he ran out of her front door.

She walked into her room and listened to Grant's quiet snores as he lay on his side, facing the bedroom window with the sheet wound around his hips.

If she got back into bed, she wouldn't have to face any of it until morning.

She must have let out a sound of some sort. He flipped over on his back and said, "What's up, Daisy?" Of course, sleepy-eyed and mussed looked adorable on him.

"Taking a little nap?" Daisy said. She put a glass of ice water down on the nightstand next to him, along with the ponytail holder he'd lost earlier. Instead of "I wrote a really smutty book about you. Isn't that hilarious?" she said, "Here's something to drink."

It seemed so easy to do, but she couldn't form the words. She couldn't tell him what she'd done. Not right now.

SHE TOOK A sip of her glass of water. "Want me to help you find the rest of your stuff? It looks like everything's here on the floor." She bent over to grab his clothes, shook them out, and laid them on the foot of her bed. He wanted her to get back into bed for round two, but it didn't look like she was in the mood. Maybe he'd pissed her off somehow. He didn't think so, but he was mystified right now. Unless he was really wrong, she seemed to be throwing his ass out of her house.

"Jeans, shirt, underwear...You're still wearing your socks, aren't you?" she said.

"My feet get cold," he said.

"I like to wear socks to bed too," she said. "I hung up your coat on the rack by the front door."

"Thanks," he said. He swallowed some more water. "Did I piss you off somehow?"

"Not at all. I know you probably have to go to the practice facility tomorrow. I have an afternoon flight, so maybe we should both get some sleep."

He could have mentioned that they were in her bedroom, where there just happened to be a bed, but she'd turned her back to rummage for something in her walk-in closet. She wasn't looking at him. To say he was confused was minimizing things. He wasn't sure what to do, other than get his ass dressed and hit the road.

The cold, dark, and rainy road back to his place, where he'd sleep alone.

He pulled his clothes on as quickly as possible. He'd grab his shoes downstairs as he went out the door. Grant finished off the water and put the glass back down on her nightstand.

She reappeared from the closet to walk him downstairs.

"Thank you for dinner," she said. "I had such a great time tonight."

"I did too," he said. "I'd like to see you again. How about Thursday night?"

"I'm working an afternoon flight from LA," she said. "If we're not delayed, that would be fun."

"Should I text you on Thursday?" he asked.

"Yes. I'd love that," she said.

He reached out to kiss her. At the last second, she moved her head, and his mouth grazed her cheek. What the hell? She'd enjoyed kissing him earlier, and now she didn't want to? He was more confused than ever, and she wasn't giving him any indication of what he'd done wrong.

"Oops," she said. "I'm a dork. Maybe we should try it again." She took his face in her hands, giving him a sweet, short kiss on the mouth. No tongue. She didn't linger. She didn't savor.

She was mad. There was no doubt about it.

"Is something wrong?" he said.

"No. Nothing at all. I had fun. I'll see you on Thursday," she said. She reached out to flip the dead bolt on her front door and pulled the door open. "Drive safely."

"Yeah. Thanks. I had fun too," he said.

He turned to wave as he walked down the cement path to her driveway. She gave him a smile that was a shade too bright. "Good night," she called out.

He got into his car, turned the key in the ignition, and backed out. Her front door was shut before he drove away.

GRANT TOSSED AND turned the rest of the night in his bed. It had never seemed so large (or so empty) before. He'd always been big on a good night's sleep. He'd bought the best bed he could afford, bedding that the salesperson at Nordstrom told him was the finest to be had, firm pillows, and a really nice down comforter. He'd wanted something so comfortable that he didn't feel like getting out of it.

He was lost in remembering every moment he'd spent with Daisy tonight. Things seemed like they were amazing even before they'd finished having the hottest sex he could remember, and then she'd pretty much booted him out of her house minutes afterward. It wasn't like her roommate was home. She'd told him herself that she didn't need to be at work until eleven the next morning. Was there a fire drill?

Once they'd resolved the condom issue, she came. He remembered her cries (and a scream). Daisy seemed to love sex, had loved what he'd done to her, and he'd enjoyed what she'd done to him in return. Everyone had had a good time, in his opinion.

He went over every moment of their evening in his mind, looking for a clue as to why she hadn't seemed to want him to spend the night. He'd never made his *this is it* speech beforehand. Maybe she knew someone else he'd been with before. But the chances of that were small to none. Seattle wasn't that big, but really. Women didn't sit around in a locker room comparing notes on guys they'd slept with. Or did they?

He yanked the pillow out from under his head, punched it a few times to get it back into shape, and settled back against the cool six-hundred-thread-count cotton sheets. She couldn't be faking all of that.

He tried to push Daisy out of his mind and concentrate on remembering the game, which now seemed like it had happened a month ago. He could go through the progression of plays in his head: What worked, what could stand some improvement, and the one or two he'd like back as a do-over. For instance, one of the receivers had missed a pass, and he'd almost gotten picked off as a result. He'd have to work on that play when he went to practice again. He'd be working on all aspects of his game, but the biggest one was doing what he needed to do so his receivers could hold onto the damn ball.

He'd loved the idea of Daisy watching him play from the team's suite.

And he was back to thinking about her again. What was it about her? She was slender, pretty, but that wasn't all that caught and held his interest. He'd always been partial to blondes, and her eyes were an interesting shade of blue/green/gray he'd never seen before. He'd dated a lot of women who could fit her description, but he'd never encountered anyone like Daisy. Someone who made him laugh, who he enjoyed spending time with. She had a life of her own, and he'd met too many women before who didn't. Maybe it was the fact she didn't need him.

If he was truthful, the fact she didn't spend every minute hanging on him made her more desirable. As far as he could tell, she was happy before she met him, and she'd be just as happy without him. He had to admit he'd like spending more time with her to see how things developed, though. He'd also like to have sex with her again. Next time, though, he'd get up and get her some water afterward, and then he'd start all over again at her toes. And work his way up.

He couldn't figure out why she'd all but thrown him out of her house. He'd always thought he wanted a woman who had sex with him and kicked him out the second he got up to pull on his pants. He realized with a shock that maybe he didn't, maybe he'd been wrong, and he should have tried harder to stay with her last night. She'd agreed to see him again on Thursday, but it wasn't enough.

He had to figure out how to entice her sufficiently enough that she'd want him to stick around for more. He was into her, but he wasn't sure if she was into him. It wasn't a good feeling, and he didn't know how to fix it.

"FML," he muttered. He'd gotten what he wanted, but it wasn't what he wanted after all.

Chapter Thirteen

DAISY SAT UP in bed and glared at the clock. Seven fifteen. Despite the fact that she'd told Grant she had to get to work today, she actually didn't. She could have spent the night and this morning with him too. She'd needed an excuse in case things didn't go well, which was ridiculous. Things with Grant had gone really well. So well, in fact, she couldn't sleep from worrying that rushing him out the door last night meant he'd be texting her today to say their date was off. When she wasn't worrying about hurrying him out the door, she was dealing with the guilt that she hadn't come clean about *Overtime Parking*. She should have told him. He most likely would have dumped her on the spot, but at least she would have been honest with him.

Guys like Grant could have almost any woman they wanted. He was handsome, interesting, fun to be around, and the fact he had money didn't hurt, either. They'd spent the night before enjoying each other. She wasn't dumb enough to imagine she was the only woman in his life. She wasn't sure how she felt about sharing him with anyone else. Mostly, she didn't want to be the hook-up he really wasn't into but didn't mind having sex with once in a while. She wanted to be his one and only, if she was brutally honest. The only way she was going to make an impression was to make him believe she could live without him. Guys as competitive as Grant would see her as a challenge.

She'd fantasized about him so many nights before, but the reality was better than anything she'd come up with on her own. They weren't dangling off the Space Needle or naked on the fifty-yard line of Sharks Stadium, but she'd had him all to herself. She'd enjoyed her crazy fantasies. Maybe he'd help her act out a few of them later. That is, if he liked the thrill of almost getting caught.

The readers of her kooky little book would have been asleep if she'd written the story of two people alone in her cozy bed while rain fell on the roof, but the memories were sweet. And she hoped she'd get the opportunity again. Very soon.

She heard footsteps in the hallway outside of her bedroom, and a rumpled Catherine poked her head around the doorjamb.

"Morning, love," her roommate said. "Did you have fun last night?"

"I did," Daisy said.

"You don't look like it." Catherine bustled into the room and sat down in the chair in the corner of Daisy's room, wrapping the bathrobe she wore more securely around her. "What happened? You don't have to tell me the good parts if you don't want to."

"Where's Declan?"

"He dropped me off on his way to the office half an hour ago. We had a nice evening," she said. "The usual. You know: A bottle of wine in front of the fire, some snuggling, and I committed acts on him that would make my mother blush." She gave Daisy an unrepentant grin. "He's tired this morning, but happy. I blame myself for that."

Catherine crossed her legs and wrapped her arms around herself, and Daisy saw something sparkly out of the corner of her eye.

Catherine was wearing a large diamond solitaire on the third finger of her left hand.

"Is there something you'd like to tell me?" Daisy demanded.

Catherine thrust her hand out. "Look what I got."

Daisy and Catherine spent the next few minutes jumping up and down, hugging each other, and crying.

"He put it under my pillow. I couldn't figure out why there was something a little hard in the middle of my pillow, so I stuck my hand under there, and—" Catherine paused for a moment and put one hand over her mouth. "He was already asleep. I had to use the light from his phone to see what was in the box, you know? I was so surprised. So surprised. And I woke him up," she said. "He put the ring on my finger, and we kissed. I have never been so happy."

Daisy ignored the bittersweet pang she felt. It wasn't the time to be sad because Catherine would move out soon and she wouldn't be seeing her as often. It also wasn't the time to wish that she was the one showing off a beautiful engagement ring and bubbling over with happiness about spending the rest of her life with the man she loved.

Right now, she wanted her friend to know how happy she was for her. She wanted to rejoice and exult. She didn't want to spoil Catherine's big moment with "What about me?" Catherine deserved all the happiness life could bring.

If she wanted the same thing, she had to find a man who loved her. Maybe that man was Grant. She wouldn't know until she took the risk of letting him know who she was, in more ways than one.

She reached out for Catherine's left hand again. "Damn, that ring's big."

"He brought it home from New York. They have an entire section of the city that's just jewelers. I love it," she sighed. "And I love him."

"Did you call your parents?"

"They are so excited," Catherine said. "My mum wants to help me plan the wedding, but we're getting married here. Maybe she could come over for a couple of weeks while I do stuff like find a dress and figure out the rest of the details. Plus, I need to get started. We're talking about getting married in June."

"June? That's not enough time. You have to find a place, and a dress takes several months to get—"

"Declan's parents want us to get married in their garden. They have acres on Mercer Island. His mum said she can rent a reception tent, and she was calling a caterer first thing this morning to see if they have bookings. I can deal with that later. We have things to do right now," Catherine said. She got up from her chair, reached out for Daisy's hand, and said, "I can't get married without you. Will you be my maid of honor?"

GRANT ARRIVED BACK in his condo an hour after a run, covered in sweat and really hungry. He needed a big breakfast, but first on his to-do list was attempting to resolve whatever had gone wrong last night.

He grabbed his phone and texted Daisy. He wasn't so great at the mushy, romantic notes. Short and to the point wasn't bad, right?

Thanks for last night. Can't wait until Thursday.

He threw some fruit, protein powder, and ice cubes into the blender for a smoothie that might hold him until he managed to find (or make) something more substantial. The text notification didn't go off while he was drinking the shake. It didn't go off while he threw a load into the washing machine and started it up. His phone remained silent while he stripped off everything else he wore and got into the shower.

Maybe she was at work already. Or maybe she wasn't interested in texting him. She wasn't ignoring him, was she?

"Get over yourself," he muttered. "Maybe she's busy."

By the time he emerged from the shower, dripping all over the tile floor of his bathroom, he had a plan. It wasn't great, but it was better than nothing at all.

He toweled off, pulled on underwear and clean warm-ups, and grabbed his phone again.

Every guy who'd played for the Seattle Sharks in the past four years had the number stored in his phone. A couple of his teammates had her on speed dial. She'd pulled their asses out of the fire many times. Now it was his turn.

He hit Dial and heard her cheery voice almost immediately.

"Crazy Daisy, Amy speaking."

"Hi, Amy. It's Grant Parker from the Sharks. I think I need your help."

He heard the sweet peal of her laughter. "I wondered when you'd finally call. What can I do for you?"

"I had a date. We had fun, but I would like to send her something. What do you suggest?" He took a deep breath. "I didn't ask her what kind of flowers she likes or anything." He hadn't asked her a lot of things. Then again, it was tough to muster up a conversation when a woman had her hand wrapped around his dick. "You met her yesterday, if that helps at all."

"It does. I really enjoyed talking with Daisy. She's great." Grant could hear the camera on Amy's phone click. "I have something here she might like. Let me send you a pic. It's roses, tulips, and those teeny daisies—Shasta daisies—in a square vase decorated with coordinating polka-dot ribbon. I know it's a risk sending any kind of daisies to a woman named Daisy, but I think she'll love it. It's cute and fun and a bit different from typical arrangements. I'll make one today and get it into the van for this afternoon's deliveries, if that works."

"I think she has a flight today. She won't be home until late, and I don't want it to sit outside."

"Will tomorrow morning work better for you?"

"I think so," he said. He sent his mom flowers a few times a year. Cam's wife had loved the baby stuff he'd sent them. He was a bit concerned, though; how many other guys had sent Daisy flowers? He didn't want to be one of a crowd. He wanted something she'd be charmed by. He had no idea what that might be, however. Not yet. He cleared his throat. "I have a question."

"Shoot," she said. He heard a voice in the background, which sounded suspiciously like the owner of the Sharks. He also heard what sounded like Amy's attempt to put her hand on her cell phone's speaker. "Matt Stephens, you are still the sexiest man alive, but I'm on a business call right now."

"Maybe you should call them back," Matt said.

"Maybe you should keep your hands to yourself," Amy said, but Grant could hear the laughter in her voice. He heard a sharp intake of breath too. "I will get you for that."

"I'll clear my schedule," Matt said. He heard what sounded like Matt swatting his wife on the butt. "Hurry home, sexy."

"May I put you on hold for a moment?" Amy said into the receiver. She probably hadn't pushed Hold hard enough. Grant heard her speaking seconds later.

"You'd better be naked when I get there," Amy called out to her husband.

"I'll call Grandma Pauline and ask her if she'd like to take the kids for tonight," Matt said. "You can't imagine the things I'm going to do to you later, Mrs. Stephens."

"Maybe I'll ask Estelle to handle things here today."

"Maybe you should."

"I love you," she called out.

"I love you too. I'm going to show you how much when you get home."

The bells on Amy's shop's front doors jingled as Matt left, and he heard a gasp from Amy a few seconds later. "Grant? Did I drop you?"

"I'm here."

"Oh my God. I hit Hold. I must not have done it right. Did you hear all that?" She was silent for a moment. "I'm so embarrassed."

"Don't be," he said. He wasn't sure what to say to make her feel better, but he blurted out, "I hope I'll find the same thing one day."

"What's that?"

"Love for a lifetime. Someone special."

"Looking for someone special is tough. I had to kiss a lot of frogs before I met my husband," Amy said. "Matt showed up late to my sister's wedding. We drank tequila, and he poured me into my bed at the hotel. I felt so embarrassed—kind of like a few minutes ago. I didn't call him, even though he asked me to. He tracked me down and kept asking me out until I said I'd go. The rest is history." She let out a laugh. "No matter what I did or who else I met, I couldn't forget about him. And he makes me feel like we just met and he can't wait to get his hands on me every day." Grant heard her sigh. "I am the luckiest woman in the world. And I know you want to make Daisy feel the same way."

"I…well, I'm kind of interested." Kind of interested? That's why he'd tossed and turned all night wondering why she hadn't let him stay over.

Amy kept talking. "So, here's the deal. We'll start small. I'll get your flowers ready to go; they'll go out tomorrow morning, and they'll be gorgeous. I will find out what else she might like—balloons, more flowers, maybe some candy or something else fun. There is nothing that makes a woman want to see you again more than knowing you thought about her when she wasn't around."

"I heard you're really good at this kind of stuff."

"I'm damn good at it. Ask your teammates," Amy joked. "Let's get your info, and I'll get to work."

Seconds later, Grant heard the chime of an incoming text on his phone.

Last night was amazing. Is it Thursday yet?

DAISY AND CATHERINE spent most of the next day making a list of wedding to-dos that resembled the checkoff lists involved in a NASA launch. The stack of bridal magazines Catherine had just bought would require hours of study.

Daisy looked longingly at her rolled-up yoga mat in the corner of the kitchen. She'd missed class again.

Maybe she could do a few poses in the living room. She was already doing some yoga breathing as she contemplated the fact that Catherine was moving out in a few short months. Money wasn't the issue. She could afford the house payment on her own. She and Catherine had become close friends, and Daisy had already been through what happened when a friend got married. Her friends spent time with their spouses. As a result, Daisy wouldn't see them or spend time with them as often. That was how it should be, and she would have to make new single friends. The fact that so many of her friends had gotten married in the past five years should have been a clue that she needed to make a change.

Catherine flipped open one of the magazines, made a face, and held up the photo of a dress. "Horrible," she said. "It looks like someone bought a glue gun, took the scissors to their down pillows, and glued them all over the skirt."

"How much does that cost?"

"They never print the prices," Catherine said. "If you have to ask, you can't afford it." She flipped a few more pages. "Now this is more like it." She held up the magazine so Daisy could see.

The dress was ivory and made of heavy satin. It was strapless and had a sweetheart neckline and a small train. The waist was accented by a front-facing bow made out of the same fabric. It would look beautiful on the tall, slender Catherine.

"You need to try that on," Daisy said. "Where can we find it?"

Catherine reached out to grab her tablet. "Let's Google it." She drew her finger across the screen to unlock it, clicked a few times, and read something.

"This isn't good," Catherine said.

"What are you talking about? If you can figure out who made the dress, we can find it. It's not a big deal," Daisy said.

"This has nothing to do with the dress. It's Grant."

"What about him? Is he okay? What's wrong?"

Catherine extended a finger in the air. "Just a second."

Daisy dropped the magazine she'd been holding onto the kitchen table and leaned back in her chair. Catherine's face had gone from radiant happiness to sadness in the few minutes she'd been staring at her tablet.

"How about a cup of tea?" Catherine said.

"No, thanks. What happened?"

Catherine let out a sigh.

"You've seen the new sportscaster at KIXI-TV, haven't you? She's made a blog post about Grant on their website." She glanced up to meet Daisy's eyes. "This isn't good."

"So, what's it about?" Daisy reached across the table to Catherine. "May I see it?"

Catherine handed her the tablet and got up from the table.

The article was entitled "Is *Overtime Parking* Grant Parker's Biography?" She glanced at the photos accompanying the article, and she was in one of them. It was a little weird to see cell phone pictures of herself with Grant at Purple and Skillet Diner on Twitter. She hadn't noticed people taking pictures. Then again, she'd been so lost in Grant she wouldn't have noticed a nuclear bomb dropping in the neighborhood.

Daisy skimmed the text. The blog post read like something from a tabloid. According to the writer, Grant had been involved with a number of women in the Seattle area. Four of them had been willing to speak out about their involvement with him, which hadn't lasted longer than a single night. They all mentioned that he'd told them he wasn't interested in a relationship, he wanted to spend the night with them, and he had no intention of seeing them again.

The Sharks wanted their fans to think that Grant's personal life was squeaky clean, and it was all a lie. The writer finished by asking the reader if he or she would want their children looking up to Grant Parker as a role model or as a man.

Daisy felt anger rising with every word she read. How was it any of the writer's concern who Grant had slept with, how often, or with how many? He was single. It was nobody else's business what another adult did in his or her personal life, squeaky-clean public image or not.

She reread the story. It sounded like a witch hunt, the kind of thing that a spurned lover would write. It had nothing to do with football or the Sharks or sports. It was a deliberate smear on someone Daisy knew wasn't perfect but who had shown he was a good person. It wasn't newsworthy. When the Sharks' front office saw it, she knew it was going to have an immediate and negative effect on Grant's career.

He'd told her how he felt about visiting the sick kids at the hospital. Would the hospital still let Grant visit the kids there, or would they think he was some kind of bad person for having casual sex with other consenting adults?

Catherine sat down in her chair again. "The kettle's on. Or should I get the vodka and a shot glass instead?"

Daisy pointed at the computer screen. "She's freaked out because he's slept with other women? It's not against the law unless he's secretly married or something. Why would she care?"

"She says that the Sharks have spent a lot of time and resources building him up as some purer-than-the-driven-snow role model. If he's exposed as nothing like that, what does that mean for his career? Even more, how is that going to affect you? You don't want the same thing to happen when you sleep with him, do you?"

Daisy glanced up from the tablet screen.

"We slept together last night."

"What? He wasn't here this morning," Catherine said.

Daisy closed her eyes and wished she hadn't been so stupid for the ten thousandth time this morning. "I kicked him out."

Catherine's mouth dropped open. "You kicked him out? Did he try to hurt you or something? What happened?"

"Of course not," Daisy said. She fidgeted a bit. "I didn't want him to think I was clingy."

Catherine stared at her. "I don't get it. Was the sex bad?"

"No." Daisy could feel the heat rising in her face as she remembered how great the sex had been. She was torn between being bothered that she now knew for sure he'd had lots of practice and being intrigued by what else he knew that they hadn't tried yet. She'd had practice too, which made her a gigantic hypocrite. She folded her hands so she'd stop picking at one of her cuticles. "I don't want him to think he doesn't actually have to pursue me now."

"But you slept with him, you silly goose. What do you think he's going to think?"

"I'm not a sure thing?"

"That's ridiculous." Catherine leaned over the table. "Explain to me how you think you're going to accomplish this."

"Mostly, I feel guilty," Daisy said. "I should have told him about the book. I couldn't get the words out."

"He's going to find out sometime. You need to tell him," Catherine said. "Come on; you can do it. Put on your big girl panties. Maybe he'll think it's funny."

Daisy dropped her face into her hands and let out a long groan.

GRANT WENT FOR another run on Tuesday morning, did a few errands, and pointed his car toward Children's Hospital for a visit. He wanted to call Daisy. Maybe a text was better. They'd been exchanging texts, but he didn't want her to think he was desperate or something. When he wasn't worrying about why she'd booted him out or that she wasn't really into him, he was sifting through the list of things he needed to accomplish before he was due at the training facility tomorrow.

He was pretty sure that the guys on the team would laugh at him for doing so, but he'd had the picture that Emma drew for him while he was in the hospital framed. He'd hang it up in his condo soon. He wasn't the most sentimental guy, but something about a little girl thinking of him when she probably didn't feel great made him want to cry or something.

Most players didn't bother with their own fan mail. They got gifts (and solicitations) from fans all the time. Once the novelty of having a complete stranger invite you to their wedding or another life event wore off (someone else named their baby after him, which he was still a little freaked out about), there wasn't a lot to monitor. Some of his teammates still read every letter. They liked the ego stroke from knowing that someone had actually sat down at a table with pen and paper and gushed over them.

He'd talked with Emma on a few occasions now. Obviously, building a friendship with a five-year-old (and her mom) was slow, but it meant a lot to him that she cared. Goofy but true. Hopefully, he could see her today.

He loved being around the kids because they didn't expect a thing from him outside of an autograph and a few minutes of his time. He relished the shy smiles and hugs he got from children who forgot how much pain they were in or how sick they were as he perched on the side of their hospital beds to talk a little. They offered their affection (and their friendship) so freely. He found himself thinking about them on days he wasn't scheduled to visit.

He'd actually called the nurses' station to check on Emma a couple of weeks ago.

"I'm so sorry, Grant," one of the nurses had said. "We can't share that information with you. It's against hospital policy."

"I don't get out of team meetings until seven or so tonight. Let's say I sneaked in there a few minutes before visiting hours are over," he said. "Will her parents be okay with it if I wanted to say hi?"

"I'll let them know," the nurse had said. "Ten minutes, Grant."

"Got it."

He had poked his head around the doorjamb of Emma's room just before eight PM that night. Emma was falling asleep in her mom's arms as her mother sang a lullaby. Grant gave her a reflexive nod. Her smile was tired, but she nodded in response.

The nurse had caught up with him as he walked away and pressed a piece of paper into his hand. "Emma's mom says to text her if you want to know how she's doing. Here's her number."

Some of the kids he visited each week had been in the hospital for months. Most of the kids recovered and went home. A few never left. He wasn't sure what to say to the parents he knew sat at their kids' bedside day after day hoping for a miracle. It took him a few visits to figure out that a gentle squeeze on the shoulder or a hug meant more to those parents than anything he could say. They were grateful that he (and his teammates) didn't avoid their child.

He was grateful that they included him.

He pulled into a parking space outside of the hospital entrance. He grabbed the tote bag of stuff for Emma he'd brought out of the car and strode to the electronic doors that led into the hospital. Four younger kids stood outside in Sharks gear. It wasn't especially warm today, and he wondered where the hell their parents were. Someone should know they were out here.

"It's Parker!" one of them cried. Seconds later, he found himself in the midst of four laughing, chattering little kids who were pulling on his pants leg and talking all at once.

"I saw you make a touchdown on Sunday!" a little girl with a ponytail and no front teeth lisped out.

"Will you play catch with us?" a little boy asked. "I got a football in my room."

"My mom said that you know Seth Taylor. He's my favorite," another little girl informed him.

"Derrick Collins said you're late," a child in a bathrobe, pajamas, and slipper socks informed Grant.

Grant crouched down next to the young man in the PJs and robe. "Do your parents know you're out here?"

"I don't think so," he proudly informed Grant.

"Well, then, I'd better get you back inside. The nurses will be worried, bro." He wasn't sure how old the kid was, but he scooped him up easily. He wasn't heavy. Most of these kids had permanent IV sites; he'd learned during his first visit to be careful so he wouldn't accidentally make more work for the nursing staff.

"I can walk," the boy told him. He had spiky, dark red hair, a dusting of freckles across his nose, and regarded

Grant through ice-blue eyes. "Derrick said some other stuff too, but my mom would take away my screen time if I said it."

Derrick was a well-known prankster among the Sharks. His wife, Holly, was pregnant with their second child. He was also under some financial duress at the moment; Holly was fining Derrick fifty dollars for every obscenity or off-color comment that came out of his mouth at home. It seemed Holly and Derrick's two-year-old son, Michael, had started imitating his daddy, which really wasn't acceptable at the play group Holly had enrolled their son in. Grant also knew that Derrick had put five hundred dollars in the swear jar recently after someone dented his Escalade in the grocery store parking lot.

"I know you can walk, buddy, but you're about to freeze out here. Come on, you guys." The kids followed him through the automatic doors and moved down the corridor toward the floor most of the young oncology patients' rooms were on. Grant noticed a couple of nurses up ahead darting from room to room. He could pretty much guess what they were doing.

"Ladies," he called out. "They're right here." He glanced down at the kids still clinging to his pants legs and chattering away. "You guys shouldn't have been outside."

"We were waiting for you."

"That's really nice, but you scared the nurses. Look at them. They're worried about you."

"We didn't go far," the little girl with the ponytail said. "It's boring being in here all the time."

"I know that," he said. "But you can't leave unless they say so."

One of the nurses came running out of the room, stopped in the corridor, and exclaimed, "Oh, thank God! You found them!" She rushed forward, dropped to her knees in front of the little group, and reached out to clasp the kids in her arms. "We were so scared. Everyone's looking for you."

"We didn't go that far," the kid in his arms said.

"Hunter, you shouldn't be out of bed at all. What got into you?" the nurse said. She had tears in her eyes. "What did you do with your IV?"

"They took the needle out to change the bag—"

"We'll put it right back in. You kids." She was in full-on mom scolding mode, but Grant could see the fear in her eyes. Other nurses were descending on the little group, and he saw a lab-coat-wearing doctor in their number as well. "I know you want to see the football players, but you can't go outside to wait for them. We didn't know where you were."

One of the little girls put her hands on either side of the nurse's face. "We're sorry, Monica. Don't cry. We didn't mean to scare you."

The other children were led away by various nurses, and Grant followed with Hunter. The kid felt so slight in his arms. Grant understood he was pretty sick, but no kid should feel like this. Hunter slung one arm around Grant's neck.

Maybe Grant should start bringing Dick's Drive-In milkshakes when he came to visit, like Drew McCoy had for months now. If Hunter could keep them down, it might help.

"So, Hunter, I want you to promise me something," Grant said.

"What's that?" Hunter said.

"Will you tell the other kids that I will do something special for them if they will agree not to sneak out to meet the football players in the parking lot?"

"What do you mean by *special*?"

Damn, this kid drove a hard bargain.

"I need to check with a couple of people first, but I can guarantee it's awesome, and you will not want to miss out. But I can't do this if even one of you guys is waiting in the parking lot on Tuesdays."

"So you want me to tell everyone else?"

"I can tell them, but you get to be the enforcer. You get to make sure nobody's out there every Tuesday afternoon."

Hunter mulled this for a minute or so as Grant followed the group back to their rooms. "I'll do it," he said.

"That's what I'm talking about." Grant walked through the entrance to the floor. "So, kid, you hungry at all?"

GRANT SET HUNTER down outside of his room and headed toward the nurses' station. This morning's rain had given way to a brilliant blue sky and bright sunshine through the hospital windows that looked over Seattle. The walls were covered with cheerful murals and joyful artwork, some of which had been created by the kids currently occupying rooms up and down the corridor. He glimpsed a couple of his teammates thirty or so feet away. If there weren't so many kids around, he'd flip off Derrick Collins for the hell of it. Right now, he was after some snacks for Hunter.

He leaned on the nurses' station as he waited for someone in scrubs to approach. Maybe they had a refrigerator he could raid or something. He could always grab something from the cafeteria.

Monica, the nurse, was heading toward him at a high rate of speed. She didn't look happy, and he braced himself.

"Do you have a minute?" she said as she came to a halt a foot or so away.

"Of course. What can I do for you?"

She reached out to touch his upper arm. "I saw that article about you during my break." She let out a sigh. "I don't care what that reporter says. You have been so kind to the kids here, and I appreciate it. I wanted you to know."

"What article?"

The hair rose on the back of his neck. There was a problem, and he needed to find out what it was so he could deal with it. The overhead PA went off, and she reached out to pat him one more time.

"I have to go."

He could feel his phone vibrating with incoming text messages. He reached into his pocket to grab his phone and pull up Google News, but he wasn't fast enough.

Harley McHugh and a camera person emerged from someone's room. Before he had time to react, she spotted him and approached. He saw the red light of the cameraman's equipment come on. Shit.

"I'd like to ask you a few questions, Grant."

"No, thanks," he said. "I'd prefer to spend my time here visiting with the kids."

"Your representation won't respond to my requests for an interview."

"I'm not willing to be interviewed here."

"Aren't your visits to Children's each week a public-relations ploy to distract the media from looking into your private life?"

He stared at her in disbelief. She was still talking.

"Wonder how these kids' parents would feel about their kids spending time with a guy who isn't a great role model by any stretch of the imagination?"

"No comment," he said. "And shut the camera off."

"I'll bet. I have five women who are willing to speak on-camera about you."

Grant put his hand over the camera lens and said, "What is your problem, Harley? This passed weird a while ago and went straight into creepy. I don't want anything to do with you. Leave me alone."

"I have a job to do," she snapped.

"You're not doing this because of your job. You're harassing me. It needs to stop."

"I'm looking for information—"

"No, you're not." Grant looked up in time to see the red light of the camera shut off. His voice dropped in volume. "We were together once. I told you at the time I wasn't interested in seeing you again. It's over. Leave me alone."

Her mouth dropped open. The cameraman let out a low whistle.

He still wanted to talk with another one of the nurses about some snacks for Hunter, but he needed to put as much space between himself and Harley as quickly as possible. He also needed to find out about the article Monica mentioned. He was willing to bet he already knew who'd written it. He saw a few of his teammates approach out of the corner of his eye.

"Didn't the nurses ask you and your camera to leave fifteen minutes ago?" Seth Taylor barked at Harley.

"No cameras on this floor without permission," Drew McCoy said. "You must have a problem with reading comprehension, Harley. Did you miss the sign at the entrance?"

"Get out," Derrick Collins told Harley and her cameraman.

"I've asked for an interview multiple times. Grant is avoiding me," Harley said.

Kade Harrison strode up to the group. "I guess he has a good reason for that. I saw that blog post. Your boss should fire you for attempting to settle a personal score like that, Ms. McHugh."

"He's nothing like his image. Our viewers should know," she insisted.

Kade moved closer to her. Her cameraman backed up in alarm.

"Your viewers should know that Parker dates and has mutually consenting sex with other adults? That's some award-winning reporting right there, cupcake. What's next? He puts his pants on one leg at a time?" Kade said.

"I'll bet he has a beer or two after a game on Sunday nights. Alert the media," Seth said.

"I heard he has an ice cream habit. Bro's entire freezer is packed with Ben & Jerry's pints," Derrick said. "He can quit at any time."

"Yeah, he's big on the ice cream. And he probably likes to walk around his house in his underwear too," Zach Anderson said.

"Bast—jerk owes me twenty bucks," Brandon McKenna called out. "He's such a cheapskate. That's the last time he plays poker with the boys and me."

"I thought you were playing for M&M's," Zach said.

"Taylor kept eating them." Brandon joined the small group and gave Harley a raised eyebrow. "I think you're done here," he said to her. He threw one arm around Grant's shoulders. "Come on. I'll teach you some stuff that will get you an ESPN *30 for 30*, buddy."

"This isn't over," she said. Harley turned on her heel and stalked away, followed by the cameraman.

"Oh, it's over, all right. Say hi to your program manager for me," Derrick called after her.

Seth Taylor slapped Grant on the back.

"Son, your tail-chasing days are over. Daisy's a great girl. You'll never find anyone else like her."

"He's dating Daisy?" Brandon said. "Daisy the flight attendant?"

"Shit, yeah," Kade said.

Brandon caught Grant's eye. "Propose now before she gets away. And you're doing an interview with me instead."

Chapter Fourteen

GRANT DUCKED INTO one of the hospital waiting rooms a few minutes later to pull up the local news station's website on his phone. It didn't take him long to find the blog post Harley had written. He sank into a chair as he read. It was worse than he thought.

He could hear his teammates talking and laughing with the kids as he sat alone and stared at his phone's screen. He'd known that the day would come when everyone would find out what kind of person he really was, and having it out in the open wasn't the worst part. He'd lied to most of the people he knew. He'd tried to be what the Sharks' front office, the coaching staff, the team, and his parents wanted, and he'd failed at all of it. He'd finally gotten to the point where he felt like he was part of the team, and he'd blown it all.

There would be more articles about him. This was too juicy for the sports media to ignore. It wasn't the fact he'd slept around. It was the fact that the team had gone all in on portraying him as some kind of overgrown Boy Scout, and it turned out he wasn't. It was bad enough that he wasn't the QB Tom Reed was. Reed wasn't perfect and never pretended to be, but people would forgive a lot when the Sharks were in the playoffs due to his play. Again.

Even worse, he didn't know why he'd kept encouraging the lies. He'd told himself so many times over the years that he didn't want to betray his parents' values and wanted to be a good example for younger Sharks fans. If he'd been who he really was this whole time, he might not have been asked to make so many personal appearances or been touted by the team as such a good example. He wasn't sure how he was going to deal with so many people's disappointment in him.

He poked at his phone's screen with one finger and scrolled through his contacts list to find Blake's number. He hit the little receiver icon next to his name.

"Hey," Blake said after the first ring. "How are you?"

"I think I need your help again."

"Your coach and the PR group would like to have a conference call with me later. I guess the shit has hit the fan."

"Yeah."

"There's not a lot we can do about the reporter besides tough it out. She'll run to her employer and her colleagues and scream that you're trying to censor her."

"I don't care about her."

"I'd ask you what we've learned from this, but I guess this may be an indelible lesson. Take a deep breath. We'll get through this."

"Maybe."

"Things will be fine. You are not the first person in history to want to keep your private life private. I'll talk to you when I have news."

"Thanks," Grant said. He heard Blake disconnect. He jammed his phone back into his pocket and sat, lost in thought.

He thought he could pull off the biggest BS campaign of all time on the biggest, brightest stage possible—that of a starting QB in the NFL. What was he thinking?

A woman's voice interrupted his troubled thoughts. Emma's mom, Malia, had tracked him down.

"Grant? How are you doing? Is this a good time?"

He got to his feet and reached out to shake her hand. "Of course. How is Emma doing? Is there anything I can help with?"

"She's still in quarantine. She'll be out in a few days. She's been asking for you." Malia grinned at him. "Thank you for the tablet and the other stuff you sent. You really didn't have to do that."

"I wanted to. I hope she'll be better soon."

"She will. Would you like me to call and leave a message at the team's headquarters when she's able to see you again?"

He texted his cell number to her as he spoke.

"How about you call me directly? Be sure and give her a big hug from me. I miss her smiling face."

"She thinks she's going to marry you when she grows up." He saw the same weary smile he'd seen on the faces of so many other parents at the hospital over the past months. "She's so excited to see you play on Sunday. We promised her that we'd turn on the TV in her room so she could watch."

"When she feels better, I'd love to host your family for a game. We'll make sure she's in a suite, so she doesn't get cold or exposed to a lot of people." He had a feeling Daisy would enjoy meeting Emma.

As Malia walked away from him, he pulled up Daisy's number and hit the Dial button. She answered on the first ring.

"I know we weren't going to see each other again until Thursday, but what are you doing tonight?" he asked.

A FEW HOURS later, Grant watched Daisy's car pull into the parking spot next to his in the small lot flanking several soccer pitches in Redmond's Marymoor Park. She waved at him as she gathered some stuff off of the passenger seat. He glanced out of the car window into the gathering darkness.

Heavy, angry-looking gray clouds were closing in overhead. The soccer fields were lit up like daylight due to two banks of floodlights on either side. Several women in team uniforms were kicking a ball around one of the fields a short distance away, while others stood on the sidelines.

He hadn't heard from Blake yet. Nobody else from the Sharks had called him, either. Actually, that wasn't true: Seth Taylor's wife, Jillian, had called twenty minutes or so ago. She'd invited him over for dinner at their house tonight.

"I really wish I could," he'd said. "I have a date."

"Bring her along. I'm trying out new recipes," Jillian said.

"Maybe another time?"

"I'd love that," she said. "Seth said it was a tough day."

"It's better now," he assured her. "Thank you. And I hope that you and Seth will come over to my place some time."

"I'll bring some food," she teased. He knew Seth's wife loved to cook. Even more, the tenderhearted Jillian would be patting him on the back and telling him everything would be okay.

"Thanks, Jillian," he said.

"Call us if you need us," she said.

The heaviness inside lightened a bit as he ended the call.

He shoved himself out of the car. He didn't make it in time to open Daisy's car door for her, but he held out his hand for the beat-up duffle bag she carried.

"That's my team," Daisy said as she indicated the group already on the field. She slammed her car door shut. "We're called Drink and Sing. Are you sure?"

"Sure about what?"

"We're not professionals. I love to play, but you do not see NFL production values out there." She let out a sigh. "There's no concession stand. And it might rain."

"I'm not going to melt," he said. "I told you that I really wanted to watch your match."

"The other team is called Beer for Breakfast."

"I like this already," he said. "Let's go."

He carried Daisy's gear bag across the field. The wind was picking up a little, but it wasn't raining yet. Daisy pulled her hair back and fastened it into an abbreviated ponytail. She pulled a thin Under Armour headband over her forehead to keep the bangs out of her eyes as they walked along.

She stopped fifty feet or so away from the group on the field.

"Will it bother you if people recognize you and want to talk?"

"No." He reached out for her hand. "What's wrong?"

"I'm really excited you're here," she said. "I hoped you'd want to see my game. But I don't want people to bug you or make things uncomfortable."

"Everything's going to be fine." He squeezed her small, cool hand. He felt her fingers curve around his in response. Just holding her hand was a thrill. "We'll have fun."

She didn't look altogether convinced. She didn't let go of his hand, though. He walked them over to the sideline and handed the bag back to her. She unzipped it, pulled out some shin guards, and stuck them into her socks. She yanked on a team-colors fleece pullover and jammed her hands into leather gloves.

"I'm ready," she told him. "Our goalie's here today, so I might be standing on the sidelines with you."

He reached out for one of her hands and kissed the back of it. "Have a great game."

"I will," she said. She joined her teammates, who were now stretching in the middle of the field.

Another guy a few feet away held out his hand. "I'm Charles," he said. He had a British accent. "Nice to meet you."

"Nice to meet you as well. I'm Grant."

"I'm a Sharks fan. I know who you are."

Grant gave him a nod of recognition.

"My wife brought her rain gear. I have a bad feeling they're going to need it."

"Has your wife been playing long?"

"She's played soccer since she was six. She had a scholarship to college, and she tried out for the Olympic team. Our house is a soccer world," Charles said. "I played at university in London."

"And you also love American football."

"My wife loves it even more than I do. She'll want to say hello later."

"I look forward to that." Grant felt a huge raindrop land on the bridge of his nose. "Maybe I should have brought some rain gear myself."

The referee was already pulling on his rain poncho. Grant reached back for the hood that unzipped from the collar of his North Face jacket. Seconds later, the clouds opened and lashed the soccer fields with a torrent of icy rain.

THE FIELD WAS a sea of wet, cold puddles and mud by the half. Drink and Sing's regular goalie slipped and pulled something in her knee; she was on her way to Evergreen Hospital's emergency room in Redmond for x-rays as soon as some of her teammates helped her limp off of the field.

Daisy's drenched uniform stuck to her body like glue. She looked like she'd rolled in the mud as well. She tried to pry chunks of turf and mud out of her cleats with one hand while hopping on one foot. Of course, she wiped out. It was a good thing she and Grant hadn't planned on going out to dinner after the match.

One of her teammates came running and pulled her out of the mud. The rain was coming down so hard it was difficult to see the other end of the field.

"Are you okay?" the teammate called out.

"I'm fine. God, it's awful out here."

"The Beer folk just lost their second goalie to some kind of sprain. Their coach is talking forfeiting."

"We only have another half. We can do it," Daisy said.

"I love to play, but if they're offering a forfeit, I'm taking it."

"Gotcha."

The ball came flying out of nowhere and smacked Daisy in the face. It was wet, cold, and muddy, and it hurt like hell. At least she managed to grab it before it got past her and landed in the goal. She took a few steps forward and booted it onto the opposing team's side. Another of her teammates tried to advance the ball. It was stuck in a huge mud trough.

There was nobody covering the opposing goal. The other team had started with fewer players to begin with and had since had a couple who'd hurt themselves and were on the sidelines.

"If we can score here, we can get the hell out!" Daisy's team's coach shouted from the sidelines. If Drink and Sing lost any more players, she'd be playing too.

Daisy could see her teammates trying to pry the ball out of the mud with their cleats, slipping and sliding in the mud and doing what they could to make that score. The bank of lights overhead couldn't compete with the howling wind and sideways rain. She'd never played a game in weather this bad, and she saw another one of her teammates bend over and clutch her knee. Seconds later, Daisy heard the roll of thunder in the distance.

The ref blew her whistle. "I'm calling this game. It's not safe out here," she yelled. "Get your stuff and get your asses home, ladies."

"Who wins?" the Beer for Breakfast coach shouted back.

"Why do you care? Let's get out of here before we drown," the ref yelled.

The two teams attempted to meet and shake hands on the side of the pitch. A Beer for Breakfast player told them, "We'll shake hands next time."

One of Daisy's teammates called back, "Let us know how your injured players are."

"I'll do that," the coach said. "Get home safe, everyone."

Grant held Daisy's elbow as they crossed the sodden, muddy field. He should have worn some cleats himself. It was slick, they were both drenched, and nothing had ever sounded as good as a hot shower.

"My place or your place?" he said.

"Mine is closer."

"Let's go then."

Grant followed Daisy's Nissan Rogue as she drove slowly through the streets of Redmond, which were awash with water. November in Seattle was all about storms, but the sheer amount of water washing over the road was worrisome. They needed to be off the road.

Daisy pulled into her townhouse development, and this time hit the garage door opener and gestured for him to drive inside. He pulled to a stop instead and hit the button to lower his window.

"Let's get inside," he called out.

Daisy paused long enough to grab her handbag out of her car's trunk. They hurried into the garage and up a small flight of stairs to a door leading to the laundry room. Grant noticed that Catherine's car wasn't in the garage as they passed.

"Catherine isn't out in this, is she?" he said.

"She's at Declan's." She yanked off her cleats and dropped them by the washing machine. "I'll deal with those later. Want me to put your jacket in the dryer?"

They probably should have gone to his place. He could call downstairs for food and a bottle of wine. He had a warm, cozy condo to relax in and a closet full of clean, dry clothing. But Grant knew she'd be more comfortable here. He could make do for one evening.

"My brother left a pair of sweats over here that might fit you," she said. "At least they're dry. I think I have a big T-shirt." He thought he saw color rising over her cheekbones. "I think you're going to have to go commando, however."

"You act like that's a bad thing."

He heard the sweet sound of her laughter. "So you'll deal?"

"Hell yeah."

They both were cold, wet, and dripping all over her laundry room floor, but he reached out to wrap his arms around her.

"Thanks for coming to my game."

"I hope you'll invite me again."

"Maybe I should check the weather report next time," she sighed.

He touched his lips to a drop of water about to roll off the tip of her nose. "It was fun anyway."

"I'll bet you say that to every woman you get caught in a rainstorm with."

"That wasn't a storm. It's some kind of apocalyptic disaster. And you're the only one I want to get caught in a rainstorm with."

She stood on her tiptoes and kissed him. Her mouth was soft, and she tasted like mint. She wrapped her arms around his neck. He wanted more, so much more. Despite the fact that he was freezing cold and was going to need some kind of power tool to get his drenched jeans off with, he felt his body respond. He pulled her closer.

"Are you freezing?" she whispered.

"Hell yes."

"Want to go lie in my tub? I have a bottle of Cabernet on the kitchen counter."

"Let's go."

They gathered up the bottle of wine, a corkscrew, and a big bag of pita snacks as they sloshed their way upstairs.

"You don't mind drinking from the bottle, do you?" she asked. "Glass and soaking tubs don't mix."

"I'll drink it out of your belly button if I have to," he said.

"I like how you think," she said.

She pulled him into her bathroom and reached out to close the drain on her soaking tub. "Do you like bubbles?"

"I like whatever you like," he assured her. "Want me to open the wine?"

"Yes. Please," she said.

A few minutes later, he'd opened the wine so it could breathe (like either of them gave a shit about that) and Daisy was helping him strip his clothes off.

"I'm not sure how we're getting your jeans off," she said as she tried to unbutton the waistband. "They're still stuck on you."

"I'll take care of that," he said. He pulled her team jersey off over her head. The pretty bra made of sheer fabric she wore was still so wet it looked spray-painted on. If he didn't get his damn jeans off, he was going to explode, but he had to pay a little attention to her reddened-with-cold breasts first. Anyone would have to.

If they could get their clothes off and get into the rapidly filling tub, they'd both be warm. Right now, though, he wanted to hold her and suck the remaining moisture off of her rosy-pink nipples.

He heard the chirp of a message waiting on his phone, which was most likely Blake. Grant could deal with the fallout from today later. He didn't want to think about anything or anyone else tonight but Daisy.

She reached behind her back to undo her bra clasp, and he put one hand over hers. "Let me," he said. She didn't resist. The bra was wet enough that he pinched the clasp together and got it off in twenty seconds. He dropped it on the rapidly growing pile of clothes on her bathroom floor.

"It's not very romantic in here," she whispered to him. "There should be candles and rose petals floating on the water or something. Mr. Bubble isn't cutting it right now."

He reached out to shut the water off. "Mr. Bubble works just fine," he said. "Let's get in the tub, and I'll show you."

They worked together to pull his jeans off and left them in a sodden heap. She shucked her uniform shorts off in record time. Minutes later, they were both naked, and after dragging a hand through the water to test the temp, he lowered himself into her tub.

He held out a hand. "It's perfect. Come on in," he said.

She stepped in, narrowly missing his junk, and settled back against him. She let out a long sigh. "I should have shut the lights off before we got in here."

"Why?"

"Dim lights. Wine." She leaned back against his chest, glancing at the open bottle of wine on the bathroom counter. "I should have grabbed that."

"Daisy, we don't need it," he murmured into her ear. He mounded soap bubbles on her belly and covered her breasts with them. "Relax."

He felt her damp and still chilly skin warming due to the hot water and his hands moving over her. He closed his eyes. She still smelled like sunshine and flowers, and he felt her heave another sigh. "Maybe we should stay in here."

"We'll have to get out when the hot water runs out," he said.

She twined her fingers through his. "I have a tankless water heater. We can hold out forever."

He wrapped his arms around her abdomen. The only sounds in her house were an occasional splash and their breathing. He let out a long breath. He was hard against her, but they had things to talk about before they got busy with each other. He wasn't sure how to start the conversation. He'd rather start the fun in Daisy's tub, carry her into her room, and have sex all night than discuss his shortcomings with someone he didn't want to disappoint. Maybe he should blurt it out and get things over with.

"Something happened today," he said. "I need to talk with you about it."

DESPITE THE HARSH circa-1990s overhead bathroom vanity light and lack of romantic accoutrements, things were moving right along in Daisy's tub. Her hair was still soaking wet, but every inch of her that touched Grant was warm and cozy. His fingers strayed dangerously close to her crotch. She let her legs fall open in invitation. She wriggled her lower back against his erection.

"We really need to talk," he murmured.

"We've got all night," she said.

His fingers moved closer to the point of no return. Actually, they moved closer to her clit. The soap bubbles might work as a makeshift lube. Then again, she was so wet that all he had to do was draw his fingertips through her labia; he'd have plenty to work with. She moved against his erection again. If she reached behind her back and between them, she could do something nice for him while his fingers moved closer and closer to the target.

She couldn't quite reach his penis. "You first," he said. His damp hair was a veil, but she could reach his mouth. She took his face into her hands and pulled his mouth over hers. His tongue slipped into her mouth, darting, stroking, and inciting. Her moan was swallowed in his kiss.

He reached between them, tipped her up a bit more against his shoulder, and slid a finger inside of her. He thrust slowly. She moved against his hand. If she opened her legs a bit more, slung one leg over the side of the tub, and wriggled a little—there. He slipped two fingers inside of her while the heel of his hand slid against her clit in the slow rhythm he set.

Her breathing accelerated. She let out another moan. She was torn between wanting the orgasm she knew was building and flipping over on her belly, straddling him, and screwing his brains out while they splashed water all over the bathroom floor. "Oh, God!" she cried out.

"Faster?" His voice was low and dark.

"Yes. Yes. Oh! Oh." She tried to spread her legs even farther. Damn bathroom wall. He picked up speed a bit.

She'd managed to tip herself almost out of the water. She kept moving. She felt the first small flutter of what she hoped would be a huge orgasm in her belly. "A few. Faster," she moaned.

"Yeah," he groaned. "Come all over me."

His fingers and the heel of his hand brought her to an orgasm so intense she screamed. She felt him jump a little in response. His fingers didn't stop, though. His movements slowed a bit, but he kept stroking his fingers in and out of her through the fireworks that burst behind her eyelids, the strong contractions she felt, the heat that spread through her.

"I'm going to make you scream again," he said.

"I…I…" She had no idea what she was trying to say. She was lost in an overpowering world of sensation and feeling. He continued to touch her gently, rub her, and whisper into her ear.

"Let go," he said.

She couldn't concentrate on anything besides his voice and his teasing, thrusting fingers. She would do anything. She flattened her other foot against the bathroom wall to offer him more access, felt his hand move a bit more quickly, and cried out as the contractions began again.

She wasn't sure what happened next. She came back to herself slowly. She slumped against him. One big hand was over her crotch as he cradled her in his other arm. She still felt fluttering in her abdomen, and she opened her eyes as she heard his voice in her ear.

"Are you okay?" he said.

She'd never been so relaxed. They'd probably made a mess out of the bathroom, but who cared? She pulled one leg back into the tub and rolled over to look into his eyes.

"I'm great," she said. She reached up to tuck some of his hair behind one ear. "I'd like to do something for you too."

Things were still twitching between her legs. Damn. If she'd known multiple orgasms were this great, she would have tried them a long time ago. Somehow, she knew it wouldn't be the same if it happened with any other man. She knew in a blinding flash she didn't want to try it with any other man, either.

"Really?" he said.

"Oh, yeah," she said. She reached out to grasp him in one fist. "Still want to talk?"

"Later," he said.

GRANT AND DAISY wrapped each other in bathroom towels and hurried into her bedroom. He was somewhat amused to watch her shut and lock her bedroom door before she put two hands in the middle of his chest and pushed him down on her bed. He'd already discovered she was surprisingly strong, and she had no problem taking charge. He wasn't objecting.

"Are you expecting someone?" he teased.

"Just making sure," she said. She reached under his pelvis, pulled his hips to the edge of her bed, and grinned up at him. "My parts might need a little rest before—well, you know." She sank to her knees in front of him. "You don't mind, do you?" She swirled her tongue around the head of his dick, and he let out a long groan. "I was hoping you'd say that," she said.

Less than three minutes later, she had him begging. She teased and taunted him with her mouth, getting him close and backing away just before he exploded. "Shit. Jesus. Daisy. I need to come," he groaned.

"Later," she teased.

"Wait until I get my hands on you—"

"I can't wait," she said before bringing him to the brink again. She reached into her bedside table and squeezed something over her fingertips, rubbing her hands together briefly. "Ready?"

"God. Fuck. YES. Shit!" he called out. He opened his eyes long enough to see what she was doing. She was licking him, rubbing him up and down while manipulating his balls with her other hand, and sweet baby Jesus, he was going to explode. "I…I can't…Fuck!" he called out.

He came so hard the edges of his vision went black, and he saw stars.

Grant heard his cell phone ringing as Daisy flopped down next to him on her bed.

"Do you need to answer that?"

"Voice mail," he said as he fought to catch his breath.

He could call them back if he was still among the living in an hour or so. Having sex with Daisy wasn't some sweet, languorous encounter. It was hot, sweaty, took every ounce of his strength, and he wouldn't have it any other way.

They hadn't gotten to the main event yet, and he was already wiped out. Maybe he was getting old or something. Right now, he wanted to scramble under the covers with her and rest.

"You wanted to talk earlier," she said. "You're not dumping me or something, are you?"

The smile on her face was playful, but he saw something else in her eyes. She was bracing herself for whatever reason. He got off the bed and pulled the blankets down so they could crawl inside. He propped the pillows against the headboard. He held out his arms so she would nestle against him.

She ran her fingers through his chest hair. "So, what's up?"

He let out a long sigh. "You might want to dump me when you hear this," he said.

"So, we're together now?"

"We weren't before?" he said. "I want to be with you. Do you want to be with me?"

"Yes," she said. She laid her hand over his heart, which was beating a bit faster at her nearness. Her scent, the softness of her skin, the sound of her voice, and the way she snuggled against him—he never wanted her to leave, he realized with a shock. He'd been searching for her, and he hadn't realized it until now. And he had to tell her the truth.

He took a deep breath. His voice, when it came, sounded shaky to his own ears. "I've been lying to everyone I know for a long time now."

He heard his cell phone ringing again in the silence.

"Want me to get that?" she said. Her voice sounded casual, like he'd just confessed to leaving the carton of milk in the refrigerator with half an inch in the bottom.

"I'll get it later," he said.

"No, let's get it now."

The ringing stopped and started again. There might be an emergency with his parents. Maybe he should get out of bed and find out who was calling and what they wanted. She hopped out of bed, disappeared into the bathroom, and closed the door slightly.

She got back into bed a few minutes later and handed him his cell phone. He had twenty-six missed calls since he'd been at the soccer field with Daisy. Ten of them were from his agent. The other sixteen were a mixture of his teammates and members of the media.

"Something's wrong," she said.

"Are you okay if I call my agent back?" He was already getting out of bed. He wrapped a towel around his midsection and padded into the bathroom. He shut the door behind him and sat down on the toilet lid. He hit Blake's number.

"Where the fuck have you been?" Blake asked.

"It's a long story," Grant said.

"Listen. There's trouble. I did my best, but there are several people in the Sharks' front office who are not happy about the story that's now been picked up by all major sports outlets. Sportscaster Barbie sure gets around." He let out another long sigh. "I did my best. I told them it was unreasonable for them to equate anything you've done with that dipshit QB they cut before, but they're not budging. I'm meeting with the front office guys and your coach tomorrow." He let out a long sigh. "Also, one of my buds in the scouting group called me earlier. They're bringing in some veteran QBs for a tryout tomorrow morning."

It took everything he had to get the next words out. "Are they cutting me?"

"No. They might be benching you, though."

"Johnny can't quarterback his way out of a paper bag, and Reed's still hurt."

"You owe Reed one hell of a fruit basket, by the way. He was on the call. He told them there were guys currently on the team who are bigger manwhores than you've ever been, and they're making a huge mistake by bringing anyone else in."

Grant couldn't seem to make his mouth work.

"I'm flying up there in the morning. Get some sleep, and we'll strategize beforehand," Blake said.

"Yeah."

"We'll get through this. If we don't, Los Angeles has already called and would like to give you a tryout."

He didn't want to play for LA. He wanted to stay in Seattle. With Daisy.

"Thanks, I think." Grant pulled breath into his lungs. "And thank you for trying."

"I'll let you buy me brunch tomorrow at that Brown Bag place. Big portions. I'll call you in the morning. My flight lands at ten AM. The meeting is at two PM."

Blake disconnected the call. Grant stared into space for a few minutes. The bathroom door opened, and Daisy walked in in some silky, flowery bathrobe. She sat down next to him on the edge of the soaking tub.

"I guess this wasn't good news," she said.

"No. It wasn't."

"Come on," she said. She held out her hand, and he took it. She led him back to her room, repositioned the pillows, pulled the blankets up to his chin, and put his phone down on the bedside table. "We can talk more tomorrow."

"I need to tell you what happened," he said.

"It's all going to look better in the morning." She shut off the bedside lamp and crawled into bed next to him. "Sleep."

Chapter Fifteen

DAISY'S ALARM WENT off at five AM the next morning. Grant wasn't in her bed. She reached out to feel the pillowcase. It was cool. In other words, he'd left sometime during the night. She could see one of the drawers in her dresser slightly ajar. He must have found the sweats and the huge Microsoft Vista T-shirt her brother left at her place once upon a time.

She sat up in bed and pulled her knees up to her chest, wrapping her forearms around them. He'd awoken in the middle of the night; they'd had sex again, and she'd had another huge orgasm. She was falling asleep in his arms when she heard him say, "We have things to talk about, Daisy."

"I have something to tell you too," she murmured.

"Then we're even," he said. She heard the smile in his voice. After the drenching on the soccer field and some pretty acrobatic sex, she could sleep for a week.

She was pretty sure she knew what Grant had wanted to tell her last night. It really didn't matter to her how many people he'd been with before or that he wasn't the Goody-Two-shoes everyone else expected him to be. She knew he was worried because he thought the Sharks would retaliate against him for some vindictive sports reporter's nonstory. Wait until he heard what she had to say.

The icy ball of fear was back in her stomach. She had to confess to him. She couldn't believe all the media about *Overtime Parking*. It must have been a slow news week or something. Plus, she knew Grant was handsome, but he was now some kind of sex symbol. He had a new nickname in the media: Quarterback Jesus.

Yikes.

The book had just hit a new best-seller list, and she'd also received a fresh new royalties deposit in her checking account. She'd transferred it to savings and resolved to find a CPA who could advise her this week.

She shoved herself out of bed. If she didn't get a move on, she was going to be late. And she was going to catch up with Grant later today and tell him. Once and for all. If he dumped her, at least she'd told him the truth. Thinking about losing him made her want to cry and cry and never stop, though.

She should have told him a long time ago. She should have told him before they'd slept together, before she'd found out what he was really like, before she'd developed feelings for him. She shouldn't have published the book in the first place. She knew how it could affect him. He liked his privacy and didn't need to be the subject of jokes and conjecture. Grant wanted to play football and not have to deal with the fallout that came from something everyone else expected him to comment on.

She'd traded with another flight attendant this morning because she wanted to work the Sharks' charter flight this weekend. She'd rather spend tonight with Grant than in a hotel room in Phoenix, but she had to work.

She heard her phone chime with an incoming text. She picked it up off the bathroom counter and clicked on the icon to open it. It was Grant.

Grant: *Let's meet up later.*

Her thumbs flew across the keyboard.

Daisy: *I'll be in Phoenix. Tomorrow.*

Grant: *Tomorrow night. I'm sorry I left without saying good-bye.*

Maybe he didn't like staying all night. Maybe he was uncomfortable. Maybe he had an appointment. Or maybe he was avoiding the conversation they needed to have as much as she was.

Daisy: *I missed you.*

Grant: *I miss you too. I taped an interview. I'll send you the file so you can see it.*

She heard another chime on her phone as the video file arrived in her in-box.

Grant: *Hopefully I don't look like an idiot. See you later.*

He must have done the interview before she showed up at Marymoor for her game; the date on the video file was yesterday. She had to leave for the airport in the next twenty minutes or so, but she could watch it before she left. The listing said that the interview would be part of Pro Sports Network's Sunday pre-game show.

She'd seen the show before because her dad and brother had watched it. Five guys with some connection to the NFL talked about that day's upcoming games, told jokes, and gave each other a hard time. The only one she recognized behind the desk was Brandon McKenna.

Brandon seemed to be the guy the other players and coaches looked to for confirmation or calm in the midst of the chaos of five highly competitive men attempting to talk over each other. He'd also built up solid interviewing skills as a result of talking with some high-profile players about the questions of the day without devolving into needless flattery to elicit information from them.

Daisy sat down on her bed, pulled her overnight bag and purse close so she could grab them up, and clicked on the video file Grant had sent.

Brandon gazed into the TV camera as Daisy watched.

"I was able to sit down with Grant Parker of the Seattle Sharks for a few minutes this week. I hope you'll enjoy this."

As the taped interview started, Grant and Brandon sat across from each other in director's chairs. Brandon reached out to shake Grant's hand and said, "Good to see you, Grant. Thanks for meeting with me today."

"It's my pleasure, Brandon," Grant said.

It was the first time Daisy had seen Grant being interviewed in street clothes. The team usually dressed him in Sharks logo stuff from head to toe. He wore a pullover sweater, beat-up jeans, and his long, sun-streaked dark hair was twisted into a bun low on his neck.

"Let's talk a little about how your life has changed in the past few weeks. You're starting for the Sharks while Tom Reed is rehabbing from broken ribs. How's that going?"

"We've won two games now, I'm really happy the second start went as well as my first. The team's really responding. Reed has been giving me some tips as well. I want to make sure things are great when he's back."

"There have been rumors that Reed has already told you he's planning on retiring from the league. What are your thoughts on that?"

"That's Tom's business. I will say, though, that it would be a huge loss to our team and to the league. He's been showing everyone how it's done for the past fifteen years."

Brandon asked Grant a few more general questions about the Sharks and their upcoming opponents, and Daisy saw him lean forward in his chair a bit. Grant put both feet on the floor and leaned forward as well.

"I'd prefer talking about football, and I know you would too."

Grant's mouth twitched into a smile. "You got that right."

"You spent a few years backing Reed up. You didn't get a lot of snaps as a result."

"It was my job. I practiced hard and did some extra work to make sure I'd be ready if I had to go into a game with little notice."

Brandon gave him the nod. "Exactly. Let's talk a little about what happens when any player becomes a starter in the league. How have you been dealing with the increased fan attention and press coverage?"

"I expected the additional attention, but the press coverage is still a surprise. It's different, and I appreciate those who like to talk or write about me and my career."

"It's appreciated until it becomes unfair or untrue, right?"

"I don't have a lot of control over what any member of the media has to say about me."

"Earlier this week, you were visiting Children's Hospital in Seattle and you were ambushed by a reporter and cameraman from a local TV station wanting to discuss rumors circulating about your private life."

"Yes, I was." Grant appeared to be thinking for a few seconds. "I'm happy to talk about football or the Sharks to any and all reporters. But I'd prefer to keep my private life private. The things that were reported about my social life have nothing to do with my career. I'm a single adult who dates. That's not news to anyone, is it? 'Local man goes out on a date with another consenting adult. Film at eleven.' Really? Who cares, besides the other person in question and me?"

Brandon grinned at him. "I remember those days. My wife says I'm dating her for the rest of my life."

"That sounds like a solid plan, Brandon." The two men shook hands again. "Actually, I'm going to break my own rule here. I've been seeing someone recently, and I'm really into her. I'm not interested in seeing anyone else besides her. Maybe that'll clear up some of the lingering questions about what I'm doing with my personal time."

Daisy clasped her hands over her mouth.

"How did you meet her?"

"We were both on an airplane at the time," he said. "She offered me a bag of pretzels or something. I couldn't resist her."

Daisy's heart started to pound. At that moment, she knew, even more than she had when she'd woken up this morning. She was in love with him. She could dream of what it might be like with him (and she had), but the reality was so much better than her fantasies. She wasn't sure he was ready to use the *L* word, but she hoped he would. In the meantime, he'd just told everyone in his world how he felt about her.

Maybe she could float to the airport. She felt like she could fly.

A huge grin spread over Brandon's face. "Does she like football?"

"She doesn't know a thing about it. I'm fine with that."

"Thanks for your time, Grant. We hope we'll talk with you again soon. Good luck on the season."

"Thanks, Brandon."

Daisy had to leave, but she had to speak with him. Right now. She reached out to grab her phone, hit Grant's number, and heard his voice.

"Did you see it?"

"Yes," she said. "You did a good job."

"McKenna does a great interview," Grant said. "I really enjoyed talking with him."

Silence fell. She could hear noise in the background. Grant must have been in the locker room at the practice facility with the other guys. She hauled breath into her lungs.

"I know it's probably dumb to ask, but did you mean what you said about just being with—oh, forget it," she said. She'd had a sudden attack of bashfulness.

"The reporter? I told you about her," he said. She could hear laughter in his voice.

"No. No. That's not it. The person you're with."

"That's you, goofball. Did you really not know?"

"Well, you could be dating someone from Alaska Airlines or something—"

"Nope. I like Pacifica flight attendants who offer me pretzels. Are you okay that I told people I'm off the market?"

"Yes," she said.

Chapter Sixteen

DAISY DIDN'T HAVE a lot of time to bask in the happiness of Grant's phone call. The next several days were jam-packed with work due to several of Pacifica's flight attendants calling in sick. Daisy and her co-workers scrambled to cover their flights as a result. She wasn't home much. The week sped by in a blur as she and Grant communicated via quick texts. When she tried to ask him about the meeting she knew had happened earlier in the week between Grant, his agent, and the Sharks' front office, he changed the subject. Maybe he'd talk about it when they saw each other. She missed him already.

Sunday morning featured gray granite-colored clouds and threatened rain. She wouldn't be at today's Sharks game, but she couldn't stop thinking about Grant as she dressed for work.

She grabbed her phone and texted, *I know you'll win. Go Sharks!*

Her phone chimed a few minutes later with *I can't wait to see you again*.

She arrived at the airport, boarded the plane an hour early, and took a quick inventory of supplies in the galley. She put sealed bottles of airline-branded water on each first-class seat, along with pillows and plastic-wrapped blankets. She'd traded flights with another charter flight attendant a few days ago so she could work on the Sharks' plane both ways next week and see Grant's game in person.

Her coworker Rachel stepped onto the plane as Daisy finished counting the available headphones for seat-back viewers. There were plenty, she noted with relief. It was always good to have some form of entertainment on any flight longer than an hour.

"How are you?" Rachel said. "I'm sorry I'm late. Traffic is a mess, as usual. You'd think that things would be clear going the opposite direction, but maybe not."

"Don't worry about it," Daisy said. "The meals are in the galley. Drinks are stocked up. Water, pillows, and blankets are ready. We're good."

"You must have gotten here pretty early."

"I was freaked out about what the traffic would be like too," Daisy said. It sounded like her cell phone was ringing again. It had rung a few times in the last ten minutes or so. She wasn't supposed to use her phone while she was at work.

"Isn't that your phone again?" Rachel said.

"It's probably my mom or something," Daisy said.

"Go take a look," Rachel told her. "I can handle the rest of the checklist."

Daisy sat down on the jump seat the flight attendants used, grabbed her phone out of her bag, and looked at the screen. Catherine had called six times in the past ten minutes, which meant something was wrong. She knew Daisy couldn't talk on the phone during a flight. The pilots were still doing their pre-check outside the plane, so Daisy hit Catherine's number and held the phone up to her ear.

"Daisy," Catherine said on the second ring. "There's a story on KIXI-TV's Facebook page. Harley, that sports reporter, she found someone in the self-publishing service's accounting department who told her you're the author of *Overtime Parking*."

"*What?*" She tried to keep her voice down. It didn't work. Rachel turned to look at Daisy.

"Yeah. She knows. Plus, she's reporting your name and where you work."

"Why would anyone care who I was or where I work? That's crazy. Didn't they have anything else in the world to report on today?"

Daisy felt fear and dread sweep over her in seconds.

"She must really hate Grant. She's a nut. Listen, I know you have to get off the phone. Call me when you get to Phoenix. And we'll handle this."

"I don't know what to do."

"Put one foot in front of the other and breathe. Call me, text me, whatever. Safe flight." Catherine ended the call.

Daisy set her phone to airplane mode, jammed it back into her purse, and slumped in her seat. Her stomach was churning already. She broke out in a cold sweat. Any hope she might have had of breaking the news to Grant that she was the author of *Overtime Parking* on her own was gone. He had his own secrets, but she knew it was no excuse. If she cared for him, she should have been honest with him. She wished she had been.

There was also the small matter of what her parents were going to think when they found out. Her brother was going to flip out, especially since he thought she was still twelve or something. Her friends. The airline, specifically the group that scheduled the Sharks' charter flights. They would think she was some kind of crazy stalker, at the least.

For the most part, though, the other people who would be hurt, angry, or shocked at the news she'd written a really smutty book weren't her biggest concern.

She couldn't stop thinking about Grant. And she had no idea how she was going to explain this to him. She was going to have a number of phone calls to make when she got to Phoenix, and none of them would be pleasant.

She grabbed her phone out of her purse again, pulled up his number, and typed.

I can explain. I am so sorry.

She shut it off, jammed it back in her bag, and got to her feet. She needed to put it all out of her mind until the flight got to its destination.

According to the manifest, today's flight was full. Typically, a full flight was a busy one. A few minutes later, Daisy was also dealing with a series of issues that made any flight miserable. Most of the time, they didn't happen all at once.

There were three customers in first class who were already drunk when they boarded the flight. Drunken passengers fell into two categories: quiet and compliant (and typically asleep for most of the flight) or loud and disruptive. Unfortunately for Daisy, all three were the latter type, and all three were VIPs. She recognized the world-famous rapper (creatively named The Revolution), his socialite wife, and his mogul mother-in-law the second she saw them. The Revolution was almost seven feet tall and probably weighed less than Daisy did. He enjoyed guy liner, significant tattooing, and the *F* word and looked like he hadn't experienced daylight in several years. The airline allowed flight attendants the ability to ask that drunken passengers be removed from any flight before departure, but Daisy also knew that denying boarding to this group would cause big issues for the Pacifica employees aboard and for her bosses.

The fun had started before the plane shoved back from the gate, when The Revolution demanded a drink.

"How about some coffee? I have a fresh pot here. I can also offer water," Daisy said.

"No. I want scotch. I want one every fifteen minutes," he said.

"I'm sorry, sir, but we don't serve alcohol until we're at cruising altitude."

"Fuck cruising altitude. I want it now. Bring her some champagne." The Revolution nodded at his wife, Prada, and reached into his seat back, producing a full chilled bottle of Roederer Cristal, which he handed to Daisy. She'd seen personnel make exceptions where celebrities were concerned, but she'd never seen someone waltz onto a plane with a full bottle of champagne before. "In a *glass* glass. Not one of those plastic cups."

"Sir, I—"

"Get it now," he barked out.

"One moment, please," she said and hurried to the galley. She set the bottle into the small sink and turned to knock on the pilots' door.

One of the pilots opened the door a crack. "What's up, Daisy? We're trying to get into the departure lineup."

"May I come in for a moment?"

"Sure."

She was admitted to the flight deck. She knew Rachel would be standing guard against the locked cockpit door. She'd better make it fast.

"We have a problem. The Revolution, his wife, Prada, and his mother-in-law, Cartier, are on the flight today. They're all drunk and disorderly. Also, The Revolution brought his own champagne."

The gray-haired pilot turned in his seat and said, "Who?"

The other pilot, a woman fifteen years younger than he was, said, "My teenage son listens to that idiot. So he's here, and he's drunk?"

"He, his wife, and his mother-in-law."

"The mother-in-law is horrible."

"Tell me about it," Daisy said. "What do we do? If we kick them off, we'll never hear the end of it. They're already demanding alcohol."

The pilot got to his feet. "I'll handle this." He glanced over at his copilot. "Please let the tower know we'll need a short delay. And I'm reopening the entry door, just in case."

"Got it," she said.

Daisy tapped on the cockpit door so Rachel would know they were coming out. The pilot strode through the door, stopped at the row where the rapper and his family sat, and said, "I'm Captain Schaefer."

He extended his hand. The rapper stared at him resentfully and didn't make a move to shake the pilot's hand.

"Okay. If that's how you want it, this is how it's going to go. The only way you're staying on this flight is if you are quiet, follow directions, do not ask for any more alcohol, and stay in your seat until we are at the gate in Phoenix. Do you understand?"

"Do you know who I am?" the rapper snarled.

"Yes, I know who you are. I'm also in charge of this flight, which means you should be more concerned at the moment with who *I* am," the pilot said.

"My Gulfstream is being repaired. We should have rented another jet," the rapper said. He got to his feet. "I don't have to put up with this shit."

"Actually, you don't have much of a choice," the pilot said. "You won't be flying anywhere else today. Enjoy your stay in Seattle." He stepped back and gestured toward the open door of the jet. "Please get your things and leave."

"I don't have to get off the plane," The Revolution said.

"We'll sue," his mother-in-law said.

"She stole our bottle of Cristal," his wife said and pointed at Daisy.

"Daisy, please call the gate agent and tell them we'll need security," Captain Schaefer said.

"You can't make us get off this flight," the rapper said.

"Yes, I can, and I am," the pilot said. Daisy heard the cockpit door open and shut behind her and the other pilot's voice in her ear. "I called the tower. The cops are on their way, and airport security is also alerted."

Two men dressed in the airline's maintenance staff's uniforms appeared at the jet's doorway. They both flashed law enforcement badges.

"Let's go," the taller guy said. "Time to leave."

"You can't tell me what to do—"

Seconds later, the rapper was on the floor in the aisle and wearing handcuffs. "I have another couple of sets," one of the police officers said to the guy's wife and mother-in-law. "Would you like to leave quietly, or would you like your own?"

The rapper was being wrestled off the plane by several people, so Daisy stepped into the galley and handed the gate agent Prada's bottle of champagne.

"I'm sure she wants this," Daisy said.

"She won't be getting it back until she's off airport property," the gate agent said.

"That's mine," Prada said and lunged for it, which started a shouting, hair-pulling melee among the rapper's wife, several passengers, flight attendants, and the law enforcement officers who were attempting to get the wife and mother-in-law off the plane.

It took almost an hour to restore order. Prada had managed to yank out a handful of Daisy's hair and had torn her uniform blouse in the guise of getting her champagne back. Daisy had also sustained a few bumps and bruises as she tried to separate people and get them back into their seats, but she could deal with those later.

She and Rachel formed makeshift ice packs out of Ziploc bags and ice for passengers. A doctor flying in coach came forward to check the passengers and crew members who got the brunt of the fight. The gate agent appeared at the door one more time.

"You guys are going to have to go in the next half hour, or the pilots are going to time out," she said. "Are you and Rachel okay to fly?"

"I can do it," Daisy said.

"Daisy, that woman beat the hell out of you," Rachel said. "She must be an MMA fighter in her spare time. Is there anyone else we can call?"

"They can't get here before the pilots time out," the gate agent said.

Daisy reached out to pat Rachel on the shoulder. "It's okay. I can handle it."

One of the passengers raised her hand. "I can help you," she said.

"Thank you for offering. That's really sweet, but we'll be fine," Rachel assured her. "Why don't you all sit back and relax, and we'll be under way quickly."

"I'll see you both tomorrow," the gate agent said. "Operations will want to talk with you all when you get there."

"I'll call them," Daisy said.

Fifteen minutes later, the flight was lining up for take-off. Daisy and Rachel were belted into their seats and listening for the engines to rev up in preparation.

"What a day," Rachel said.

"And it just started," Daisy said.

The pilot got on the overhead speaker when the plane reached altitude and said, "I'd like to thank everyone for their patience while we dealt with a problem earlier. As a result, I'd also like to offer a free drink to everyone over twenty-one on this flight. It's on us. So relax, enjoy, and it looks like a smooth flight to Phoenix. Thanks again for flying Pacifica Airlines."

Daisy and Rachel handed out drinks, snacks, served the in-flight meal, and cleaned up afterward. The adrenaline pumping through her wore off as the flight continued. By the time they were an hour outside of Phoenix, she wasn't feeling well at all.

"Are you okay, Daisy?" Rachel said as they stowed the last of the glassware and dirty silverware from the meal.

"I feel like crap," Daisy said. "It's just another hour. Maybe I can take a hot bath at the hotel."

"I think you need to be seen by a doctor," Rachel said.

"Later," Daisy sighed.

"We're done. Everything's cleaned up. Sit down for a few minutes, and I can handle it."

Sitting down made things worse. She ached all over. Her ankle had been throbbing since a passenger fell on it, and the pain was worse than it had been earlier. She would have to walk through the airport to get to the curb and catch the crew shuttle to the hotel. Thinking about what would greet her on the ground in Phoenix didn't help her aches and pains.

GRANT'S SUNDAY AFTERNOON was as bruising as Daisy's. His first two games as a starter had gone well; his teammates made an extra effort to work together, and the Sharks won easily as a result. Today's game was a study in frustration. His wide receivers were dropping a pass for every one that they caught. The offensive line was struggling to keep Atlanta's defense off of him so he would have time to pass in the first place. He tried to scramble out of the pocket and almost got pantsed by Atlanta's gigantic defensive end. The guy wagged his finger in Grant's face and shouted, "There's more where that came from, asshole."

Grant saw two flags hit the turf out of the corner of his eye. Taunting. Even better, the guy was dumb enough to make his comments (and the obscene hand gestures) in full view of two game officials.

"Thanks for the fifteen yards and the first down. I appreciate it," Grant said as the guy's coach screamed at him from the sidelines.

The Sharks defense wasn't having a great day, either. Atlanta's quarterback was mobile, had pinpoint passing accuracy, and shredded most defenses with ease. The Sharks trailed at halftime by ten points.

"At least it's only ten points," Zach Anderson said as they headed to the locker room. "We can catch them."

"We're not helping ourselves at the moment," Drew McCoy told him.

"And we're going to let them win?" Derrick Collins shouted. "These guys aren't good! We beat the shit out of them the last time we played them. What the hell is wrong here? Let's fix it and win this thing!"

The coach and his assistants spent the next ten minutes drawing diagrams on the whiteboard and adjusting their previous game plan to contain the defensive end who had spent the entire game tormenting Grant, for starters. "They're vulnerable. They burn energy in the first half, and they always come out flat after halftime. Let's take advantage of it," the coach said as he gestured for the players to form a circle. Every man thrust his hand in to grab his teammates' hands. Everyone yelled "Go Sharks" on the count of three, and then it was time to jog back onto the field for the second half.

Kevin smacked Grant on the ass. "You can do this. Don't let them get in your head."

"Got it," Grant said. "Want some work?"

"You know I do."

"Then you're getting the ball. Let's see what you can do with it," Grant said.

"Shit, yeah," Kevin told him.

Grant took the snap for the first play from the line of scrimmage, handed it off to Kevin, and stepped aside as Kevin blasted a hole through Atlanta's defensive line. He easily evaded men who outweighed him by almost a hundred pounds as he clutched the ball to his abdomen with both hands. He was chased down the field by those defensive players, who couldn't do a thing when Kevin strolled into the end zone, spiked the ball, and did a little dance to celebrate.

Grant ran to congratulate Kevin as the Sharks' offense headed to the sidelines following a successful point-after kick.

"Good job, bro."

"Someone around here has to score a few points," Kevin said.

"Let's try that at least one more time today," Grant said.

"You got it."

The Sharks' defense seemed to rally as a result of being within a field goal of tying the game. Kade managed to escape from Atlanta's double-teams and pulled their quarterback to the ground a few plays later. The ball popped out of the quarterback's hands, flew into the air, and Clay Morrison grabbed it. After a split second of confusion, Clay took off for the end zone. The defensive line guys didn't typically run the ball. Clay wasn't fast, but it wasn't possible for the other team to bring him down, even with three guys pulling on his jersey.

"Run, you magnificent bastard!" Reed yelled from the sidelines.

"Move dat ass!"

"Get it!" Seth Thomas shouted at Clay.

"He's going to need some damn oxygen," the trainer said to nobody in particular.

Clay managed to make it to the end zone without pulling a hamstring or needing an ambulance. The game officials signaled touchdown, and he collapsed to the turf under five of his opponents.

"Their QB probably broke a nail," Derrick said.

Grant watched his teammates pull Clay up off the turf, loop their arms around him, and walk him back to the Sharks' sideline. Clay wasn't letting go of the ball. His smile was ear-to-ear—well, what anyone could see of his smile, due to the huge chunk of turf stuck in the face-mask of his helmet.

Grant jogged over to the knot of players surrounding Clay and stuck out his hand. "Good job," he said. "I'm proud of you."

Clay leaned forward and smacked his helmet into Grant's in response.

Two hours later, the game was over. The Sharks won by one point. If Grant was quick about it, he could make it into the locker room and grab a shower before he had to talk with the media.

He wasn't quite fast enough.

Harley McHugh and her cameraman were feet away from him—too close to pretend like he didn't see them. He couldn't walk away without creating more of a problem, so he nodded at her and tried to swerve away. It didn't happen.

She stuck her microphone in his face. "Talk to me about today's game, Grant."

Oh, so now she wanted an actual interview about football? He pasted a smile he didn't feel on his face. "The first half was tough. Our coaches made some great adjustments during halftime, though, and I'm pretty happy about our victory."

"Sources are telling me that Tom Reed asked to be put into today's game when you couldn't move the offense during the first half."

Grant wanted to snap at her. Tom had said nothing of the kind. He'd been talking through the microphone in Grant's helmet about the play choices and some strategies to try to get Atlanta's defense off of his back. Tom also had told Grant before the game that the team specialist recommended that Tom be placed on injured reserve. In other words, he wasn't going to heal up before the season was over. The team had tried out a few healthy veteran QBs to back Grant up, and they had no choice but to sign one now.

"Tom was actually going over some plays with me. He wants to win."

"Our viewers would also like to see Reed in the next few games. We'll look forward to that."

In other words, she was trying to piss him off. He told himself to take deep breaths and let her comments roll off of his back.

"It's always great to have Tom on the field." He gave her another nod. "Thanks for the interview. I need to get back."

"One more thing, Grant." The hair stood up on the back of his neck as her eyes narrowed. She was practically purring, and it wasn't because she liked him. "Were you surprised to learn that one of the flight attendants who work on the Sharks' charter flights actually wrote *Overtime Parking*? We confirmed this morning that Daisy Spencer is the book's author. You know Daisy, don't you? Haven't you had several dates with her over the past few weeks?" Harley gave him an insincere smile. "Were you lying when you said you had no idea who wrote the book?"

"Excuse me?"

"Did you help her write it? It really raised your profile around the league, didn't it?"

"No! What are you talking about?"

"How do you think the Sharks will react to this knowledge? Should be interesting!" She turned her back to Grant and said, "This is Harley McHugh reporting from Sharks Stadium. Back to you, guys."

"That can't be true," Grant blurted out. "You made it up. Daisy—Daisy would never do anything like that."

"The truth hurts, doesn't it, Grant?" Harley snapped as she walked away from him.

Grant strode through the tunnel to the Sharks' locker room. He heard fans calling out to him, but he couldn't respond. He kept walking.

This could not be true. He was reeling like someone had sucker punched him in the face. Daisy. Daisy, the woman he was falling for and the only woman he wanted to pour his heart out to. They hadn't been seeing each other for more than a few weeks, but he knew there was something about her that kept drawing him closer. She accepted him as he was, not some carefully constructed, media-friendly version. It took him a while to warm up to people, to trust people before he revealed his true self, and he'd trusted her. How could she do this to him?

She wasn't some crazy stalker. She couldn't be. His knowledge of the sweet, funny, and sexy Daisy was totally at odds with a woman who would write such a detailed and graphic description of everything she'd like to do to him, every place she'd like to do it, and if they were observed by others while doing it, so much the better. "Can't be," he muttered to himself.

He was so fucking confused. And sad. If she'd really done this, why hadn't she told him? Did she think he'd never find out? He heard about that damn book in the media every day. He actually had women come up to him on the street and ask if he'd sign their e-readers. If they didn't approach him in person, they sent fan mail (and Tweets) so explicit he was embarrassed. He'd thought he was open-minded about sex. Some of the things women said to him—he'd love it from Daisy, but not from strangers.

Daisy liked to give him shit about the stuff he couldn't do according to his contract, kiss him until they were both trembling, and wasn't afraid to take charge when they ended up in her bed. She wasn't some desperate weirdo. At least he didn't think she was. It hadn't escaped his notice that guys all over the restaurant stared at her whenever he'd been out with her. If his observations were correct, she would have no problem getting a date with any single red-blooded male. She couldn't have done this. She hadn't lied to him the entire time they'd known each other, had she?

If she'd really written that damn book, why wouldn't she have told him?

Grant rounded the corner to the hallway outside of the locker room. He wanted to get in the shower, get dressed, and get his ass on the bus back to the Sharks' facility. Daisy was working another regularly scheduled commercial flight today. He could catch up with her when he got home, no matter what time it was.

Matt Stephens leaned against the wall outside of the locker room. Matt was typically a pretty easygoing guy. Today, he didn't look happy. Even the reporters gathered in the hallway were keeping their distance.

"Parker. Follow me."

"Of course," Grant said. The reporters had come to life and were shouting questions as he followed Matt a few doorways down the hall.

"Did you know Daisy Spencer wrote *Overtime Parking*?"

"Did you pay her to write it?"

"Are you romantically involved with Ms. Spencer?"

"Are you splitting the proceeds from the book?"

"Don't answer them," Matt said to him in a low voice. He tapped at a closed door. One of the assistant coaches opened it for them.

Grant glanced around to see the head coach, several of the assistant coaches, some front office people, and a couple of people from the Sharks' PR group. The PR employees were typing away on their laptops. Tom Reed pulled up a folding chair to the conference table everyone else sat around.

Matt pointed at the empty chair in the middle of the table. "Have a seat, Parker."

Grant sat. It wasn't comfortable in his sweat-drenched uniform, but he wasn't going to argue with Matt right now. He pulled off the gloves he wore and laid them on the tabletop. Matt placed both fists on the table. He leaned forward.

"We have some things to talk about. We need to get to the bottom of this before we go home."

Grant gave him a nod of acknowledgement.

The Sharks' head coach shoved a chilled bottle of Gatorade across the table to Grant. "Maybe you should explain to us how long you've known that Daisy Spencer wrote that book about you."

"I didn't know. Harley McHugh told me a few minutes ago."

"It hit ESPN just before our game started. She's running an interview tonight with five women from the Seattle area who said that you've been physically involved with them as well. I'm not sure what's up that reporter's ass, but why is she singling you out for this?"

"She claims that the team should know 'the truth' about Grant and stop portraying him as this clean-cut role model," Matt said. "I understand this is not my business, and you are an adult, Parker, but I need you to tell me right now that you were not romantically involved with Ms. McHugh at any time."

Grant swallowed hard. He was going to need a vat of Gatorade instead of a bottle.

"I slept with her. Once. A year or so ago."

"Did you know what she did for a living?"

"No. I met her at a bar. She indicated interest. We had consensual sex. It was one night, and I never saw her again."

Matt folded his arms across his chest. "You had dinner with her a few weeks ago."

"I sat at her table during the windstorm last month in the restaurant in my building. We weren't on a date. I sat there because there wasn't another table. She started asking me questions about the team and my personal life. I excused myself as soon as I could, paid the bill, and left."

"No romantic involvement?"

"None. Not interested."

"How long was it until you figured out you'd been with her?"

She wasn't memorable, but he knew that saying it in front of a woman sitting across the table from him wasn't going to win him any friends. "It was one night. I wasn't interested in pursuing her again. I didn't think there was a problem."

"The other women you've been physically involved with—did you make sure they consented to any sexual activity?"

Grant stared at Matt in shock.

One of the PR people glanced up from her laptop. "Matt."

"I won't have a rapist playing for the Sharks, Trudy." Matt didn't break his stare. The PR employee inclined her head. "I'll deal with HR if they have a problem with my asking these questions." Matt straightened up and folded his arms across his chest. "Yes or no. If you're lying to me, Parker, I'll cut your ass."

"I met some of the women I've been with at bars in the Bellevue area, but I know the difference between yes and no, Matt. And I don't sleep with nonconsenting women."

"You'll stake your job on that?" Matt said.

"Yes, I will."

Matt appeared to be thinking this over for a minute or so. He jammed his hands into his pants pockets.

"When did you decide it was a great thing to do to screw over the PR group as well? And when were you going to tell us about it?" Matt said.

Grant rubbed one hand over his face. "I didn't do this on purpose—"

"Bullshit, Parker. We told your agent the other day you were already skating on thin ice, and now this happens? Do you want to start for this team? Did you think about the impact of your actions at all?"

Matt and Grant stared at each other. If Grant didn't give a shit about his future (or where he'd end up playing after Matt cut him before they got to the team plane), he would have asked Matt how he would feel about having his private life dictated by a pro team's PR department. It wasn't his fault their former backup fucked up so badly. He hadn't driven drunk. He'd never hit a woman in his life, and he never would. He'd never done anything (besides sleep around with other consenting adults) that anyone else would raise an eyebrow over.

Celibacy wasn't written into his contract. Not even for eight million dollars a year. Matt was still glaring at him, but he must have decided to take another tack.

"How did you meet Ms. Spencer?" Matt said.

"She handed me a bottle of water and some pretzels or something on a team flight."

"Did you know she'd written a book about you?"

"No."

"Has she ever talked with you about writing anything?"

"No. We've talked about her job, my job, the usual stuff people dating each other talk about."

Grant was going to have to spend some time thinking about what all this meant later, but mostly, there was one thing that was going to happen when he could get out of his uniform, get a shower, and get into street clothes: he was calling Daisy. He wanted some answers.

"She doesn't seem like a stalker," one of the assistant coaches said.

"Her bosses didn't want her working our team flights. It seems the airline awards charter flights to flight attendants with a lot more seniority than Daisy has, but she filled in one day for someone who was sick, and I told her bosses that I wanted her on our team flights permanently," Matt said. "She does a great job. She takes care of us, and she's been patient when another flight attendant would have gone storming into the terminal and quit her job."

"The pillow fight incident," one of the assistant coaches said.

"Nerf football in the back of the plane while Daisy and her coworkers were trying to serve dinner," another assistant coach said.

"She was laughing," Trudy said. "She wasn't mad."

"That and a few more. Let's not talk about some of the guys getting their hands on the in-flight announcement mic again, either. Plus, she makes sure everyone has what they need."

"She also let Jonathan help her pass out the water bottles. He's still talking about it," Matt said. "I can't believe she's some nutty stalker, or she's the greatest actress known to mankind. The airline told me that her employment record with them is stellar. My kids love her. Amy has been talking about her since they met too." Matt shoved one hand through his hair. "What the hell is going on here?"

The room fell silent for a few moments.

"That sports reporter is acting like the world's caving in," Matt said. "She's making a hell of a lot of trouble for no good reason." He rubbed one hand over his face. "What's her end game?"

"She wants a scoop," Trudy said.

"That book brought practice to a standstill for a few days," the head coach said.

"We've been answering questions about it ever since," an assistant coach said. "It's a distraction. And the media questions at our practices over the next few days will be nonstop."

Trudy glanced up from her laptop. "I can write a statement for both Matt and Grant on the subject. Matt's will be something to the effect of, 'It's been a pleasure for us to fly with Pacifica, the official airline of the Seattle Sharks. We have been very pleased with Daisy Spencer's job performance on behalf of our team. We had no knowledge of and nothing to do with this book. We wish Ms. Spencer the best. Grant Parker is an adult, and we don't involve ourselves in the personal lives of our players.'"

"The press is expecting us to come out there and tell them Grant's had the starting job taken away, Tom is playing next week, the team is disgusted and appalled at this latest development, blah blah blah," Matt said.

"We're not releasing any information right now. We're making a short statement, and we'll figure out how to handle the fallout later," Trudy said. Matt locked eyes with her.

They stared at each other for a minute or so. He finally nodded and said, "Fine." Despite the fact that Grant pretty much thought Matt was an asshole right now, he was surprised to see that a team owner would allow his public relations professional to shape the team's message.

Trudy glanced over at Grant. "Your statement will be something to the effect of 'No, I didn't know anything about this book before my teammates told me about it—'"

"Actually, I did," Grant said.

"How did you find out?"

"I was on a date. The woman left her e-reader in the sheets. I grabbed it, turned it on to see if it still worked, and saw it on her bookshelf," Grant said.

Matt raised an eyebrow.

"Let's not tell everyone that's how you found out about it," Trudy said. "Let's go with 'My teammates told me about it.' You will be thanking the team for standing by you in your statement, and you are not confirming or denying any personal relationship with Ms. Spencer. You will not be taking questions after you read your statement. Got it?"

"I told Pro Sports Network in a pre-taped interview this week that I was dating someone. We've been photographed together."

"We'll let the press dig into that. We're not giving any more information about it," Matt said. "I need to meet with you and your representative tomorrow morning at the practice facility." He nodded at Grant. "You're excused."

"I need to make a call before the press conference," Grant said. The hair on the back of his neck stood at attention. It matched the cold sweat trickling down his spine and the fact he wanted to barf. He knew that getting benched was the best thing he'd hear tomorrow morning. He was fairly sure that he would hear he'd been cut, and the team would be starting a combo of Johnny and one of the free-agent veteran QBs they'd tried out the other day.

He was also starting to wonder if he really wanted to stay with the Sharks. He was going to spend every day earning his credibility as a player and as a man back. He realized he should have been truthful about himself and his life, but he wondered if things might be better somewhere else.

Talking to Daisy would be the filling in his shit sandwich. He'd earned (and probably lost) the starting job he'd been working to achieve for several years now in less than a month.

"You'd better find out if she's some kind of nutjob before you see or talk to her again, Parker," the head coach warned.

"I need to talk to the airline," Matt said. He glanced at Grant. "Go get dressed. We have a press conference to do."

DAISY LIMPED OFF of the plane in Phoenix. She wasn't sure she could make it through the Jetway leading to the terminal, let alone walk to the airport shuttle outside. Her ankle had swollen to approximately twice its normal size and was painful. She reached out for the handrail that ran along the wall and leaned against it as she took small steps.

One of the airline's maintenance guys (who always seemed to be around; she wondered how many of them were actually law enforcement after her experience earlier that day) reached out for her elbow.

"Let me help," he said. "Lean on me. Did you hurt yourself?"

"There were some drunken passengers and a brawl. Just a typical workday," she said as she smiled at him.

"We heard about that," he said.

"We're famous already?"

"It was on the national news."

Daisy shook her head.

"Take it easy. We'll get there." He wrapped one arm around her shoulders. "I can carry you if you'd like."

"No, thank you," she said. "It's only a few more feet."

Another gate agent hurried over as she sat down in the passenger waiting area. "I can call first aid," she said.

"That would be great."

Two hours later, Daisy had spent some time in the emergency room of the hospital closest to the airport. Her ankle had been x-rayed. The diagnosis: a bad sprain, which meant she couldn't work in the morning and most likely would not be working for several days. She called her bosses in Seattle, who put her on the next flight home that night.

"You should have been checked out before you left Seattle," the scheduler said.

"I didn't think I was hurt this badly."

Her boss let out another sigh. "Put some ice on your ankle and keep it elevated as much as possible. Give me a call tomorrow morning to let me know how you're doing."

"I will," Daisy said. "Maybe we could talk about my bestselling book then too."

She hoped that her boss would brush it off or make a joke. It didn't happen.

"Daisy, this isn't a great time to tell you this, but there's already been a conversation about the fact you won't be continuing on the Sharks' charter flights. I know that's hard to hear."

"The money was nice."

"Since you'll be on sick leave until you get a doctor's release, I'm not sure if there will be repercussions for your regular flights as well."

"I was afraid that might happen."

"Listen," her boss said. "Your service to Pacifica has been exemplary. The biggest conversation will be about how this makes the airline look. We don't have a lot of control over what our flight attendants do in their spare time, but the airline would want something that wasn't an issue for public relations."

"I understand."

"Again, we'll talk about this later. Go home and get better. I will see you soon."

"I look forward to it," Daisy said.

Good-byes were exchanged, and Daisy hit End on her phone. She had another hour before she could board the flight back to Seattle and several more phone calls to make. Maybe she should start with the easiest one.

She pulled up her contacts list, hit the one that read "Mom," and listened to the ringing. She heard her mom say hello just before the call went to voice mail.

"Mom," Daisy said. "How are you?"

"I left my phone in the laundry room," her mom said. "I should have put it in my pocket. How are you doing? How is Phoenix?"

"Actually, I'm on my way back to Seattle."

"What happened?"

"I sprained my ankle, so I'll be home for a few days."

"Honey, that's awful. What time does your flight land?"

"It'll be after midnight. I'll take a cab home, and maybe Catherine can drive my car home tomorrow from the parking garage."

"Do you want to come here for the night? There're no stairs, and you can have your old bedroom."

NOELLE GRANHAM

Chapter Seventeen

GRANT'S PERSONAL AND professional life had just blown apart with tremendous force, but he wasn't going to be able to get out of the post-game press conference. He clutched a copy of the statement Trudy had written for him. Matt had made it clear there would be more discussions about his future with the Sharks tomorrow morning. He wanted to get through tonight's press conference as quickly as possible.

"Hello, everyone. I'd like to read a statement."

He read the few sentences offering an apology and expressing regret for his actions aloud while making eye contact with several of the reporters around the room. The media were still going to ask questions about Daisy and *Overtime Parking*, but he didn't have to answer them. He could still hear the shouted questions as he walked out of the room and hurried to where the team bus was boarding. He settled back into his seat and pretended to watch some game film on his tablet while he thought about Daisy.

He hadn't had a lot of experience with stalkers, but some of his teammates had. He'd never met the woman who'd broken into his house a couple of seasons back and claimed he was the father of her twins. He'd met a few women over his career who made his alarm bells go off, though. He'd put as much distance between himself and them as quickly as possible and gone about his life.

He couldn't figure out how he'd been so wrong about Daisy. Had she done this as a joke? One of the articles he'd pulled up on his tablet stated she'd done well financially with the book; she could make even more writing a sequel. She wouldn't do that. Would she? His thoughts circled through his mind like a puppy chasing its tail. He couldn't figure out why she'd done this or why she hadn't told him in the first place.

Had she slept with him because she wanted to see how reality measured up to her imagination? They couldn't get enough of each other, and she couldn't fake that. The thought that she was using him for whatever reason was worse.

He wouldn't get answers until he talked to her. He couldn't believe he'd started this day with so much hope, and it had all turned to ashes.

DAISY LIMPED UP the front walk of her mother's house after midnight, dragging her rolling suitcase. Her mom had left the porch light on so Daisy would not trip over the small step leading to the front door. The ibuprofen the emergency-room nurse had given her was wearing off. She was exhausted and in pain, and she wanted somewhere soft to lie down.

The front door opened as Daisy's mom reached out to her. "There you are."

"Mom," Daisy said. Seconds later, tears were flowing down her face.

Her mom stepped out onto the front porch, wrapped her arms around Daisy, and patted her on the back. "It's okay, honey."

Daisy wanted to tell her mother that it may not be okay ever again, but right now, she couldn't get the words out.

"What happened?" her mom said. It was only a few steps from her parents' front porch into the living room. The Spencer family's living room was formal and was typically used when her parents had guests for dinner or someone important came to visit. The furniture wasn't especially comfortable, even though she knew her parents had spent a small fortune furnishing and decorating it after her dad was named a vice president of the bank. Right now, though, sitting on the couch (instead of limping into the much more comfortable family room) would work.

Daisy pulled off the coat she wore and laid it over the back of one of the slipper chairs that flanked the couch. She kicked off the low-heeled pumps she wore to work and finally had a seat. Her mom picked up a couple of the silk cushions that probably cost more than five credit hours at the University of Washington, put them on the coffee table, and helped Daisy prop her foot up. She sat down and took Daisy's hand in both of hers.

"Tell me about it. Don't leave anything out."

A couple of hours later, Daisy's mom had helped her into the guest room, gotten her into bed, and propped her ankle up on a pillow. Daisy put her cell phone on the bedside table.

"Everything will be better tomorrow," Claudine said. She made sure there were extra pillows and tucked the blankets around Daisy like she had when her daughter was a child.

"Mom, Grant probably thinks I'm harmful or something. Why did I do this? He's probably really mad at me, plus I'm in trouble at work…I should have taken it down before anyone saw it." She let out a sigh. "Have you ever done something so stupid?"

Claudine brushed the hair off of Daisy's forehead. "I know it's hard to believe right now, but it might not be as bad as you think it is," she said. "We all do things we probably shouldn't. The best people learn from those decisions. Everyone else keeps making them over and over."

"I guess I shouldn't write that dinosaur erotica, then," Daisy muttered.

Her mom laughed out loud. "How much did you say you made from the proceeds of that book? Maybe I should write it."

"Daddy will freak out."

"Daddy won't care when he gets a look at the royalty statements," Claudine said.

Daisy tried to imagine her Junior League, country club, and St. Mark's Cathedral member mom publishing something explicit enough to shock everyone who knew her.

Claudine leaned over, kissed Daisy's forehead, and said, "Good night. If you need help getting to the bathroom or anything else, I'm right next door."

"I love you, Mom."

"I love you too, sweetheart. And don't worry. I think it's all going to work out."

Claudine shut the door with a gentle click as she left.

Daisy picked up her phone off of the nightstand and turned it on. There was a text from Grant.

I need to talk with you ASAP. Text me when you get this.

It was two thirty AM. He wouldn't be awake, but she couldn't ignore him. Tears rose in her eyes as she considered what to say. She tapped her response onto the screen.

I need to talk with you too. I'm at my parents' house in Redmond. Let's talk later this morning.

Her phone chimed ten seconds later.

What time? I'll meet you.

She stared at the screen. She wasn't exactly mobile right now. She needed a set of crutches and a lot of ibuprofen. Hopefully, her mom would be okay if she told Grant to meet her here.

Come over after practice, she wrote, typing in her parents' address and the code to their security gate.

See you then, he replied.

Daisy sent him one more message: *I'm so sorry.*

He didn't respond. She stared at her phone, hoping he'd say anything at all.

Daisy rolled onto her side, pulled the pillow around her face so her parents wouldn't hear her, and cried.

Around nine the next morning, Claudine walked into Daisy's room with a latte and a set of crutches. Daisy tried to wiggle her toes. Everything hurt. It was the worst morning ever as far as she was concerned.

"One of my bridge partners has crutches you can borrow. Her husband broke his leg in two places during ski season last year," she said. "He's fine now, but I don't think he's going skiing again. Did you sleep well?"

The only good thing about yesterday's adventures was the fact Daisy had slept like a rock after she cried her eyes out. "I did. How are you this morning?"

"I cancelled my appointments so I could hang out with you," her mom said.

"Mom, I'll be fine. You didn't need to do that. It's really nice of you, though." Daisy's phone chimed with an incoming text. Time to confess. "Grant texted me really early this morning and said he wanted to meet me so we could talk."

"What did you tell him?"

"Is it okay if he meets me here? If you don't want to deal with it, we can go somewhere else."

"Of course, he's welcome."

"There might be yelling," Daisy said.

"Let me go find you something to wear. I'll be right back."

Three hours later, Daisy was on the family-room couch in one of her mom's Lululemon exercise outfits with yet another ice pack over her propped-up ankle and the TV remote in her hand when she heard the front doorbell. Her mom had even brushed her hair and insisted that she use a little mascara.

Like she wasn't going to cry it off.

"I'll get it," her mom called out.

She heard Grant's voice, but she couldn't quite make out what he and her mom were talking about. A minute or so later, he walked into the family room with a bouquet of flowers. She wanted to run into his arms—that is if she could run. He wasn't smiling. Despite the flowers, her heart sank.

"Hi," she said.

"Hi," he said.

"Would you like to sit down? Can I get you anything?" she said. She couldn't really get off the couch, but she could at least offer.

"No, thank you," he said. He glanced around. "Your parents have a beautiful home."

"Thanks," she said.

He laid the bouquet on the coffee table near her injured ankle. "I heard you got hurt. These are for you."

She reached forward to pick up the flowers and breathed in their scent. "They're beautiful. Thank you."

Daisy's mom peeked around the corner. "Honey, I have some errands to run. I'll be back in a while, okay? Grant, it was nice to see you. Stay as long as you like. Help yourself if you'd like something to drink or eat."

"Thank you, Mrs. Spencer."

"Call me Claudine. I'll see you later," she said. Daisy heard the garage door open and the sound of her mom's car backing out.

"How did you hear I got hurt?" she said.

"It was on the national news. Some of the morning TV shows were talking about the fact you must have had the worst day ever between being revealed as the author of *Overtime Parking* and getting hurt while trying to break up a fight."

"You watch morning TV?"

"When I'm on it," he said. It was like a knife to her gut. He let out a long breath. "So, I have some questions for you."

She stifled herself before blurting out, "I'll bet." She pulled breath into her lungs. "Grant, I am so sorry. I should have told you about the book when we met. I actually should have never clicked Upload, but mostly, I should have been honest. I'm not sure I could ever apologize enough."

"Do you have any idea what the past month has been like for me because of your book?"

"You said in the media that you were flattered," she said.

She knew the second the words left her lips that she should never have said it. It was stupid. She owed him the most abject apology she could muster up. He was right—she couldn't imagine what it must have been like to deal with the fact that the sports media were a hell of a lot more interested in talking about *Overtime Parking* than Grant's passing statistics and touchdowns scored. He had worked so hard to become a starter, and instead of being able to bask in that achievement, he'd become the butt of so many stupid jokes because of her book. The last thing she should be doing was anything but apologizing.

"What was I going to say? 'Some person I've never met wrote something about me that I'm never going to be able to live down'? The only way to get people to stop talking about it was to laugh it off. I can take a joke like everyone else, but, Daisy, this is my career. Everything I do or say is spread all over social media, written about, and talked about on TV, whether I like it or not. How would you feel if someone did the same thing to you?"

She put the bouquet of flowers back onto the coffee table. She couldn't look at him. Even worse, he didn't yell. His voice was quiet. There was so much hurt and anger in his expression, and she couldn't face it. She'd done this. She hadn't thought through the consequences of anyone deciding to actually read her crazy little book, and it had ended up being a lot worse than she could have imagined. She folded her hands in her lap. Her ankle throbbed, she couldn't run away, and she wished she was anywhere else in the world right now.

"My parents were here for the first game I started for the Sharks," he said. "I wanted them to meet you. I thought you were different than any other woman I ever went out with. I thought they would be proud."

"Why did you think I was different?" she said.

"You have your own life, and you have a career. You don't depend on anyone else to make your decisions. I knew I had to work to get your attention. You're smart, friendly, and outgoing. I thought they'd think I made a good choice."

"I'm so sorry—"

"I wonder if I ever knew you," he said, and her heart broke. She fought back the tears that rose in her eyes. "I mean, we slept together. We talked for hours. I trusted you. I thought you cared about me. Who are you, anyway? Are you the woman I met, or did you conceal yourself in some attempt to be who you're not? I understand that we haven't been together long, but I can't understand how you could do this to me."

"I'm that woman you were getting to know. I'm still that same person."

"But I'll never know if you were out with me for me or because you wanted to find out if I lived up to your fantasies." He let out another long breath. "I might play football for a living, but I'm just a guy," he said. "I want to be with someone who is interested in all of me, not just the famous part. I know I'm kind of quiet and sometimes don't have a lot to say. I hoped you'd want to be with the real me. I hoped I could find out more about you. I wanted to stay with you."

Hoped, he'd said. In other words, there was no way out of this.

"I'm sorry," she blurted out. She felt hot tears roll down her cheeks. "I didn't mean to hurt you. It was silly and stupid, and I should have kept it to myself. I didn't realize this would have such an effect on you and your career. I really enjoyed spending time with you too. I wanted you most of all. More than your career and more than the book. Please believe me."

She brushed more tears off of her face with both hands. She needed to face this without falling apart. She could cry later, when he was gone. She would be back to first dates again. Or maybe she wouldn't date for a long time after this. Maybe she needed to take a hard look at what she really wanted in life. She wanted Grant, but he no longer wanted her.

"I really care about you," she said. She summoned the courage to look into his face. He still wasn't smiling. The look in his eyes was sad and resigned. "Would you please take another chance on me?"

He ignored her words.

"I keep trying to decide if you have some weird fixation on me."

"I wrote down a bunch of my fantasies. That's all."

"Involving me. Were you ever going to tell me you wrote that?"

"Yes. Eventually." The hot tears were streaming down her cheeks now.

"After we fell in love? After we were married? At the baptism of our first child? When?"

She bit her lip.

"So you weren't going to tell me," he said.

"I knew I had to tell you. I tried so many times. I couldn't say it. I realize it wasn't fair to you, and I should have told you a long time ago. But I wasn't sure what would happen when I did."

"How hard would it have been? 'Hey, Grant, funny thing. You know that book you keep hearing about? I wrote it. Isn't that hilarious?' I had to tell people the truth about my life, but you couldn't be truthful with me? How many other things have you lied to me about?"

He folded his arms across his chest.

She swallowed hard. "I haven't lied to you about anything else. I'm so sorry. Please believe me."

"I'm sorry too," he said. "I don't think we should see each other anymore."

She nodded. There really wasn't anything else to say. She'd apologized, but there wasn't an apology that would help with something like this.

He took a deep breath and stared into her face again. "And by the way, as of this morning, I'm benched. The team has signed another vet QB, and Johnny's starting on Sunday."

"Oh my God. That's awful. Are they crazy?" Tears rose in her eyes again. It wasn't original, but it was all she could think to say. Were they nuts? The team wouldn't win with anyone else, and the thought that she was part of that decision left her shaken. What could she say to him that would be enough?

He reached out to pick up his jacket and slipped it on.

"It was nice to see you," she said. "Thank you for the flowers."

He nodded at her. She reached out for her crutches so she could walk him to the door.

"No, don't. I can find my way out," he said.

He got to his feet and walked away without another word. She heard the front door shut behind him, his car driving away, and then silence.

GRANT SPENT THE rest of the afternoon and most of the evening sitting on his couch in front of the TV.

Something was on. He wasn't watching it. He thought about calling downstairs for some food, but he wasn't hungry. He opened a beer, but he didn't drink it. He kept remembering the look on Daisy's face as he'd talked to her. The longer he'd talked, the sadder she'd looked, and he couldn't help but recall her tear-streaked face.

He knew the difference between women who cried to manipulate men and women whose tears came so seldom that they shook one to the core. Daisy hadn't cried because she thought he was going to buy it. She'd cried because she knew she'd made a mistake.

He'd told himself he was going to state the facts—her book had caused trouble for him professionally. He'd had enough of people giving him a bad time about it. He hadn't been able to remain calm and factual, though. He'd asked her if she was a stalker, and he knew damn well she wasn't. She'd done something and hadn't realized the impact it would have on his life. The teammates who had given him so much shit had told him they were a bit envious. After all, they joked, most guys would love to know that a woman desired them that way, even if they weren't into her.

His anger and hurt were fading into something much worse. The longer he thought about it, the more he realized he was full of shit and a real asshole to boot. He'd lied too. Maybe she should be mad at him for riding his high horse when he still hadn't explained that he should have been truthful about his own life. To everyone, including her.

After several hours staring blankly at the TV, he realized it wasn't the book at all. Sure, the book didn't help, but the other guys in the league who had had something similar happen laughed it off.

The problem was him. He didn't believe that a woman like Daisy would care for him when she found out that he wasn't such an exciting guy when he wasn't wearing a football uniform. She wasn't going to stick around for someone more introverted. She should be where there was excitement and variety, new things to see and new places to go. She deserved a guy who wanted to join in on every experience with her. The compass tattoo on her hip was perfect. She'd always find her way home, wherever that might be for her. She was everything he'd ever wanted but knew he could never hold onto, like starlight.

And he'd hurt her. He'd hurt her as much as he believed she'd hurt him. Did that make him better somehow? Maybe it just made him an asshole.

The difference between what he wanted and what he thought he could have engulfed him. He'd lost the job he'd been fighting to get for years now. He'd met the woman he wanted to build a relationship with, and he'd walked away from her.

He couldn't imagine what was next.

Chapter Eighteen

One month later

GRANT COULDN'T STOP thinking about Daisy. It wasn't like he didn't have anything else to do these days. The team had benched him, and Johnny's performance on the field was abysmal, but they couldn't move forward with their new backup QB, either. The vet had torn his ACL two plays into the game last week. Terrell, the free safety (and emergency QB), had ended up taking the field. Terrell still had a hell of an arm, but the coaching staff had to dumb down the offense so badly to get through the game, that the Sharks had lost 45-3.

Grant was the Sharks' starting QB again, at least through the regular season. Or at least as long as the team continued to win.

He heard the chirp of a voice mail message left on his phone. Daisy had called a few times since the last time he'd seen her. Things hadn't gone so well for her lately, either. According to Matt, she was not only removed from the Sharks' charter flights, she'd been suspended by the airline. She'd also removed *Overtime Parking* from online.

The first couple of messages she'd left weren't anything like the sweet, funny Daisy he knew. "I wanted to call and apologize to you again for what I did. I am so sorry. I don't think I can figure out a way to say it enough," she'd said. He'd always heard the smile in her voice before. Now she sounded like she wanted to cry.

She called and left a message on Thanksgiving, wishing him a happy holiday and saying she hoped he was having a really nice celebration. His conscience was on fire. She wasn't pestering him or asking for a thing. She wished him well, and he was acting like a gigantic asshole by not accepting her apology.

Everyone else was accepting his apologies these days.

Mid-December during football season meant twelve-hour days at the practice facility—watching film of the Sharks' future opponents, meeting with his coaches and teammates, and going to practice. The Sharks were in the playoff hunt. When he wasn't in official meetings, he was in the unofficial kind: sitting in front of his locker with Tom Reed, who was sharing the secrets of his long pro-football career. That is when he wasn't giving Grant all kinds of shit about every subject under the sun. He'd told Grant he was retiring at the end of the season. The actual statement was, "I'm out of here, asshole. Try not to fuck things up for yourself again, will ya?"

Today's subject was a particularly painful one. If it had been anyone else but Tom, Grant would have been looking for some type of revenge.

"Did you call her yet?" Reed said as he shoved his feet into a pair of cross trainers. "You're wasting time." He grabbed Grant's phone out of his locker and looked at the screen. "She sent you a text. You need to answer her."

They both knew who *she* was. Grant had gone back to Daisy's parents' house about a week after he'd told her they couldn't see each other anymore and knocked on the door. He wanted to talk. He actually wanted to apologize for the fact he knew he'd hurt her too, but more than that, he wanted to see her. Nobody had answered.

He'd also stopped by her place, where Catherine answered the door.

"She's not here," Catherine said.

"Will you tell her I was here?"

"I'll consider it." And the British, very proper Catherine shut the door in his face. Catherine's reaction was calm in comparison to that of some of his teammates' wives and Amy Stephens when they discovered that he had broken up with Daisy. The guys got it. The women, while sticking up for him publicly, told him privately that they really liked Daisy and they wished he'd reconsider.

His favorite reaction: Amy Stephens had sent him a bill for flowers from Crazy Daisy and written across the front of it, *"Apologize to each other and move on. Love, Amy."*

Grant picked up the water bottle next to him on the bench and took a long swallow.

When he wasn't thinking about telling Daisy what a stupid asshole he was, he was getting told by guys like Tom to man up and make his move.

"You think I snapped my fingers, and my wife came running? Oh, hell no. I had to put on my track shoes and chase her."

"So you think I should pursue a woman who actually published a book saying she wanted to boink me on the top of the Space Needle?"

Tom Reed rolled his eyes. "Seriously? Some guys would think that was a benefit. I get that you're still pissed, but she's apologized over and over. How long are you going to make her grovel?"

"I'm not making her grovel—"

Tom stared at him. "Don't kid a kidder. Back to how I met my wife. There were so many other guys who wanted to date her, and I was one more. I set myself apart from the pack by finding out what she liked and listening to what she was talking about. Not the *uh-huh, yes, dear* listening, the kind of listening when you bring up something she told you a week later. She kept talking to me; I kept listening to her and bringing her little things, like a flower or one of the peanut-butter cookies she liked from the coffee place down the street from our college campus, and she finally agreed to go out with me. I still bring her a cookie when I stop by the coffee place to get her skinny latte. Every time, she acts as if I handed her a fistful of diamonds." Tom leaned forward and poked Grant in the chest with one finger. "You want to build something that will last a lifetime, you start small. You can't forget her, and she can't forget you. That sounds like something you might want to look into. What does she like to do? What makes her happy? Get out of your head and start talking."

"I stopped at her house. She wasn't home."

"A month ago. Text her. Start the conversation. Come on, Parker. You persisted until you were a starter, and now you've earned your damn job back. Are you giving up this easily? Be a man. Talk to her."

Grant heard the chime of an incoming text on Tom's phone.

Tom whipped the phone out of his pocket, glanced at the screen, and said, "I'm out of here. Gotta go see about my girl. Later."

DAISY'S SPRAINED ANKLE healed, and she went back to work about a month later, after a meeting with her bosses. After some good-natured razzing from her coworkers, she settled back into her weekly flying routine. She really enjoyed her job, but she wanted something to do on her time off that distracted her from thinking about Grant.

She'd tried to call him a few times to apologize again and say she understood why it wasn't going to work with them. It was best to let go, especially when he didn't return her calls. She knew she'd always care about him.

He'd meet a wonderful woman someday, ask her to marry him, and move on with his life. She needed to move on with hers. As a result, she'd sat down at the kitchen table in her house during her month-long suspension one day with her tablet and keyboard, opened the word-processing program, and typed the first sentence of what she hoped would be a funny and interesting memoir of her life as a flight attendant.

She kept writing. Some days were a struggle to get any words on the page at all. Other days, the words poured out of her faster than she could type them. It was a good distraction from reality. She wanted to keep flying. She also wanted to publish something that she could actually admit she'd written it. The more she wrote, the more she realized how much she wanted to keep writing. Maybe she should take an online creative writing class or something.

The day the doctor gave her permission to go back to work, she got back in her car and drove to Children's Hospital. She'd met with a CPA and paid the taxes on the royalties for *Overtime Parking* a week ago. She'd gotten the last (big) chunk of royalties after she'd pulled the file off of the server. It was nice, but the money was burning a hole in her bank account (and her conscience). She knew what Grant would have done with the fifty thousand dollars. As a result, a cashier's check for that amount was riding around in her handbag.

The writing wasn't the only thing she aspired to do. She'd heard Grant talk before about how going to the hospital to visit the kids was the highlight of his week. She knew they accepted volunteers. It would be nice to feel like she was giving back to the community by volunteering once a week or so.

Daisy parked her car and walked into the hospital's administration office.

"May I help you?" the receptionist at a long, low desk asked.

"Hi, I'm Daisy Spencer. I talked with someone about volunteering here the other day, and I have an appointment. And I have a donation to the hospital, as well."

"We're happy you're here, Daisy. You've been highly recommended to our board by a friend who prefers to remain anonymous." Her eyes twinkled.

"A friend?"

"Oh, yes. You'll need to fill out some paperwork and have your picture taken. We'll do a background check as well. If you come with me, we'll get this started," the receptionist said. "Would you like a tax receipt for your donation?"

"Sure," Daisy said. She reached into her handbag and pulled out the long, white sealed envelope with the check inside. She was led along a corridor to a series of office doors. The receptionist stopped in front of one of them and indicated a chair in a waiting area. "Why don't you have a seat, and I'll get that tax receipt for you."

"Thank you so much."

Daisy glanced around at the colorful artwork on the walls and winter sunlight streaming through the windows. The small waiting area even had a fish tank. Plump, colorful fish swam through a variety of scenery. She took a deep breath and felt herself relax. Hopefully, the volunteer organizers wouldn't mind if she asked not to volunteer on Tuesdays.

The receptionist skidded into the waiting area again with a look of surprise on her face.

"This check is for fifty thousand dollars. Did you mean to give us this much money?"

"Yes. I'm happy to," Daisy said.

"I wanted to make sure," the woman said. "Thank you so much."

"Thank you. I really admire what Children's does for so many kids. I hope the money will help."

The woman hurried away again, and a few minutes later, a boy in fuzzy blue pajamas, slipper socks, and a picture book in one hand padded into the waiting area. He walked over to the fish tank and stood transfixed as he watched them.

"Do you like the fish?" Daisy asked.

"Yeah. This tank is bigger than the one by my room. There's more fish," he said. He turned to face Daisy. "What's your name?"

"I'm Daisy," she said. "What's your name?"

"I'm Alex," he said. "My dad's name is Alex too."

"That's pretty cool," Daisy said.

"Yeah," the boy said. He scrambled up on the empty chair next to Daisy's. "Will you read this to me?" He held out a well-used copy of Goodnight, Goodnight, Construction Site. "It's my favorite."

"I'd be glad to," she said. She took the book and opened to the first page.

Alex leaned against her arm so he could see the pictures as she read. She was so absorbed in the little boy's enjoyment of the story that she didn't glance up when someone else walked into the waiting room.

"Daisy," Grant said.

She hadn't seen him for a month, but she was never going to forget the sound of his voice. Her heart began to pound.

Alex was off the chair and threw his arms around Grant's neck in seconds.

"Hey, buddy. Good to see you," Grant said. "How are you feeling?"

"I'm okay. The medicine's icky."

"I know. Want to hear the rest of the book?"

"Yeah," Alex said.

Grant sat down in Alex's chair, pulled him up onto his lap, and glanced over at Daisy. "I'm so glad to see you," he said.

"Me too," Daisy whispered. Tears blurred her eyes. She blinked them back as she fought for control. Crying in a public place wasn't her favorite thing. The volunteer coordinator was going to think she was some kind of nut or shouldn't be working around sick little kids.

"Why is she crying?" Alex asked. Daisy felt Alex's chubby little hand on her cheek. "Don't cry," he said.

"It's my fault, Alex. Want to look at the fish some more?" Grant said.

"Yeah." Alex scrambled off of Grant's lap and went back to watching the fish.

Daisy swallowed hard. There were better places for all of this to happen, but before he walked out of her life again, she needed to speak up. He reached out and took her hand in both of his.

"I'm so sorry," she said. "I didn't mean to do anything that would hurt you. I wasn't thinking, and I'm just so sorry. I understand why you were so mad at me. I deserved your anger and hurt."

He reached out to stroke her face. "I should have called you a long time ago. I've accepted your apology a thousand times in the last month, and I should have been man enough to tell you that." He brushed a tear off of her cheek with his thumb. "Will you accept my apology for not making this right a long time ago? I was a real asshole myself."

Alex turned to face them. "You said a bad word, Grant. My mom would make you have a time-out."

"That's true, buddy. I'll have to talk to your mom about that."

Alex went back to watching the fish. Daisy was still trying to blink back the tears.

"Yes," she said. "But you should have been mad—"

He put a fingertip over her lips. "Maybe we should start over. You know—Daisy, the beautiful woman who works next door to Purple in Bellevue, and Grant, the guy who works in a cubicle somewhere." He stuck out his other hand. "Nice to meet you, Daisy."

"Nice to meet you too," she whispered.

"I miss you all the time," Grant said.

"I miss you so much too," Daisy said.

"I don't want to be without you anymore," he said. "Let's try this again. You know, dinner, a movie, maybe some skydiving?"

"No jet car barbecue?"

"I'll work on it," he said. His voice dropped. "I don't care where we go, as long as we're together." He reached out, took her face in his hands, and kissed her. His mouth was warm on hers. He tasted of mint. Maybe it wasn't the best thing to use tongue in front of a four-year-old, but Daisy didn't object. "Stay with me," he whispered.

She heard an office door open and someone call out, "Daisy Spencer?" She pulled her mouth off of his and said, "I gotta go."

"I didn't mean to interrupt," the woman said and grinned. "I never knew the waiting room was a good make-out spot."

Daisy reached out to wipe her lip gloss off of Grant's mouth. "Sorry about that."

"They were kissing," Alex told the woman. "My mom and dad kiss. And they say 'I love you.' A lot."

"Maybe on our second date," Daisy said. "It's still a bit soon." But she couldn't stop the smile that spread over her mouth.

Grant grinned at Daisy. "There's no time like the present. I love you, Daisy Spencer."

"I love you too, Grant Parker."

"Now you have to get married," Alex said. "You say you love each other, and you get married."

"I love this kid," Grant said.

"Maybe on our third date," Daisy said.

"Perfect. Let's do that," Grant said.

INTERCEPTING DAISY 261

Epilogue

Fourteen months later

GRANT PARKER ATTEMPTED to open his eyes and let out a groan. He was facedown on a beach. Somewhere. If he could get his eyes to focus, he might be able to figure out where he was.

He flipped over onto his back and let out another groan while the sun stabbed him in the face. It had to be just after sunrise. His head was pounding, and he had to piss like a racehorse. He tried to brush sand off of his face, only succeeded in getting it in his eyes, and swore extravagantly as he tried to a) get rid of the sand and b) piece together why he wasn't in a warm, comfortable bed.

He'd gone out for drinks last night with his dickhead teammates and his soon-to-be father- and brother-in-law. He remembered a few of them and several rounds of mai tais or some other drink with an umbrella in it. They hadn't tasted like they'd had alcohol in them. There'd been music and beautiful women doing the hula, and the guys had been giving him shit because tomorrow was his wedding day.

Tomorrow. *Tomorrow.* As in this morning. *Fuck!*

The wedding was at eleven AM or some other ridiculous time he'd tried to talk Daisy out of. She'd given him that smile he loved and said, "I don't want to wait all day to become your wife. Let's get married, have brunch with our friends, and go surfing."

He'd signed another contract the month before (with a stunning number of zeroes), after the Sharks won the big game. He wasn't sure how to tell her that surfing was now on the *banned activities* list, as well. At least those writing his contracts hadn't said a word yet about bedroom-related activities, which could be more dangerous with Daisy than the items they'd already listed in the contract.

"How about some snorkeling instead?"

"Deal," she'd told him.

A few minutes after that, she'd scampered out of his master bathroom wearing her new swimsuit. She'd wanted to model it for him. He'd had to take it off of her, they hadn't left his room for several hours as a result, and he'd forgotten all about the fact he'd agreed to an eleven AM wedding until he got the invitation in the mail a month later.

He patted himself down as he worked up the courage to open his eyes again. He was going to have no choice at some point, but right now, he'd prefer waiting until he felt a bit more human. His fingers brushed the cell phone in his pocket. Thank God. He felt a credit card or a room key in the opposite pocket. He jammed one hand beneath himself to discover his wallet, still securely buttoned into his back pocket.

Okay. He could get back into his hotel room if he could open his eyes and get to his feet—that is, if he was still on the same island he'd arrived at so he could marry Daisy.

"Sir. Sir," a voice above him said.

"Yeah?" he managed to croak out while slightly opening one eye. A guy wearing a uniform slowly came into view.

"You're going to have to go back to your room."

"I realize this probably isn't a great way to start off our acquaintance, but where am I?"

"You're on the beach at the Turtle Bay Resort. On Oahu." The guy reached out a hand. "How about coffee? It's on me."

Grant was at the right place. They hadn't put him on an inter-island flight and dumped his ass in the sand on Kauai or something.

"How did I get out here?"

"You told your buddies you wanted to sleep on the beach last night."

"I must have been shit-faced."

"Coffee," the guy said. He helped Grant to his feet. "You can get your revenge on them later."

Grant felt a bit wobbly and wondered if he was about to barf, but the world stabilized a little as he dug his toes into the sand.

"I'm getting married later."

"Congratulations. Now let's go get that coffee."

DAISY AWOKE TO a knock on her hotel room door.

"Ms. Spencer? Room service," a cheery voice called out. "May we come in?"

"Go ahead," Daisy responded.

She was going to have to get in the bathroom and take care of things before the hair and makeup people arrived at eight thirty, but she could relax with a mimosa and some breakfast before the insanity began. They'd wanted a small, intimate wedding and ended up planning a 150-guest extravaganza on a Hawaiian beach after Grant informed her that he'd invited the entire team, as well as the coaches and their wives.

Her parents almost stroked out when they calculated how much the wedding would cost. Daisy still had some royalties from *Overtime Parking*. She'd also signed a contract with a publishing house for her flight-attendant memoir. She and Grant could afford to pay for their big day themselves.

"We'll pay for it," Grant told them as he squeezed Daisy's hand. "Will it work for you to pick up the tab for the rehearsal dinner, Mr. Spencer?"

"Call me Gerald. The rehearsal dinner is on us," Daisy's dad told him.

Shortly afterward, he'd started calling Grant *son*, and they went out to hit a bucket of balls at the driving range and drink beer with Daisy's brother while Daisy and her mom immersed themselves in the minutiae of planning a wedding. She knew Grant's joining their family was a done deal when her brother invited him to some gaming exhibition. It turned out Grant loved being included.

Daisy scrambled out of bed when several women followed the rolling carts of food and drinks into her room.

"Hey, bride, it's time for breakfast," Catherine called out. "I brought some people with me. You're okay with that, aren't you?"

"I'm great with it," Daisy said. She found herself inside a knot of women still in bathrobes and slippers, talking and laughing as they hugged her. The food carts kept rolling in. She'd ordered breakfast for five people; the kitchen must have gotten a different memo.

"We heard there are mimosas," Megan Reed told her.

"We'd like you even if there weren't free drinks," Delisa said.

"Daisy, I checked on the flowers already. They're perfect," Amy Stephens said.

"Thank God I can drink this time. I could have a lot more fun when I'm out with the girls if my husband would stop getting me pregnant," Holly Collins said. She patted her slightly rounded abdomen. "He walks into the room, raises an eyebrow, and I miss a period. Mama needs a mimosa, damn it."

"Oh my God. We need to get that guy a hobby," Cameron Anderson teased. "Then again, my husband says practice makes perfect." Her voice dropped. "He wanted to reenact every scene in Daisy's book. Let's just say we came up with another plan when we almost got caught red-handed in our own backyard by Grandma."

Sophie Carlson burst out laughing. "I hate it when that happens."

Kendall McCoy's hand strayed to her abdomen. Twenty-five women turned to stare at her in response.

"Well?" Jillian Taylor said.

"Of course, I'm pregnant. Couldn't you tell when I was sneaking into the airplane bathroom all the way over here?"

There were hugs and congratulations, and Kendall took the glass of ice water Holly Collins pressed into her hand.

"You could have had an upset stomach," Emily McKenna said.

"It's been upset for three months now." Kendall took a sip of water. "Drew spends every night with his hand on my belly waiting for the baby to move so he can feel it. He says he wants another little girl like Tessa, but I think I'd like a little boy like him." She heaved a sigh. "I'm going to have to tell Matt eventually so we can start the planning for my maternity leave."

Amy Stephens cleared her throat and tried to look mysterious.

"Okay, what do you know?" Emily asked her.

"Matt came home a couple of weeks ago and said, 'I think Kendall might be expecting. She's drinking herbal tea instead of lattes, and she's been falling asleep on the plane rides home from games instead of working. Plus, she's using the ladies' room a bit more often these days.'"

"What did you tell him?"

"He knew I was pregnant before I figured it out," Amy said. "It pissed me off. How can I surprise him with anything when he already knows?"

Daisy heard the tap-tap-tap of a piece of flatware against a glass. "Ladies," her mom said, "the breakfast buffet is served." She patted Grant's mom, Martha, on the back. "Daisy told me that you and your husband do not drink. How about some freshly squeezed orange juice instead?"

Daisy moved in their direction. "I'll get it for you, Mrs. Parker," she said.

She still wasn't sure what to call her mother-in-law. "Mrs. Parker" felt so formal. Calling her by her first name felt too informal. Maybe they could talk about it later and come up with a nickname or an endearment. Daisy knew Grant's parents were trying hard to fit in. They had been so kind to her already.

"Oh, yes." She reached out to kiss Daisy's cheek. "I'm so excited I'm getting a daughter."

"And I'm getting a second mom," Daisy said. "Would you stay with us while I'm putting my dress on and stuff later? I would really like you to be here."

To Daisy's surprise, Martha's eyes filled with tears. "I would love that."

A FEW HOURS later, Daisy's father helped her out of the golf cart that stopped a hundred yards or so from the bamboo archway festooned with flowers, vines, and tulle that looked out over the Pacific Ocean. The sun shone brightly in a startlingly blue sky. The center aisle had been covered by a white cloth runner, scattered with rose petals and small shiny green leaves, and flanked by 150 white wooden chairs for their guests. The breeze smelled like plumeria. She could hear the ocean waves against the sand, the soft sounds of a guitar, and the low hum of conversation among the guests waiting a short distance away. The skirt of her wedding gown rippled around her as she smoothed it with both hands.

She'd wanted something beautiful enough to get married in but casual enough for a barefoot walk on the beach with Grant later. The silk chiffon gown had an Empire waist, an illusion bodice covered in delicate white-on-white embroidery, short sleeves, small fabric-covered buttons down the back, and a slight train. It was gorgeous, she could move in it, and it wasn't itchy. Anywhere. She wore lace ballet flats threaded with blue ribbon bows, a penny in her shoe, and her grandma's pearl bracelet. She'd decided to skip the veil.

Her mom had pinned a wreath of rosebuds and tiny white orchids into her hair. She carried a bouquet of white cattleya orchids and rosebuds tied with a white double-faced satin bow.

Her dad held out his arm for Daisy to slip her hand through. "Ready, kitten?"

She was shaking. It wasn't that it was nerves—well, maybe it was nerves. She wanted to marry Grant. She was crazy in love with him, to be honest. At the same time, this was the rest of their lives. What if they got tired of teasing each other about all the activities he wasn't allowed to engage in while he still played for the Sharks?

What if he got sick of dealing with her flight schedule? What if she got tired of a refrigerator full of Gatorade and protein bars?

"I'm a little nervous," she said to her dad in a low voice.

"Everyone who gets married is nervous. If you weren't nervous, I'd worry about it." Her dad kissed her forehead. "Are you nervous because you're thinking about the rest of your life with one person, or are you freaking out because you've never done this before?"

"Maybe both." She heard a golf cart approaching behind them and the *toot-toot* of the ridiculous little horn all golf carts came equipped with.

"I heard there was a wedding," Tom Reed called out to them as he drove past. "Free booze." Catherine had one hand through the hand-holds on her side, but she was laughing.

Catherine and Tom got out of their golf cart twenty-five feet or so ahead. Catherine had on a floor-length sleeveless soft yellow chiffon gown, which was made by the same designer as Daisy's and outlined the slight baby bump she was sporting these days. She was already holding her bouquet of white cymbidium orchids. Tom wore a linen shirt, slacks, flip-flops, a boutonniere, and a big grin.

"Let's get this show on the road," he said to Catherine. "Shall we?" He extended his arm to her. "How are you feeling?"

"I might be able to get through the next hour without being sick," she said. "Let's get them married."

"I love that idea."

Daisy heard applause from the guests as Catherine and Tom stepped onto the aisle runner. She knew that Cam was already waiting at the altar with Grant; Grant had decided he wanted two best men. She wanted to see Grant, but she needed to stay hidden for just a few moments more. Plus, she had some things she'd like to discuss with her dad.

"There's no such thing as a perfect marriage, but there are plenty of happy ones. Your mother and I are pretty happy. Your brother's pretty happy with his wife," her dad said. "There's no reason why you won't be happy too."

"What if we get sick of each other or fall out of love? What happens then?"

Her dad stroked her cheek. "Then you remember all the reasons you fell in love with him in the first place. You have a lifetime to discover everything about him that you love. I'm still discovering new things about your mother, and we've been married for forty years."

"I think she has a crush on Grant," Daisy said.

"Everyone has a crush on Grant, kitten, but he's marrying you today, isn't he?"

"That's true."

"Then come on. Let's go show everyone how beautiful you look."

Daisy and her dad stepped onto the cloth runner as her mom got to her feet. The rest of the guests followed. She glanced from side to side, trying to take in all of the guests, the beautiful day, Catherine's smile at the little archway. Her dad patted her hand as she finally recognized the song the guitarist was singing, and they began making their way along the aisle.

Grant had asked to choose the song she walked down the aisle to. "You'll love it," he'd said.

"It's supposed to be some big, formal bridal thing."

"We're getting married on the beach. I'm not wearing a tux. It's not going to be a big, formal thing."

"Please tell me I'm not walking down the aisle to 'All About That Bass.'"

"People wouldn't forget it, would they?"

She'd tried to find out what his plan was, but he was maddeningly silent. He even told the guitarist they'd hired for the ceremony music not to tell her.

He'd chosen "Here Comes the Sun," the Beatles song she woke up to every morning. She'd been listening to it since she was a little girl. The words of the song fit them perfectly. For a couple who'd made their home in rainy Seattle, the return of the sun was always an event. They'd each lived a long, cold, lonely winter before meeting each other and falling in love. Even the warmth of the Hawaiian sunshine could never compare to the joy in her heart when she spotted Grant at the end of the aisle.

He wore a pale ivory long-sleeved linen shirt and linen pants and had an orchid pinned to his collar. His long, dark hair blew in the breeze. His smile was dazzling. He stepped forward and reached out his hand to her.

Her dad kissed her cheek and whispered, "Be happy, kitten. We love you."

"I love you too, Daddy," she said.

She felt her dad step away from her, but she didn't look back.

She took Grant's hand as the minister said, "Dearly beloved, we are gathered here today to share in the happiness when two hearts are joined together in love. Please be seated."

Grant turned to face her as she handed off her bouquet to Catherine so she could take both of his hands in hers. She looked up at him.

"You look so beautiful," he whispered.

She felt overwhelmed. She clutched his hands and whispered, "You look beautiful too."

"I can't wait to marry you," he said.

"I can't wait to marry you, either." She let out a sigh. "I'm such a dork. Maybe I'll be able to come up with something more original to say the next time we get married."

The minister cleared his throat.

"'I do' has worked well at every wedding I've performed so far, so let's start," he teased Daisy. He turned the page of the small black book he held open.

"Daisy and Grant, you are about to enter into a relationship that will determine and shape the rest of your lives. None of us knows what lies ahead when we speak the promises in our wedding vows, but we step forward in faith, believing that our lives together will be full of happiness with our beloved. After today, you will belong to each other. You will be one according to the law and according to the love you share. You will start your life together with the self-sacrifice that comes from true love, the belief that you always want the best for each other.

Your love will grow stronger and deeper as the years go by. If your actions are guided by unselfishness and love for each other, you can expect a happy, lasting marriage." He paused for a moment. "No pressure."

Daisy could hear Derrick Collins's deep voice from the back of the seated guests. "Amen, brother."

Grant squeezed her hands in both of his. "I love you," he whispered. "Have I told you how beautiful you are yet?"

"I love you too," Daisy said.

"Do you, Grant Parker, take this woman, Daisy Spencer, to be your lawfully wedded wife?"

"I do," Grant said.

"Do you, Daisy Spencer, take this man, Grant Parker, to be your lawfully wedded—"

"I do," she blurted out. "I do. I do."

"Well, then," the minister said through his laughter. "Let's try this again: your lawfully wedded husband."

"Yes," she said. "I do. For all of my life."

Author's Note

I TOOK A lot of liberties with my descriptions of what the life of a flight attendant is like. I hope the flight attendants (and other airline employees, past and present) who may read my book will forgive my artistic license, especially since you have a really tough job, and it wasn't my aim to add to this. I'm also pretty sure the nightmarish scenarios I dreamed up for poor Daisy pale in comparison to your stories. If you'd ever like to share them with me, I'd love to hear them! There's a contact form on my website, which is http://www.juliebrannagh.com.

Again, thank you for your hard work.

Go Sharks!

Be sure to score a copy of every book in
Julie Brannagh's Love and Football series!

BLITZING EMILY
A Love and Football Novel
_____

All's fair in Love and Football…

Emily Hamilton doesn't trust men. She's much more comfortable playing the romantic lead in front of a packed house onstage than in her own life. So when NFL star and alluring ladies' man Brandon McKenna acts as her personal white knight, she has no illusions that he'll stick around. However, a misunderstanding with the press throws them together in a fake engagement that yields unexpected (and breathtaking) benefits.

Every time Brandon calls her "Sugar," Emily almost believes he's playing for keeps—not just to score. Can she let down her defenses and get her own happily ever after?

RUSHING AMY
A Love and Football Novel

For Amy Hamilton, only three F's matter: Family, Football, and Flowers.

It might be nice to find someone to share Forever with too, but right now she's working double overtime while she gets her flower shop off the ground. The last thing she needs or wants is a distraction…or help, for that matter. Especially in the form of gorgeous and aggravatingly arrogant ex-NFL star Matt Stephens.

Matt lives by a playbook—his playbook. He never thought his toughest opponent would come in the form of a stunning florist with a stubborn streak to match his own. Since meeting her in the bar after her sister's wedding, he's known there's something between them. When she refuses, again and again, to go out with him, Matt will do anything to win her heart…But will Amy, who has everything to lose, let the clock run out on the one-yard line?

CATCHING CAMERON
A Love and Football Novel

Star sports reporter Cameron Ondine has one firm rule: she does not date football players. Ever. She tangled with one years ago, and it did not end well. Been there, done that.

But when Cameron comes face-to-face with the very man who shattered her heart—on camera, no less—her world is upended for a second time by recklessly handsome Seattle Shark Zach Anderson.

Zach has never been able to forget the gorgeous blonde who stole his breath away when he was still just a rookie. They've managed to give each other a wide berth for years, but when their jobs suddenly bring them together again and again, he knows he has to face his past once and for all.

Because as they spend more time together, he becomes less focused on the action on the field and more concerned with catching Cameron.

COVERING KENDALL
A Love and Football Novel

Kendall Tracy, General Manager of the San Francisco Miners, is not one for rash decisions or one-night stands. But when she finds herself alone in a hotel room with a heart-stoppingly gorgeous man—who looks oddly familiar—Kendall throws her own rules out the window…and they blow right back into her face.

Drew McCoy should look familiar; he's a star player for her team's archrival, the Seattle Sharks. Which would basically make Drew and Kendall the Romeo and Juliet of professional football…well, without all the dying.

Not that it's an issue. They agree to pretend their encounter never happened. Nothing good can come of it anyway, right?

Drew's not so sure. Kendall may be all wrong for him, but he can't stop thinking about her, and he finds that some risks are worth taking. Because the stakes are always highest when you're playing for keeps.

HOLDING HOLLY
A Love and Football Novella

Holly Reynolds has a secret. Make that two. The first involves upholding her grandmother's hobby answering Dear Santa letters from dozens of local school children. The second...well, he just came strolling in the door.

For the last two years, Holly has not been able to stop thinking about gorgeous Seattle Shark Derrick Collins. His on-field exploits induce nightmares in quarterbacks across the NFL, but she knows he has a heart of gold.

Derrick has never met a woman he wants to bring home to meet his family, mostly because he keeps picking the wrong ones-until he runs into sweet, shy Holly Reynolds. Different than anyone he's ever known, Derrick realizes she might just be everything he needs.

When he discovers her holiday letter writing, he is determined to play Santa too. And as the pair team up to bring joy to one little boy very much in need, they discover the most precious Christmas gift of all: love.

CHASING JILLIAN
A Love and Football Novel

Score a touchdown with Julie Brannagh's latest Love and Football novel about discovering who you are and finding love along the way.

Jillian Miller likes her job working in the front office for the Seattle Sharks, but lately being surrounded by a constant parade of perfection only seems to make her own imperfections all the more obvious. She needs a change, which takes her into foreign territory: the Sharks' workout facility after hours. The last thing she expects is a hot, grumbly god among men to be there as witness.

Star linebacker Seth Taylor had a bad day—well, a series of them recently. When he hits the Sharks' gym to work out his frustration, he's startled to find someone there— and even more surprised that it's Jillian, the team owner's administrative assistant. When he learns of Jillian's mission to revamp her lifestyle, he finds himself volunteering to help. Something about Jillian's beautiful smile and quick wit makes him want to stick around. She may not be like the swimsuit models he usually has on his arm, but the more time Seth spends with Jillian the harder he falls.

And as Jillian discovers that the new her is about so much more than she sees in the mirror, can she discover that happiness and love are oh-so-much better than perfect?

GUARDING SOPHIE
A Love and Football Novella

---

*Hearts beat and sparks fly when two people
find shelter in each other.*

Seattle Sharks wide receiver Kyle Carlson needs to escape
and Noel, Washington is the perfect place for him to do
it and figure out his next step. He likes the seclusion and
predictability of the small town...until the biggest surprise of his life turns up in the local grocery store.

Sophie Hayes has her own reasons for disappearing without a trace and moving to Noel. This mountain town
makes her feel safe for the first time in a long time. But
her quiet routine is threatened when Kyle walks back into
her life. Growing up in the same Florida town, she always
had a little thing for the sexy football player. This tie to
her old life, though, could mean she has to run again,
even if her heart wants to stay.

When the reason she fled shows up in Noel, Kyle and Sophie,
with a little extra help from his teammates, must decide to
stay and fight for the life, and love, they've found together.

About the Author

JULIE BRANNAGH has been writing since she was old enough to hold a pencil. She lives in a small town near Seattle, where she once served as a city council member and owned a yarn shop. She shares her home with a wonderful husband, two uncivilized Maine Coons, and a rambunctious chocolate Lab. When she's not writing, she's reading, or armchair-quarterbacking her favorite NFL team from the comfort of the family room couch.

Discover great authors, exclusive offers, and more at hc.com.

Give in to your Impulses . . .
Continue reading for excerpts from
our newest Avon Impulse books.
Available now wherever ebooks are sold.

THIS EARL IS ON FIRE
THE SEASON'S ORIGINAL SERIES
by Vivienne Lorret

TORCH
THE WILDWOOD SERIES
by Karen Erickson

HERO OF MINE
THE MEN IN UNIFORM SERIES
by Codi Gary

An Excerpt from

THIS EARL IS ON FIRE
The Season's Original Series

By Vivienne Lorret

Vivienne Lorret's Season's Original series
continues with an earl whose friends are
determined to turn him into a respectable
member of society . . . and the one
woman who could finally tame him.

Liam Cavanaugh grinned at the corrugated lines marking his cousin's lifted brows. It wasn't often that Northcliff Bromley, the Duke of Vale and renowned genius, showed astonishment.

Bending his dark head, Vale peered closer at the marble heads within the crates. "Remarkable. Even seeing them side by side, I hardly notice a difference. The *fellows* will be fascinated when you present this to the Royal Society at month's end."

"It was pure luck that I had the original as well." Liam shrugged as if he'd merely stumbled upon the differences between a genuine article and an imposter.

Vale turned, and his obsidian eyes sharpened on Liam. "No need to play the simpleton with me. You forget that I know your secret."

Liam cast a hasty glance around the sconce-lit, cluttered ballroom of Wolford House, ensuring they were alone. Fortunately, the vast space was empty aside from the two of them and a dozen or more large crates filled with artifacts. "By definition, a secret is that of which we do not speak. So lower your voice, if you please."

No one needed to know that he actually studied each piece of his collection in detail—enough that he'd learned how to spot a forgery in an instant.

"Afraid the servants will tell the *ton* your collection isn't merely a frivolous venture? Or that your housekeeper's complaints of dusty urns and statues crowding each room would suddenly fall silent?" Vale flashed a smile that bracketed his mouth with deep creases.

Liam pretended to consider his answer, pursing his lips. "It would be cruel of me to render Mrs. Brasher mute when she finds such enjoyment in haranguing me."

"She may have a point," Vale said, skirting in between two crates when a wayward nail snagged his coat, issuing a sharp *rip* of rending fabric. He stopped to examine the hole and shook his head. "Your collection has grown by leaps and bounds in the past few months. So much so that you were forced to purchase another property to house it all."

"The curse of immense wealth and boredom, I'm afraid."

His cousin's quick glower revealed that he was not amused by Liam's insouciant guise. Then, as if to punish him for it, he issued the foulest epithet known to man. "You should marry."

Not wanting to reveal the discomfort slowly clawing up his spine, Liam chuckled. "As a cure for boredom?"

Vale said nothing. He merely crossed his arms over his chest and waited.

It was a standoff now. They were nearly equal in regard to observation skills, but apparently Vale thought he had the upper hand.

Liam knew differently. He crossed his arms as well and smirked.

If anyone were to peer into the room at this moment, they might wonder if they were staring at matching wax figures. The two of them looked enough alike in build and coloring to be brothers, but with subtle differences. Vale's features were blunter, while Liam's were angular. And Vale's dark eyes were full of intellect, while Liam's green eyes tended to reveal the streak of mischief within.

"Marriage would do you good," Vale said.

Liam disagreed. "You're starting to sound like Thayne, always hinting of ways to improve my social standing."

The Marquess of Thayne was determined to reform Liam into the *ton*'s favorite pet—the Season's *Original*. In fact, Thayne had been so confident in success that he'd wagered on the outcome. *What a fool.*

"I never hint," Vale said.

Liam offered his cousin a nod. "True. You are a forthright, scientific gentleman, and I appreciate that about you. Therefore, I will give you the courtesy of answering in kind: No. I should *not* marry. I like my life just as it is." He lifted his hands in a gesture to encompass his collection within this room. "Besides, I could never respect a woman who would have me."

Vale scoffed. "Respect?"

"Very well. I could never *trust* a woman who desired to marry me. Not with my reputation. Such a woman would either be mad or conniving, and I want neither for a wife."

He'd nearly succumbed once, falling for the worst of all deceptions. After that narrow escape, he'd vowed never to be tricked again.

"Come now. There are many who care nothing for your reputation."

That statement only served to cement his belief. If his despoiled reputation were the only thing keeping him far afield of the *ton's* conniving matchmakers, then he would make the most of it. And the perfect place to add the crème de la crème to his list of scandalous exploits would be at Lady Forester's masquerade tonight.

After all, he had a carefully crafted reputation of unrepentant debauchery to uphold.

Liam squared his shoulders and walked with his cousin to the door. "If the Fates have it in mind to see me married before I turn sixty, then they will have to knock me over the head and drag me to the altar."

An Excerpt from

TORCH
The Wildwood Series
By Karen Erickson

USA Today bestselling author Karen
Erickson continues her Wildwood series
with a hot firefighter who knows that
enemies make the best lovers . . .

Wren Gallagher wasn't the type to drown her sorrows in alcohol, but tonight seemed as good a time as any to start.

"Another Malibu and pineapple, Russ," she said to the bartender, who gave her a look before nodding reluctantly.

"That's your third drink," Russ said gruffly as he plunked the fresh glass in front of her.

She grabbed it and took a long sip from the skinny red straw. It was her third drink because the first two weren't potent enough. She didn't even feel that drunk. But how could she tell Russ that when he was the one mixing her drinks? "And they're equally delicious," she replied with a sweet smile.

He scowled at her, his bushy eyebrows threaded with gray hairs seeming to hang low over his eyes. "You all right, Wren?"

"I'm fine." She smiled but it felt incredibly false, so she let it fade before taking another sip of her drink.

Sighing, she pushed the wimpy straw out of the way and brought the glass to her lips, chugging the drink in a few long swallows. Polishing it off like a pro, she wiped her damp lips with the back of her hand as she set the glass down on the bar.

A low whistle sounded behind her and she went still, her breath trapped in her lungs.

"Trying to get drunk, Dove?"

That too-amused, too-arrogant voice was disappointingly familiar. Her shoulders slumping, she glanced to her right to watch as Tate Warren settled his too-perfect butt onto the barstool next to hers, a giant smile curving his too-sexy mouth as he looked her up and down. Her body heated everywhere his eyes landed and she frowned.

Ugh. She hated him. His new favorite thing was to call her every other bird name besides her own. It drove her crazy and he knew it. It didn't help that they ran into each other all the time. The town was too small, and their circle of mutual friends—and family members—even smaller.

Tate worked at Cal Fire with her brothers Weston and Holden. He was good friends with West and her oldest brother, Lane, so they all spent a lot of time together when they could. But fire season was in full swing and Tate had been at the station the last time they all got together.

She hadn't missed him either. Not one bit.

At least, that's what she told herself.

"What are you doing here?" Her tone was snottier than she intended and he noticed. His brows rose, surprise etching his very fine, very handsome features.

He was seriously too good-looking for words. Like Abercrombie & Fitch type good looking. With that pretty, pretty face and shock of dark hair and the finely muscled body and *oh shit*, that smile. Although, he wasn't flashing it at her right now like he usually did. Nope, not at all.

"I'm assuming you're looking to get drunk alone tonight?

I don't want to get in your way." He started to stand and she reached out, resting her hand on his forearm to stop him.

And *oh wow*, his skin was hot. And firm. As in, the boy's got muscles. Erm, the man. Tate could never be mistaken for a boy. He was all man. One hundred percent, delicious, sexy man . . .

"Don't go," she said, her eyes meeting his. His brows went up until they looked like they could reach his hairline and she snatched her hand away, her fingers still tingling where she touched him.

Whoo boy, that wasn't good. Could she blame it on the alcohol?

Tate settled his big body back on the barstool, ordering a Heineken when Russ asked what he wanted. "You all right, bird?" His voice was low and full of concern and her heart ached to say something. Admit her faults, her fears, and hope for some sympathy.

But she couldn't do that. Couldn't make a fool of herself in front of Tate. She'd never hear the end of it.

So she'd let the bird remark go. At least he hadn't called her Cuckoo or Woodpecker. "Having a bad day," she offered with a weak smile, lifting her ice-filled glass in a toasting gesture. At that precise moment, Russ delivered Tate's beer, and he raised it as well, clinking the green bottle against her glass.

"Me too," Tate murmured before he took a drink, his gaze never leaving hers.

Wren stared at him in a daze. How come she never noticed how green his eyes were before? They matched the beer bottle, which proved he didn't have the best taste in beer, but she'd forgive him for that.

But, yes. They were pretty eyes. Kind eyes. Amused eyes. Laughing eyes. Sexy eyes.

She tore her gaze away from his, mentally beating herself up. He chuckled under his breath and she wanted to beat him up too. Just before she ripped off his clothes and had her way with him . . .

Oh, jeez. Clearly she was drunker than she thought.

An Excerpt from

HERO OF MINE
The Men in Uniform Series
By Codi Gary

The men of Codi Gary's Men in Uniform
series work hard and play hard . . . but
when it comes to protecting the women
they love, nothing stands in their way.

Tyler Best didn't believe in fate.

Fate was an excuse people who'd experienced really bad shit or really astounding luck used in order to explain how their lives tended to twist and turn. Fate was a fantasy.

Tyler was a realist. He didn't rely on some imaginary force to direct him. He'd taken chances and gotten knocked on his ass a few times, but he kept going because that's what life was. You didn't give up when it got hard.

Even in the face of devastating loss.

Tyler stared at the picture of Rex, his military dog, and the ache in his heart was raw, even eight months later. Rex had been his for three years before getting killed in combat. While Tyler was overseas, away from his family and friends, the dog had been his best friend, bringing him great comfort. When he'd lost Rex, he'd almost quit working with dogs. It had been difficult to be around them.

Yet, here he was, waiting to be led back to the "last day" dogs at the Paws and Causes Shelter. It was his first time here, as it was relatively new. Most of the time he visited Front Street Animal Shelter or the one off of Bradshaw, but new rescues and shelters were being added to the program every day.

Ever since he'd become the head trainer for the Alpha Dog Training Program, a nonprofit created to help strengthen the connection between military personnel and their community, he'd become the last hope for a lot of dogs. If they passed their temperament test, they'd join the program. Not all of them did, and on those days it was hard to remember all the lives the program saved. It was hard to walk away from a dog's big soulful eyes when Tyler knew the only outcome was a needle filled with pink liquid death, but he couldn't save them all.

Just like he couldn't save Rex.

"Sergeant Best?" a woman called from behind the reception desk.

Tyler stood up and slipped his phone back into his pocket. "Yes, ma'am."

"You can go on through. Our tech, Dani, is waiting in the back to show you around. Just straight back; you'll see the double doors."

"Thank you." Tyler opened the door, assaulted by high-pitched barks of excitement and fear. As he passed by the kennels, he looked through, studying the dogs of all shapes and sizes. He wasn't sure why he was so melancholy today, but it had been coming on strong.

He pushed through the double doors and immediately realized the man and woman inside were arguing. Loudly.

"No, he has more time. I talked to Dr. Lynch, and he promised to give him until the end of the day in case his owners claim him." This was shouted by the woman with her back to him, her blonde ponytail swinging with every hand gesture.

"Don't be naïve. You've been here long enough to know

that he won't be claimed." This was said by the thin, balding man in the lab coat, who was pushing sixty and had the cold, cynical look of someone who'd been doing his job too long. Tyler had seen it on the faces of veterans who had found a way to steel themselves against the horrors that haunted them. But once you shut that part off, it was hard to find it again. "Even if they come looking, they'll just tell you to put him down anyway. If they had the money to pay for his care, then they could afford a proper fence. All you're doing is putting off the inevitable and wasting valuable pain meds."

He tried to sidestep the blonde, who was a good head shorter, but she planted herself right in his path. When she spoke, her voice was a low, deadly whisper. "If you make one more move toward that cage, I will body check you so hard you'll forget your own name."

Tyler's eyebrows shot up, and he crossed his arms, hoping like hell the guy tested her. He really wanted to see her Hulk out.